Stephen Dobyns is the author of twelve novels and seven books of poetry. His fiction includes *The Two Deaths of Señora Puccini* and a series of detective novels featuring Charlie Bradshaw of Saratoga Springs, all published by Penguin Books. His most recent collection of poems is *Body Traffic* and is also available from Penguin. Mr. Dobyns is a professor of English at Syracuse University.

SARATOGA HEXAMETER

Stephen Dobyns

PENGUIN BOOKS

PENGUIN BOOKS
Published by the Penguin Group
Viking Penguin, a division of Penguin Books USA Inc.,
375 Hudson Street, New York, New York 10014, U.S.A.
Penguin Books Ltd, 27 Wrights Lane,
London W8 5TZ, England
Penguin Books Australia Ltd, Ringwood,
Victoria, Australia
Penguin Books Canada Ltd, 2801 John Street,
Markham, Ontario, Canada L3R 1B4
Penguin Books (N.Z.) Ltd, 182–190 Wairau Road,
Auckland 10, New Zealand

Penguin Books Ltd, Registered Offices:
Harmondsworth, Middlesex, England

First published in the United States of America by
Viking Penguin, a division of Penguin Books USA Inc., 1990
Published in Penguin Books 1991

1 3 5 7 9 10 8 6 4 2

PUBLISHER'S NOTE
This is a work of fiction. Names, characters, places, and incidents
either are the product of the author's imagination or are used
fictitiously, and any resemblance to actual persons, living or
dead, events, or locales is entirely coincidental.

A portion of this book originally appeared in
The Gettysburg Review in slightly different form.

Grateful acknowledgment is made for permission to reprint an
excerpt from *If You Call This Cry a Song* by Hayden Carruth.
Copyright © 1983 by Hayden Carruth. Reprinted by permission of
The Countryman Press, Inc., Woodstock, Vermont.

THE LIBRARY OF CONGRESS HAS CATALOGUED THE HARDCOVER AS FOLLOWS:
Dobyns, Stephen, 1941–
Saratoga hexameter/by Stephen Dobyns
p. cm.
ISBN 0-670-82568-9 (hc.)
ISBN 0 14 01.1691 5 (pbk.)
I. Title.
PS3554.O2S264 1990
813'.54—dc20 89-40676

Printed in the United States of America

For Hayden Carruth

It is not music, though one has tried music.
It is not nature, though one has tried
The rose, the bluebird, and the bear.
It is not death, though one has often died.

—Hayden Carruth

SARATOGA
HEXAMETER

1

The music was a rag by Scott Joplin—a piece that always reminded Charlie Bradshaw of the up and down movement of many musical yo-yos. Neglected for over fifty years, the rag had been rediscovered by Hollywood and now could be heard in supermarkets, dentists' offices, restaurants, and, in this particular instance, a carnival merry-go-round parked in a small shopping center in the city of Cohoes, about seven miles north of Albany. The shopping center itself was dark which was not surprising since it was past ten o'clock on a drizzly Sunday night, the last day in July. In fact, almost everything was dark—the only lights coming from several streetlights, the headlights of Charlie's Renault Encore, and, strangely enough, the merry-go-round. Charlie shut off his engine and got out. The music grew louder. It was the only noise anywhere except for the creak and groan of the merry-go-round itself as it circled and circled. Charlie pulled his tan raincoat around him, then hurried across the lot toward the chain link fence that surrounded the carnival—half a dozen rides, some games, and a popcorn wagon. Above him the Ferris wheel loomed wet and desolate with several of its seats rocking in the wind.

Charlie had come down to Cohoes from Saratoga Springs for a meeting with Blake Moss, an Albany private detective. Moss had called that morning saying he had some work for him. He wouldn't elaborate except to remark that it concerned poetry.

"What kind of poetry?" Charlie had asked and thought he heard Moss chuckle over the wire.

"You know, ta-TUM, ta-TUM, ta-TUM. I need your advice about it."

"And this is a job for a private detective?"

"You bet."

Moss had asked to meet Charlie at nine-thirty outside of this small carnival parked in a Cohoes shopping center. Again he had been mysterious, saying only that he had wanted to show Charlie something. For days afterward Charlie kept wondering if Moss had said "something" or "someone," but he was almost sure he had said "something."

Charlie didn't like Moss, which was probably one reason he was late. Moss was a liar and an inveterate gambler who could no more walk by a poker game than he could walk by a ten dollar bill lying on the sidewalk. And even though many of Charlie's best friends were gamblers, they weren't whiners and Moss was also a whiner— always complaining about his losses and how something had conspired against him to keep him from winning, a win that he saw as rightfully his.

But unfortunately Charlie needed the work. His small house on Saratoga Lake had developed a leaky roof over the winter and all the pots and pans and patching no longer helped. Of course, he could have taken a job at the Bentley, his mother's hotel in downtown Saratoga, but Charlie had done that once before and swore never to do it again. It had been like spending his days in a straight jacket. Still, as he approached the open gate of the carnival, he wondered if at fifty-two he wasn't too old to go traipsing about on rainy July nights. Right now his friend Victor Plotz, who was hotel detective at the Bentley, was probably sitting in front of a fire with his feet up and sipping an expensive brandy. Most likely there was an attractive woman nearby as well. But then Charlie thought that if getting wet on a cold July night was the cost of his freedom, it was cheap at the price. After all, many of his heroes had worked alone: Billy the Kid, Gentleman George Leslie, Willie Sutton.

But the primary mystery concerned the merry-go-round. Why was it going round and round? And why was the music playing? The parking lot was deserted except for Charlie's Renault and a dark Alfa Romeo Milano which Charlie assumed belonged to Blake Moss. Across the street were a row of non-descript two-story buildings, darkened storefronts, a sub shop, a unisex beauty parlor and a Midas Muffler garage. There was no sign of Blake Moss. Charlie paused by the entrance of the carnival and glanced around. The Joplin rag started up again and Charlie found himself whistling along under his breath.

"Moss," he called, "are you in there?"

There was a padlock and chain on the gate but the padlock was dangling open. Charlie passed through the fence. He could feel the rain spattering against his bald spot and wished he had brought a hat. On his right was a kiddie ride of miniature race cars designed to let the dimmer toddlers imagine they were taking part in the Indianapolis 500. Charlie made his way around it and continued toward the carousel which was clearly the center of all activity.

Apart from his disinclination to see Moss, Charlie was also late because he had been with Janey Burris, a woman whose very name made his pulse beat faster. Janey was a registered nurse. She was supposed to work that night but at the last moment her job had been cancelled and she had shown up Charlie's house at the lake around eight thirty. And then they had talked. It seemed they were always talking. And before Charlie had realized, it was past nine-thirty and he still had a twenty mile drive ahead of him. But he also knew that if he had any real interest in seeing Moss, he wouldn't have forgotten. And what had he and Janey talked about? Maybe politics, maybe the weather. Charlie could hardly remember, but before him he could see her animated face and hear her laugh.

The merry-go-round was on the other side of the tilt-a-whirl. Charlie knew all these rides although he hadn't been on any for nearly forty years. Through the shell shaped disks of the tilt-a-whirl he could see the horses rising and falling and the little scarlet wagons where the more timorous children could sit with their mothers. The merry-go-round was old and the colors had faded. Charlie wondered if some glitch caused by a decaying part hadn't made the whole thing to start up accidentally. But then who had opened the gate?

It was at that moment that Charlie saw Blake Moss. He was sitting in one of the little scarlet wagons and as the wagon went up and down, Moss's head bobbed up and down as well. Perhaps Moss wasn't sitting so much as slouching. Actually he seemed asleep. Charlie hurried forward. As a private detective he had come to distrust the appearance of sleep. There was always so much death about.

Grabbing a pink and chartreuse horse, Charlie swung himself onto the platform, then began to make his way back toward Moss. Within the merry-go-round itself the Joplin rag was quite loud, almost aggressive and military, and many of the notes were being struck off-key. Then it occurred to Charlie that all the horses were race horses. It was a matter of posture rather than design: they were stretched out, elongated as if running fast. Even the scarlet wagon in which Moss appeared to be sleeping was drawn by a pair of purple race horses. Charlie wound his way toward it, catching hold of the horse rods for support. The surface of the platform was slick with rain and Charlie had to take care not to be thrown down between the plunging multicolored hooves. Moss leaned back in the seat with his arms spread out along the top. He wore a dark raincoat and dark suit. His blond hair was mussed and there was a small bruise with a trickle of blood on his forehead. Then, as Charlie got closer, he saw that Moss's eyes were open. He's watching me, Charlie thought.

"Moss," he called.

And then Charlie realized that Blake Moss was dead.

In the second floor lounge of the Phoenix Colony, Alexander Luft was pontificating. It was something he was good at. Expressing his ideas in a positive and aggressive manner was to Alexander Luft what water is to a flounder: it was his natural element.

"The linear," he was saying, "is a prosaic mode. The artist's approach in a poem should dance. It should shimmer with a multitude of directions. The surface of the poem should be as multi-faceted as one of those baroque churches one finds in Vienna—all sparkle and dazzle. And the artist's treatment of his subject should zigzag and circle like a hare evading a hound."

"But wouldn't that make the poem difficult to understand?" asked a young woman, a photographer who read few poems and who found in Alexander Luft's words good reason to read even fewer.

"That is why we have critics," said Luft, touching his fingers to the strangled knot of his necktie. "The critic is like the conductor of a symphony who guides the musicians toward a correct interpretation of the score. In such a way the critic guides the reader."

Six people, all artists of one kind or another, were sitting on the over-stuffed couch and armchairs. All were guests of the Phoenix Colony, an estate on the outskirts of Saratoga Springs where artists came for periods of a week to several months to pursue their various crafts or just to sit and rebuild the interiors of their heads. Most were watching Luft, who had stood up in preparation of returning to his room. It was late Sunday evening and he was tired. Luft was not an artist but a critic and he had been invited to the Phoenix Colony for a six-week stay in order to work on his biography of Wallace Stevens. But it had been a troubled time and he wasn't sure if he would remain. The room was shadowy, the only light coming from a lamp with a Tiffany shade on a dark mahogany table. On the walls were Piranesi prints showing massive blocks of crumbling stone.

"What about Walt Whitman?" asked a man with a beard, a poet of sorts. "He seems pretty linear."

"Whitman was a cretin, a misdirected autodidact," said Luft, taking a step toward the hall. "Those few poems of his which have any merit were produced purely by accident."

"What about Dante?" asked a woman. "He marches down through hell and up to heaven. What could be more linear than that?"

"In my opinion Dante is a much over-rated writer," said Luft. "His reputation owes far more to politics and squabbles within the Catholic church than to ability. Basically he was a novelist who never discovered his proper medium. But now I've said enough. We critics need our periods of repose if we are to make sense of the intuitive projectiles flung at us by you artists." Luft chuckled. He was a big man in his fifties whose thick graying hair fell in waves to his collar. Apart from those occasions when he swam in the Phoenix Colony pool, he was never seen without a suit and tie. "Good night, good night." He lifted a hand above his head in a casually dramatic wave and moved off down the hall. He knew they didn't like him. Even the painters and composers were suspicious of him. He, after all, sat on the panels and chaired the committees that awarded fellowships and grants. He had the ear of the prize-givers. He wrote the reviews that made a book or sent it sliding into the yawn of oblivion. And of course he had his favorites.

Luft didn't see himself as hungry for this power, nor did he feel he abused it. The passing of judgment was only part of his job. He was a critic, a professor at a major university in New York City, and he took his work seriously. There were many poets, a confusing jumble of names, and people turned to him to sort them out, to list and to categorize, to raise up the best and cast down the scribblers. This was his duty.

He had not expected to be fawned upon at the Phoenix Colony, but he had expected to be treated with respect. But of the thirty or so guests, at least half a dozen were poets and most of those were triflers. Certainly they were not people whom Luft would have expected to find at a serious artists' colony. It almost hurt him to see them, for how could it be an honor for him to be invited to the Phoenix Colony if they were here as well? He realized of course that a place like the Colony would accept a certain number of unknowns—young artists whose work showed potential but who had not yet achieved public success. But several of these poets were men and women whom Luft had reviewed. Surely the book was already closed upon them. But here they were pursuing their bogus craft like legitimate artists. And most likely they had complained and told stories about him until the other artists had grown suspicious even though he was probably more committed to poetry than any of them.

But considering his work and why he had come to the Phoenix

Colony, none of that mattered. Indeed, it even hardened him. And if it was friends he wanted, there were many among the critical establishment who took pleasure in his company.

Luft opened the door to his room—a large bedroom with windows looking out on the great lawn. His studio or workspace was through a door to his left on the other side of the bathroom. Many of the guests had cabins in the woods as studios or had studios in other buildings, and of course the painters and visual artists all had regular artists' studios with north light and turpentine smells. Luft felt lucky to have a studio adjoining his bedroom. He disliked all useless movement. Besides, it suited his purposes to have his studio so close.

He passed through the bathroom—a long, narrow room with marble floors and a six foot tub. He wanted to see his desk and think about what he had worked on earlier. The studio was dark. He fumbled for the top of the articulated lamp that hung over his computer, then flicked on the switch. The effect was dazzling. Everything was red. Luft gasped and staggered back. His desk was covered with blood and his papers were floating in it—a scarlet, brilliant blood that shimmered and sparkled in the light of the lamp. But even more shocking than the blood was the single bare foot, a bloody foot which rested on the keys of his portable Kaypro: blood was spattered over the keyboard and splashed across the screen, while that blood-stained foot stood in the midst of it all. A metrical foot, Alexander Luft told himself.

Then he stumbled back toward the door and began to scream.

The woman on the other side of the small marble table had what Victor Plotz thought of as a fine pair of hooters—large soft breasts which seemed to recline upon her chest, leaning heavily against the purple fabric of her diaphanous gown. The woman was about fifty and her name was Mrs. Bigalow. She was a widow. Victor was partial to widows—women who had regained their single state through nothing more complicated than death. And Mrs. Bigalow's breasts had seen a lot of life: children, lovers, a husband or two. They weren't the hard ignorant breasts of a twenty-year-old, the chest muscles of a cheerleader. They were pillowy and welcoming and Victor imagined resting his head between them.

"Like another cognac, Mrs. Bigalow?" he asked.

"I really shouldn't." Mrs. Bigalow smiled. Twenty years ago she had been a beautiful woman and Victor thought there was still much beauty about her. Her eyes were large and blue with large dark pupils and as she looked at Victor she blinked slowly several times.

"Just a taste," said Victor and he raised his hand to summon the waitress.

They were sitting in the bar of the Bentley, which was fairly deserted on this rainy Sunday night: a few ballerinas, a few jockeys' agents and several middle-aged couples who had come for the start of the races on Wednesday. Victor had been pleased to learn that Mrs. Bigalow had signed on at the Bentley for two weeks and that this was her first night. He had spotted her at once. She was, Victor thought, idly in the market for an adventure and he was only too happy to oblige.

The waitress brought two more Hennessys and Victor told her to put them on his bill.

"It must be exciting to be a hotel detective," said Mrs. Bigalow.

"It can be," said Victor, "and dangerous, too. Sometimes there's a lot of money in the safe. You'd be surprised how many desperate characters there are even in a civilized place like Saratoga."

Mrs. Bigalow sipped her brandy. The fire in the large fieldstone fireplace snapped and crackled. "I feel better just knowing you are here," she said.

Victor reached across the table and patted her hand. On her wrist was a diamond bracelet that sparkled in the candlelight. Victor looked at it speculatively. He was about ten years older than Mrs. Bigalow and thought himself thoroughly capable of exploring her charms. He was a large man, not fat or particularly tall but solid. He wore a three-piece gray suit which exactly matched the frizzy hair which rose above his scalp like a dust ball. His face seemed a collection of over-sized features, as if nose, mouth, teeth, jaw, ears had all been bought secondhand from a used parts place. It was not a handsome face but it showed a lot of character.

"Just last year one ruffian threatened me with a shotgun," said Victor. "Super Sunday, I'll never forget it."

Mrs. Bigalow leaned across the table. Her decolletage seemed as big as a birdbath and Victor imagined dabbling within it. "You must tell me," she said.

Victor glanced around the room. "Perhaps some place more intimate."

Mrs. Bigalow leaned back in her seat and seemed to stiffen. Victor wondered if he had gone too far, but no, it had just been a small jolt of adrenaline which had caused her movement.

"Give me ten minutes," she said. "Room two eleven." She rose from her chair and glided toward the door. Victor watched her go, exhaled a long breath, and poured the rest of her brandy into his snifter. What he liked about women was that they made his heart beat fast. He began to imagine how they would spend the remainder of their evening and perhaps a number of evenings to come.

Victor's thoughts were interrupted—rudely, he felt—by the arrival of Raoul, the manager of the Bentley, who plopped himself down in the seat recently vacated by Mrs. Bigalow.

"Working hard?" asked Raoul with a smile which signified neither friendship nor good humor.

Victor stirred in his chair and glanced at his watch. "I like to make our guests feel secure in their surroundings, to let them know someone responsible is watching over their interests." He did not like Raoul whose whole appearance and metaphysical being struck Victor as slicked-back and prissy. Raoul's shiny black hair made him look like a young Don Ameche, while his fastidiousness had led Victor to think of him as a machine which ran on talcum powder and Vitalis.

"You would do better," said Raoul, "to circulate among the floors rather than to chat up the female guests."

Victor finished the last of his brandy. "I was just about to do so," he said, getting to his feet. "I need to stretch my legs." He nodded to Raoul and strolled into the lobby where, despite the hour, several people were checking in. August was the busiest month, the month that paid for everything else, and Victor felt himself ready for it both as a detective and as a militant hedonist.

The Bentley was an over-sized Victorian hotel in downtown Saratoga Springs which had been purchased some years before by Charlie Bradshaw's mother, who had raised the money through the sale of a successful race horse and then by investing wisely in several roulette wheels in Atlantic City. Once in command, Mabel Bradshaw had completely remodeled the dilapidated building until now it was a museum of Victorian design. Victor found it dark and fussy, but he appreciated the clientele who tended to be big tippers and sometimes, like Mrs. Bigalow, older women interested in adventure.

It was as he was thinking of adventure that Victor began to hear a woman screaming on one of the upper floors. For a moment the lobby went silent, then everybody began talking and calling to one another at once. Victor turned to the stairs and broke into a run. He was aware of a lot of commotion behind him and of doors opening and slamming. The screaming continued, an angry indignant wailing over and over. Victor thought that the voice bore certain resemblances to Mrs. Bigalow's. But was that possible?

Unfortunately, however, the voice was indeed Mrs. Bigalow's. Furthermore, she was distraught, not to say unreasonable. Victor ran into her room and immediately regretted it.

"Somebody has broken in here and stolen my great aunt's diamond necklace," she said, giving Victor an angry shove. "What sort of hotel detective are you, anyway?"

Victor stumbled across the carpet and regained his balance by sitting down abruptly on the king-sized bed. Although this was exactly where he had imagined being, the circumstances were cruelly different. He glanced around. Drawers had been pulled out and clothing was scattered across the rug, including the most delicate and revealing of Victorian lingerie. Raoul had hurried into the room and now stood near the television set attempting to console Mrs. Bigalow. He kept trying to clasp her hand and she kept jerking it away. Squeezed together at the door, a crowd of guests looked on with moon-shaped faces which bore expressions of alarm and trepidation. Victor felt something crinkle beneath him and found he was sitting on a piece of paper. He pulled it out from under him. It was a poem.

> *They are but fools*
> *Who leave their jewels*
> *Where thieves like me can take them.*
> *But they make me rich*
> *So I won't bitch—*
> *For their kindness I do thank them.*

2

The Cohoes police lieutenant unbent the paper clip until it was a straight piece of wire, then delicately inserted it into his ear. "People die of heart attacks all the time, Mr. Bradshaw," he said.

"But who turned on the merry-go-round?" asked Charlie. He couldn't take his eyes off the paper clip which seemed to have gone into the lieutenant's ear farther than humanly possible. Charlie thought that if the paper clip had gone that far into his own ear, he'd be dead.

"Perhaps he was signaling for help, perhaps he felt funny and started up the merry-go-round as the only way to attract attention." The lieutenant—his name was Melchuk—removed the unbent paper clip and inspected the tip, which appeared clean. He was a thin man in his thirties with thick black hair which seemed to rise up like some jungle weed out of the collar of his white shirt. Charlie couldn't get a handle on him, couldn't decide whether he was stupid or just unusually calm.

"What about the bruise on his forehead?"

"He could have fallen."

"Do you really think that Blake Moss suffered a heart attack?" asked Charlie.

The lieutenant moved some papers around his desk as if that very action encouraged thought. They were in his office and on the wall behind him were pictures of eight black-haired children of different ages. It was ten thirty Tuesday morning and Charlie had arrived a few minutes earlier, although of course he had talked to Melchuk Sunday night as well. A patrol car had driven up shortly after Charlie had discovered Moss's body and Charlie had had a lot of explaining to do, explanations which had led to his introduction to the police lieutenant. The merry-go-round had apparently been running for about half an hour and people had called the police to complain. Melchuk had also been suspicious and took Charlie back to head-quarters where he called the police in Saratoga to find out just who this Bradshaw guy was. The Cohoes police department was in the same building as the city hall, on the corner of Ontario and Mohawk several blocks from the Mohawk River: the boundary between Saratoga and Albany counties. It was a small department, about thirty men.

"The state police couldn't find any evidence that any one else had been around," said Melchuk. "The body went to the coroner and the autopsy was done at the medical school. Some of the arteries to his heart were pretty well clogged. I mean, look at Moss. He smoked, he drank, he was overweight. The fact that he was forty-five means nothing. On top of that, he was diabetic."

"But do you really think he died of a heart attack?" repeated Charlie. On Monday Charlie had expected to hear from the Cohoes lieutenant but he had been out of his office all day, partly dealing with the confusion at the Bentley and partly trying to avoid it. He dreaded the thought of being caught up in an investigation in which he was responsible to his mother and had spent a lot of time trying to reassure everyone that Victor was the man for the job. Late in the afternoon Charlie had checked his answering machine and found no word from Melchuk. He called the lieutenant and learned that Moss's death was "under investigation." Melchuk's voice had sounded so detached that Charlie had decided to pay him a visit the next morning.

"Aren't the circumstances a little suspicious for a heart attack?" added Charlie.

"I don't know," said Melchuk. He was trying to rebend the wire into its original paper clip shape and wasn't doing a very good job of it. "The autopsy also showed that he was suffering from insulin shock: hypoglycemia and low acetone. I figure he started to go into insulin shock and the stress of it brought on the heart attack."

"Did the toxicology turn up insulin?"

"Yeah, but not enough to kill him."

"Did the scan turn up anything else?"

"It's not like a menu, Bradshaw. You got to know what you're looking for. They looked for insulin and they found it. I don't know what else they looked for."

"What's happened to the body?"

"We're holding onto it for a while."

"Will you have another autopsy?"

"Right now there's no reason to."

"What if it wasn't a heart attack, what if he was murdered?"

Lieutenant Melchuk stared at Charlie as if trying to decide how to respond. He looked as if he hadn't had much sleep and that he hadn't laughed or found anything funny for about five years. "There was no sign of murder. Okay, okay, so that doesn't mean anything. But the trouble is we need a motive. We need someone who wanted him dead. And even then it would be circumstantial. I mean, what I like is someone hauling off and shooting another guy. Then you know where you stand." He looked disappointedly at the bent wire and tossed it into the waste basket.

"So what have you done?" asked Charlie.

"I sent a sergeant over to his office to talk to his secretary and another guy to talk to the carnival owner. Also we're checking the shopping center and nearby houses. The trouble is I can't spend a lot of time on it. Like I don't know for sure that any law was broken except for busting into the carnival and turning on the merry-go-round. What do you think he meant that he had some work for you and that it concerned poetry?"

"I have no idea," said Charlie, "but maybe I'll look into it." He was beginning to have a clearer idea about Melchuk and suspected he might need some help.

"What are you going to do?"

"Go talk to his secretary."

"And who's paying you for this?"

"I was an hour late on Sunday night," said Charlie, deflecting the question. "If I'd been on time, Moss might have been okay."

"Private dicks with consciences don't make any money," said Melchuk.

As Charlie got to his feet he tried to think of a snappy reply, but he felt too tired. He hadn't gotten home from Cohoes until three in the morning. Then for the past two mornings he had woken up at six, thinking of Moss. He kept picturing him in that little scarlet wagon on the merry-go-round with his head bobbing up and down as if to the Scott Joplin rag.

"Just don't ship that body off to some funeral home," said Charlie. "You might have to look at it again."

Blake Moss's office was in a shopping center on the north side of Albany. At one time it had probably been a shoe store or yarn shop, but for three years, according to his secretary, it had held Blake Moss Enterprises. Originally there had also been branch offices in Schenectady, Pittsfield, and Kingston but these had somehow fallen by the way. Moss's big problem had been his gambling and the time it took from his more conventional occupations. Whatever profits he made as a detective had been funnelled into his losses as a gambler.

Moss's secretary, Mrs. Hatcher, was unattractive, ill-natured and probably underpaid. Charlie guessed she had a history of lots of little jobs from which she had been let go through no choice of her own. With Moss she had most likely arrived at a compromise—he would keep her, but pay her as little as possible. It was certainly money that was on Mrs. Hatcher's mind this Tuesday morning: her lack of it and how the world had conspired to cheat her.

"You'd think he could have put off dying until he'd come across with my check," said Mrs. Hatcher who stood behind her typewriter rather, Charlie thought, like a Roman charioteer might stand behind his chariot.

Charlie buttoned the single remaining button on the jacket of his blue seersucker suit and could feel his damp shirt stick coolly to his back. The air-conditioning was on full blast and it had been hot outside. "His lawyer should take care of that," said Charlie.

"What lawyer? You think he could afford a lawyer? Just Friday afternoon he said, 'Oh, Mrs. Hatcher, I'll have to give you your check on Monday.' I wouldn't be surprised if he knew he was going to die. And now the police want me to keep his office open for a couple of days just to answer phone calls. Nobody calls, nobody ever calls. And who'll pay me, that's what I want to know?" Mrs. Hatcher was about Charlie's age and he wondered what she had been like at the shared moments of their lives. She too had probably put streamers on her bike after Germany surrendered in '45. She too had probably cha-cha-cha'd to "Hernando's Hideaway" during high school sock hops. Now she was rectangular and brick-like with a no-nonsense purple suit and permanented gray hair that looked so rigid and strict that even to glance at it was a scolding.

"I'm sure it will be taken out of his estate," said Charlie.

"Blake Moss was in debt up to his hairline," said Mrs. Hatcher, "and even if there're a few cents left over, it will be months before I get it. I have half a mind to take this typewriter and I would if it worked right, but he was too cheap to get it fixed."

Charlie stared down at the typewriter, not knowing quite where else to look. It was an IBM that had seen better days. Other than the typewriter and a current self-help paperback about stock market investments, the desk was bare.

"I'm the one who found Blake on Sunday night," said Charlie, plunging into his subject. "He had asked me to meet him but didn't say why and I wondered if you had any idea."

"Do you gamble?" asked Mrs. Hatcher.

"Not really."

"Then I can't say. Mr. Moss and I spoke as little as possible."

"Do you know what cases he was working on?" Charlie wished Mrs. Hatcher would sit down. She was as tall as he was—about five ten—and he kept thinking she wanted to hit him.

"Are you just going to ask the same questions as the police?"

"Not necessarily," said Charlie. He hadn't decided exactly what he was doing at Moss's office, apart from avoiding the mess at the Bentley, but no matter how guilty he felt about being late for his meeting with Moss, he saw no point in duplicating the efforts of Lieutenant Melchuk.

Mrs. Hatcher was thrusting a sheet of paper at him and shaking it so it fluttered. "Here are the cases he was working on. I gave the same list to the sergeant from Cohoes."

Charlie glanced at the paper. It seemed that Moss was doing a lot of insurance work. "And had he said anything about poetry?" Charlie asked.

Mrs. Hatcher stared at Charlie as if he had made an off-color suggestion. "Poetry?"

"He said that the case he was working on concerned poetry."

"In all our time together," said Mrs. Hatcher, "Mr. Moss never said a word about poetry. He was not that sort of man."

"What about friends," asked Charlie. "Do you know who his friends were or business associates or girlfriends or who his bookie was?"

"I knew nothing of that side of his life. He had an address book and the police took it. Other than that I feel that Mr. Moss had few friends."

Charlie wondered if Moss would have kept his bookie's number in his address book. "But people called him," said Charlie. "His bookie, a girlfriend or two. You must have written down their numbers."

"Perhaps I did."

Mrs. Hatcher was staring at Charlie fixedly and at first he couldn't understand her intention. Then he withdrew his wallet and placed a twenty dollar bill on her paperback about stock market investments. Mrs. Hatcher's fingers closed around the bill and she slipped it between the pages of her book. Then she took a pad from the desk, wrote down two names and two telephone numbers, ripped off the top sheet, and gave it to Charlie.

"The first I believe is a gambling associate and the second is a woman. Both have been calling."

"Did you give these to the police?" he asked.

"They telephoned after the police had been here."

Charlie stepped back toward the door. It was too cold in the office and the air smelled of disinfectant. He wanted to get back outside. "I'll check with you later," he said. "Someone else might have telephoned."

Mrs. Hatcher appeared not to have heard and for a second Charlie wondered if she had been struck deaf and dumb. Then he took another twenty from his wallet and laid it on the paperback. Again she took the bill and slipped it into the book and it struck Charlie that the book had eaten his twenty dollar bill.

Mrs. Hatcher looked at him and twisted her mouth into a facial contortion which Charlie belatedly realized was a smile. "Trust me," she said.

Charlie knew the bookie, Pinkie Schwartz, or at least knew him by reputation. Steady and dependable, that was how he was described. It occurred to Charlie that people looked for the same qualities in a bookie that they looked for in a dentist or a tax accountant or an undertaker. Nothing flashy. Although not a gambler himself, Charlie had a fascination with gambling—horses, cards, numbers, dice. He knew that with little effort he could turn his life over to that sort of speculation. It had happened to his father; it had happened to one of his cousins. And Charlie believed he knew what it was like to be driven by such a passion, to let something else make all the decisions in his life. The temptation was sometimes so powerful that it was like a big man standing behind him. In the same way, Charlie felt he could turn his life over to drinking or romance—as if his life were a cramped house that he longed to escape from. But he also knew that such a capitulation would only create wreckage and he had a fear of wreckage. So he lived at the borders of gambling, of a fast life that he could see into but was careful to avoid for himself. But perhaps that was no longer true about romance since the image of Janey Burris would often sweep across his mind and carry everything away with it. Wasn't it because of his wish to be with her that he had been late to his meeting with Blake Moss?

As for horse racing, this Tuesday was August 2 and tomorrow was the beginning of four weeks of thoroughbred racing at the flat track in Saratoga—flats by day, trots by night. Charlie wanted to be there.

He was not a good handicapper. No matter how much he studied the horses, he was still an impulse bettor who leapt to his decisions because of the cheerfulness of the jockey or the beauty of the horse. Indeed, he was often more successful if he didn't go to the track, if he made his choices in a darkened room with nothing but the official program and a copy of *Racing Form*. But he loved the track, loved all the little conversations with his fellow handicappers that invariably began with the question: "Well, whaddaya think?" and each year he gave himself about one hundred and fifty bucks and six visits or for as long as his money held out. But this year he wasn't even sure he'd make the opener, or that's what it looked like, what with Blake Moss on one hand and that mess at the Bentley on the other.

It was noon. Before driving downtown to look for Pinkie Schwartz, Charlie stopped at a sub shop and bought himself a turkey Italian, a type of sandwich that always made him feel vaguely cannibalistic. He bought turkey because all this rushing around was going to make him miss his daily swim at the Saratoga YMCA and he imagined that turkey had fewer calories than the pastrami for which he yearned. And he went to a small sub shop because he disliked the chains—the McDonalds and Wendy's, great corporations with executives who lived in dark over-sized Tudor houses in the suburbs of midwestern cities. At Mack's Sub Shop the money went to Mack, but, as Charlie drove across Albany, drops of olive oil dripped from his sandwich onto the pants of his rumpled seersucker suit and he thought he would have been smarter to skip lunch altogether.

For that matter, perhaps he would have been smarter simply to stay in Saratoga. Charlie couldn't decide how much his activities in Albany had to do with Blake Moss and how much with the Bentley being robbed. He had already talked to his mother and knew how upset she was. And he had also talked to Harvey Peterson, Director of Public Safety in Saratoga, and knew there were no leads, no witnesses, and no sympathy. "Of course you got robbed," Peterson had said. "My advice is to get rid of that Plotz guy. He's a loose cannon."

"What do you mean?" asked Charlie.

"I mean he's big trouble."

Charlie had yet to speak to Victor. Every time he called the hotel he was told that Victor was busy chasing down a lead. Then that morning Charlie learned that his cousins wanted to speak with him: three older and successful Saratoga businessmen who had spent their lives trying to convince Charlie that he was the moral equivalent of used chewing gum. No wonder he had run down to Albany. And now here he was with olive oil stains on his pants.

Pinkie Schwartz had an office in a run-down building on Steuben, a few blocks behind City Hall. Ostensibly, Schwartz sold insurance but the walls of his office displayed pictures of race horses and basketball players and there was a large poster which advertised discounted vacations in Las Vegas showing happy chorus girls kicking up their legs. Schwartz was a small porky man with wisps of gray hair over his mottled dome and a shiny blue suit which fitted him like Saran Wrap. He leaned across his newspaper littered desk and gave Charlie a limp handshake, offering only the tips of three fingers.

"I know you," said Schwartz, "you used to be a cop in Saratoga."

"For twenty years," said Charlie, sitting down on a straight chair.

"You busted me once in a crap game, me and my pal Maximum Tubbs. How's he getting on?"

Charlie had no memory of the event, although Tubbs was now a good friend. He was an elderly gambler who had known Charlie's father. "We play a lot of gin rummy for nickels."

"He must be getting soft," said Schwartz.

"I've got some questions about Blake Moss," said Charlie, again noticing the olive oil stains on his pants. It looked like he had peed himself. He crossed his legs, trying to cover the stains.

"I just read that he passed away," said Schwartz, patting one of the newspapers on his desk.

"He might have had some help," said Charlie. "He told me he was working on something that concerned poetry. Did he talk to you much? Do you have any idea what that might have been?"

Schwartz began looking through the newspapers. "Poetry, that's a coincidence," he said. "And you're Bradshaw too. You related to that lady who owns the hotel that got robbed?"

"What about it?" asked Charlie.

Pinkie Schwartz held out the newspaper. "You seen the *Saratogian*?" The phone began ringing. Schwartz answered it and began taking down numbers for the daily double the next day at Saratoga.

Charlie put on his reading glasses and an inauspicious headline emerged out of the blur: BENTLEY HOTEL ROOM ROBBED. Then he saw the poem.

> *They are but fools*
> *Who leave their jewels*
> *Where thieves like me can take them.*
> *But they make me rich*
> *So I won't bitch—*
> *For their kindness I do thank them.*

A diamond necklace worth twenty thousand dollars had been stolen from the room of a Mrs. Bigalow. Police had no clues and no suspects. Chief Peterson was quoted as saying that security at the hotel had been lax.

Charlie had known that an article would appear but he hated to see it on page one and he felt badly about those harsh words concerning hotel security. "Oh, no," he said. "Poor Victor."

Schwartz hung up the phone. "I take it you know the folks involved."

"She's my mother," said Charlie.

"Something like that doesn't do a hotel any good," said Schwartz. "Funny about the poetry, though."

"What about Blake Moss?" asked Charlie. Despite his question, Charlie was still brooding about the robbery at the Bentley. Was it fair to be down here in Albany while his best friend was getting yelled at in Saratoga? He would have to talk to Victor as soon as he got back.

Schwartz had retrieved the newspaper and was standing over it shaking his head. "Blake Moss, I been taking his bets off and on for about two years. He was never what you'd call a chummy guy. Like he acted like a soldier, maybe a general. Bossy, you know what I mean? For the past year he's been on the phone to me about twenty times a week. Sometimes he wins, sometimes he loses. Mostly he loses." Schwartz sat back down, took out a cigar, and began licking it from one end to the other. "In the past week or so he's only called a couple of times. He said he'd been having trouble getting to the phone. I asked if he'd got himself a pretty girl and he said no, he'd been spending all his time with old folks."

"Did he say what he meant?" asked Charlie.

"I didn't ask. The less you know, the less you get in trouble." Schwartz held the cigar up to the light to make sure it was wet all over, then he struck a match and lit it. A smell like burning socks filled the small office.

"And he didn't say anything about poetry?" asked Charlie.

"Not to me he didn't. Maybe he knew something about that hotel robbery."

"It seems unlikely," said Charlie, wondering if it really was. "I mean, the robbery hadn't occurred yet."

"But maybe he knew about it."

They talked about this for a while, then Charlie told Schwartz that the Cohoes police might drop by for a chat and Schwartz said he didn't care a green pickle if they did. Some of his best friends were cops. Then they talked about the opening day at the track and how they both would like to be there, sitting in the clubhouse with their feet up and going over the program. Post time was in twenty-four hours. A crowd of thirty thousand was expected. The stakes race was the Schuylerville and Schwartz said he had a hot tip on a two-year-old filly named Dipsi-Doodle.

"I never get out of this damned place," said Schwartz. "Why don't you come back tomorrow and we'll hear it on the radio. I'll get a six pack."

Charlie got to his feet. The smell of the cigar was turning his stomach. "Maybe I will if I'm not working and I can't get to the track." He took out his wallet. "Here's ten bucks for Dipsi-Doodle to win."

Schwartz held the edges of the bill with his fingertips as if it were too hot to handle, then he snapped it several times. "You don't want to make it a hundred?"

"I'd be nervous all day," said Charlie.

Blake Moss's girlfriend taught aerobics at the Albany YMCA. Her name was Patti Bifcatelli.

"They call me Patti Beefcake, but I don't care," she told Charlie, flexing her muscles and making her skin ripple beneath her pink leotard. They stood in a corner of the gym. The air smelled of chlorine from the pool and it again reminded Charlie that he had missed his daily swim.

"I wanted to talk to you about Blake," said Charlie.

Patti covered her face with both hands, then dragged her fingers across her cheeks, pulling down her eyes and distorting her features. The gesture was more dramatic than woeful. Her fingernails were dark purple and extended the length of each of her fingers by about an inch. Although sad, Patti Bifcatelli didn't seem stricken. She was a dark brunette in her early thirties whose body was so well conditioned that it appeared to have been made from hard pink plastic.

"Wasn't that a shame? The cops from Cohoes called me yesterday morning. I haven't been able to do a thing since. Who would have thought it, a heart attack at his age?"

"I was supposed to meet him on Sunday night," said Charlie, deciding not to mention the possibility of murder. "He said he wanted to talk to me about something concerning poetry. Do you have any idea what that might have been?"

Patti wrinkled her brow. Several men were playing basketball and the sharp squeak of their shoes on the gym floor sounded like demented birds. Charlie was keenly aware of the olive oil stains on his crotch and he stood slightly bent with his hands hanging forward just to cover them.

"You know, Blake told me he was going to a poetry reading last week. I was surprised. I mean, he never seemed like that kind of guy. And after that he was sort of hard to get a hold of. He even broke a date. I knew he was working on something important because he'd told me, but I never had any idea what it was."

There were mirrors along the wall and, catching sight of himself, Charlie saw that by leaning forward and holding his hands in front of himself, he was standing exactly like a gorilla. He straightened up and folded his arms. To hell with the stains. "What had he told you?" he asked.

"He said I might be seeing him around town with another woman but I shouldn't worry because it was connected to a case he was working on. Actually I didn't care. I mean, Blake had been getting too serious and I was looking for some way to put distance between us. He'd even started sending me flowers, can you believe it?" As she talked Patti Bifcatelli kept stretching and bouncing on her toes, making her hard body even harder.

"Do you know anything about this woman?" asked Charlie.

"Nothing except that he called her Betsy."

"And do you know where she worked?"

"I have no idea."

"Did he say anything about spending a lot of time with old people?"

"No, why should he say anything like that?"

"He'd mentioned it to someone. Do you think he went with this Betsy to the poetry reading?"

"Maybe. I mean, I can't see Blake going to a poetry reading by himself."

It occurred to Charlie that he had never gone to a poetry reading either. He simply couldn't imagine it. "Did he ever talk about the poetry reading again?"

"No. I hardly saw him after that. He'd gotten real busy. But when he first mentioned it, it wasn't because he thought it was important or anything. It was just that he saw it as an odd thing for him to be doing."

After leaving Patti Bifcatelli, Charlie began to check out the cases that Moss had been working on. Mostly he did it from the phone in the lobby of the YMCA but it was frustrating work because the person he wanted often wasn't there or he got an answering machine. In each instance the Cohoes police had been there before him. Charlie talked to insurance investigators, adjusters, and a woman with a runaway husband. No one knew anything about poetry or Betsy or old folks. What struck Charlie, however, was that none of these clients had heard from Moss for the past week to ten days. Clearly, Moss had been working on something else during that time, but whatever it was, it wasn't on the list that Charlie had received from Mrs. Hatcher.

As he kept calling, Charlie was constantly aware of the smell of chlorine from the pool and even that the pool was open. But he hadn't brought his suit or goggles and in his impoverished state he couldn't justify buying new ones. At one point he went downstairs to look at the pool: six lanes and nearly empty. Charlie sighed and returned to the phone booth. He imagined that the fat globules of Albany already knew he had missed his swim and were floating toward him from all over the city just to stick themselves to his body.

Charlie was also tempted to call the Bentley and ask about the robbery. But he saw the Bentley as a place that was trying to over-complicate his life, entangle him with the wishes and complaints of his mother and cousins, lead him to pursue a course of action where he could do nothing right, where he would be so nervous and anxious that he would stumble into one blunder after another. Better to stay away, he thought, better not to get involved.

Around four Charlie drove out to the mall at Colonie where Moss had been investigating a series of thefts from a department store. It was one of those cases where the thief was most likely an employee and morale was terrible. The clerks snapped at each other and looked at Charlie suspiciously. Again no one knew anything about poetry or old folks. They hadn't seen Moss for over a week.

Afterward Charlie called Lieutenant Melchuk from a booth outside a shoe store. Melchuk wouldn't say much, just that his men had learned nothing to raise suspicions about Moss's death. "As far as we're concerned," he said, "it's still a natural death." He promised to keep one man working on it. Melchuk didn't ask what Charlie had learned and Charlie said nothing about Pinkie Schwartz or Patti Bifcatelli. Maybe it was a natural death, thought Charlie, maybe Moss really had a heart attack. But again he wondered what Moss had wanted to show him and whether it had been a person or a thing.

Also from the mall Charlie telephoned Mrs. Hatcher, hoping to get her before she left at five. She had apparently been on her way out the door and was not pleased to hear from him.

"So did anyone call?" asked Charlie.

Mrs. Hatcher made a sort of hissing noise. "New York Telephone said they'd cut off service if he didn't pay his bill by Thursday."

It occurred to Charlie that she was teasing him in a rudimentary way. "And who else called?"

There was a slight pause. "A woman, if you want to know."

"Was it Betsy?"

Charlie could feel Mrs. Hatcher's disappointment. "If you're so smart, why bother me?"

"I thought you might have her phone number."

Mrs. Hatcher said nothing for a moment. "She called half an hour ago. I didn't tell her he was dead."

"And her phone number?"

Mrs. Hatcher gave it to him. It was an Albany exchange.

"Did she say anything else?"

"Only to tell Mr. Moss that she had called. She seemed to think he was an accountant."

"Okay," said Charlie, "I'll talk to you tomorrow."

There was another hiss and the phone went dead.

Before Charlie could call the number, he had to get more quarters, which meant buying some inexpensive item in the drug store. He bought a pack of spearmint sugarless gum, then thought he should have bought spot remover instead. When he got back to the phone, a teenage girl was giggling into it. Charlie had to wait ten minutes. He chewed his gum, looked at the shoppers, and thought about how he disliked malls. There was something about the lights which made his eyes burn.

It was after five when he at last made his call. The phone rang six times, then was answered by a tremulous voice. Charlie asked for

Betsy and was told she had left for the day. He asked for her home phone number. The tremulous voice explained that it was unlisted and couldn't be given out.

"And who am I talking to?" asked Charlie. "I mean, where does she work?"

"This is Long Meadows," said the voice. "Miss Thomas is our social director."

"And what is Long Meadows?" asked Charlie.

The person on the other end of the line seemed to have trouble breathing. "It is a retirement community," said the voice. "We are mostly very quiet here."

3

Victor leaned forward over his Jack Daniels Manhattan so his gray tie trailed across the glass. There was a sadness in his eyes which Charlie hadn't seen before. "The worst thing, Charlie, is that Mrs. Bigalow moved out. You should have heard what she said about me."

Charlie felt sympathetic. He too had often felt a victim of romantic feelings. It was Tuesday evening and they were sitting in the bar of the Bentley. "You liked her?"

"She had hooters designed by John Philip Sousa. A tuba would of felt chagrined."

"But what about the theft?" asked Charlie, trying to keep the exasperation out of his voice. "Have you made any progress?"

Victor sighed. "There's not much to do. The police poked around but didn't bother to fingerprint. You know what the locks are like here. It would take two seconds to get through a door. The thief was probably in and out in no time. Your mother's had two cancellations since the robbery and some old couple checked out. That poem in the paper didn't help matters." Victor noticed the tip of his tie floating in his glass, removed it, and began sucking it noisily.

Charlie had seen his mother earlier. Mabel Bradshaw had not been happy and wanted him to drop everything and come back to the hotel. Charlie had refused. It amazed him that even though he had been an adult for more years than he cared to calculate, whenever he was with his mother he became a sullen teenager again. He hated working in the hotel. But the difficulty was that Mabel Bradshaw didn't trust Victor. Although charmed by him, she doubted his skills as a detective. Her three nephews, Charlie's cousins, supported her in this. They, after all, had been trying to get Victor out of the hotel for years. He wasn't the right class and he talked too loudly. These men all felt that the renaissance which Saratoga had enjoyed since the early seventies owed a lot to their efforts. For Charlie his cousins had always been trouble.

At best Charlie had gotten his mother to agree to hire an assistant for Victor, Rico Medioli, an ex-con whom Charlie had employed years before when he was head of security at Lorelei Stables. Rico was now upstairs patrolling the halls. He was about five foot five and not only had the shape of a bowling ball but the hardness as well. Charlie imagined Rico silently rolling along, eager to bash any intruder who crossed his path. Charlie had also convinced his mother to install new locks which could be opened with an electronically coded plastic card and which could be changed with each new guest. Those, however, wouldn't be going in for at least a week.

"What about back doors and side doors?" asked Charlie.

Victor smoothed his gray tie down against his gray shirt and avoided looking Charlie in the eye. "Hey, Charlie, security was lax, just like Peterson said. I mean, we'd never had any trouble. Now we got this place as tight as a drum. Drop the whole fuckin' place into Saratoga Lake and it would float. That robbery was a one-shot deal and after a week or so people will forget about it."

Charlie disliked speculating optimistically about the future. It always brought bad luck. As he sipped his Rolling Rock, he wanted to touch wood but the bar at the Bentley was art deco and everything was plastic.

"By the way," said Victor, "did Chief Peterson get a hold of you?"

"No, what did he want?"

"He said he wanted to talk to you about the Phoenix Colony. Isn't that the place for artists? Maybe some beautiful bimbo painter wants you to pose nude."

"Maybe," said Charlie. He considered calling Peterson, then decided to wait. If Peterson really wanted him, he'd find him soon enough.

"So what about this Albany thing?" asked Victor.

"I'll go down tomorrow and talk to this Betsy at Long Meadows."

"And that's some kind of retirement place?"

"Right."

"I could use some of that myself. Who's paying you?"

"I guess I am."

"You living off your credit cards again?" asked Victor.

"Just about." Charlie didn't want to talk about money.

"I thought Moss tried to kill you once."

"He didn't really try, he just wanted to."

"Hey, he's dead and you're still hitting the bricks. Send him some flowers and let it go."

"It's more complicated than that," said Charlie, getting to his feet. It was nine o'clock and he wanted to see Janey Burris before it got too late.

"Complications keep you poor," said Victor.

Janey Burris lived on the west side of Saratoga near the train station. A few minutes after leaving Victor, Charlie parked his Renault in front of her large run-down Victorian house and hurried up the walk. Although Janey had a husband—a man named Dumkowski—he had disappeared a year and a half earlier and his only contact since had been a postcard from a small town in western Australia.

"He always liked sheep," Janey had said.

Charlie had been struck that the front of the postcard had shown a whole field of sheep.

This evening Janey was in the kitchen reading a mystery novel about Navaho Indians while her three daughters—ages seven, nine, and eleven—were in the living room watching the last of some TV show on whales. The walls of the kitchen were covered with her kids' brightly colored watercolors. Animals were the big favorites, especially horses and spotted dogs, but there were also several houses, and a picture of their mommy in her white nurse's uniform.

"Actually," said Janey, "I've been fixing to smash that TV for a year. I keep using it as a baby sitter. Who ever heard of Dan Rather as a baby sitter? You feel like some whiskey?"

"I don't mind if I do," said Charlie sitting down at the kitchen table. It had a white enamel top and was bare except for Janey's book and a stethoscope.

Janey nodded toward it. "I brought it from the hospital so the kids could hear their hearts but they use it mostly on the cat."

Janey walked to the cupboard. She wore blue gym shorts from the Saratoga YMCA and a yellow T-shirt advertising a 10-K race she had run in that summer. Janey was a thin attractive woman in her early forties with short black hair that stuck out in all directions. Pouring out a double shot of Jim Beam green, she dropped in a couple of ice cubes and set it on the table. As she got him his drink, Charlie told her what he had been doing in Albany: the bookie, Patti Beefcake, and the police. When he talked about Moss, Charlie again thought of the merry-go-round, could even hear the Scott Joplin rag.

"Is there any chance that Moss really had a heart attack?" asked Janey.

"I suppose it's possible. It just seems unlikely. I'll go back tomorrow but I can't keep this up for long. I mean, I'm broke."

"I bet your mother would hire you to find the guy who robbed the hotel."

"Working for my mother would give me an ulcer," said Charlie, wondering if it were true. "You ever heard of Black Bart?"

"Sounds like the name of a cigar," said Janey, sitting down again. As she passed behind Charlie she had ruffled his hair and he was smoothing it down again.

"His real name was C.E. Boles and he was from Decatur, Illinois. Then he changed his name to C.E. Bolton when he was living in San Francisco. He started robbing stages when he was older than I am and robbed twenty-eight owned by Wells Fargo and a bunch of others too. All this was in California between 1875 and 1883. He'd always stop the stage at the top of a steep hill when the horses had slowed down. He'd be wearing a long white linen duster and had a flour sack with eye-slits over his head. He'd say, 'Throw down the box' and he'd point a double-barreled shotgun at the driver just to show he meant business. He never shot it, though. He made about forty thousand out of Wells Fargo. One August in 1877 he robbed the stage near Fort Ross and the posse later found a poem in the empty strong-box. It said,

> *I've labored long and hard for bread*
> *For honor and for riches,*
> *But on my corns too long you've tread*
> *You fine haired sons of bitches.*

"He signed the poem 'Black Bart, the PO EIGHT.' I don't think anyone knows what 'PO EIGHT' means. Anyway, why leave a poem?"

"Are you thinking of the person who robbed the hotel?" asked Janey. She had finished her whiskey and was sitting on the table swinging her leg.

"Sure. Why did he leave a poem?"

"Maybe as a joke."

"There's something too serious about it."

"Maybe he was a frustrated artist."

"Or just frustrated."

"Speaking of frustrated," said Janey, reaching out and touching Charlie's hand, "let's put those kids to bed so we can neck."

At eight o'clock Wednesday morning Charlie drove down to the Long Meadows Retirement Community in Loudonville just north of Albany and when Betsy Thomas arrived at nine he was there to meet her. She was a tall woman in her mid-thirties who wore a long khaki skirt and a long sleeved white blouse with ruffles around the collar. Her dark hair had a lot of gray and she wore no jewelry and very little makeup. She was rather plain looking and seemed to want to make herself look older than she really was. She still had not heard about Moss's death.

"A heart attack." Betsy Thomas put her hand over her mouth and sat down abruptly on the couch in her office. "But I'd just seen him that afternoon. We'd gone on a picnic out to Peebles Island. I'd made deviled eggs." Her face suddenly grew wrinkled, as if folding in on itself, and her eyes filled with tears. She took a lacy handkerchief from the pocket of her skirt and began wiping her eyes.

"I'm sorry," said Charlie. "I was supposed to meet him that night. When I got there, he was dead."

"Had he been sick?" Betsy Thomas blew her nose and sat up straight, trying unsuccessfully to push her grief away.

"No, but he was diabetic. The police think he went into insulin shock and then had a heart attack."

"He'd told me about the diabetes. It was a great trial for him."

"Had you known him long?" asked Charlie.

"Less than a month, but we had become very close." Here she stopped for a moment and stared down at her hands, while Charlie waited. He hated to see people cry. It made him feel so ineffectual.

It turned out that Moss had first met Betsy Thomas at a Friendly's Restaurant in Troy where she went for dinner by herself several times a week. She had seen him there almost three weeks ago. Then he appeared at her church, St. Michael's, and when he again went to Friendly's he recognized her and spoke to her. Betsy Thomas didn't know he was a private detective and Charlie didn't tell her. They had eaten together several times at Friendly's. Moss told her he was an accountant who had recently moved to Troy. He was a widower and quite shy, she said. They began to eat together regularly, went to several movies, and of course they met at church as well. Moss had also taken an interest in Long Meadows and had come to several activities here.

"He told me he'd been to a poetry reading," said Charlie.

"Yes, he loved it and he took such an interest in the participants." Betsy Thomas lowered her head as her voice choked again. On the walls of her office were many framed drawings and watercolors, mostly landscapes and pictures of flowers. They were rather primitive and Charlie assumed they had been done by people at Long Meadows. They reminded him of the watercolors of Janey Burris's kids and, as he thought about Janey, his heart took a little leap.

"He said there was one person whose poem he especially liked," said Charlie, getting back to business.

Betsy Thomas nodded energetically. "That must have been the little colors man. Blake spoke to him and asked to read the poem again. He was quite impressed by it."

"Colors man?" said Charlie.

"Ted Davis, he used to work at racetracks and take care of the jockeys' silks. And I guess he was a jockey as well. He's quite small."

"He told me about a jockey," said Charlie.

"Personally, I was surprised by how much Blake knew about the track, but he said he was a great reader and that it all came from Dick Francis, you know, the mystery writer?"

"I know the name," said Charlie. "And this Ted Davis is also a poet?"

"I don't know about that," said Betsy Thomas with a smile. "I'd organized a poetry contest among the residents, then a local Albany poet picked the five best poems. The winner received a copy of the Norton Anthology and everyone had the opportunity to read his or her poem. I think Ted Davis came in second."

"What was his poem about?" asked Charlie.

"We had a nurse who worked here who was very popular. She had a fatal accident. It was very sad. She fell down the back stairs and hit her head. All the guests were upset about it."

Charlie found himself suddenly attentive. "How terrible," he said.

"Yes, it happened late one evening and apparently she lay there for nearly an hour before she was found. The back stairs are very steep and residents are especially asked not to use them. She fell, then hit her head on the newel post supporting the banister. The doctor said that death must have been instantaneous. Mr. Vinner, he's the owner of Long Meadows, he was heartbroken."

"And when was this?" asked Charlie.

"Nearly a month ago, at the very beginning of July."

"Did the police look into it?"

Betsy Thomas seemed surprised. "Oh, it wasn't a matter for the police."

They both sat silently for a moment as if struck by the cruelty of fate, while Charlie wondered if his suspicion of death was unwarranted. After all, people died from natural and accidental causes all the time. It was only a side effect of Charlie's profession that led him to doubt the normal course of events, as if in a well-regulated world death could be stopped entirely, as if it were only murder that kept people from being immortal.

"I would like to talk to Ted Davis," said Charlie. "I'd hate to have him learn about Blake's death from a newspaper."

"That's very kind of you," said Betsy. "He's probably in the morning room right now. He likes to read the Racing Form right after breakfast. I'll take you there."

They left her office and went down a thickly carpeted hall toward the main part of the building. On the walls were photographs of group activities: elderly people having fun at Ping-Pong, dances, touring a local art museum, making crafts. Soft music came through speakers in the ceiling and it was almost with shock that Charlie realized it was the same Scott Joplin rag he had heard Sunday night. This version was being performed by an orchestra and while the music still reminded Charlie of musical yo-yos, they were very slow yo-yos.

The retirement community was in a Victorian mansion which had been renovated and expanded so that apart from the sitting rooms and parlors at the front of the house, the building seemed completely modern. Betsy Thomas told Charlie that the owner, Mr. Vinner, had taken it over five years before. There were seventy-five residents mostly in small apartments, although there were also rooms for those who needed special care. At the moment they had a staff of eighteen, but they were short-handed. Generally they had a staff of twenty.

"Long Meadows offers total care," said Betsy Thomas. "Usually there is a nurse on the premises twenty-four hours a day and several nurse's aides, as well as a doctor here in the morning. When a resident can no longer look after himself or herself, they move from the apartment to a room or small ward."

"So people die here?" asked Charlie.

"People die everywhere, Mr. Bradshaw. Some of our residents who have passed on have died here and some have died in a hospital. No one lasts forever."

Ted Davis was a wizened and diminutive old man whose face closely resembled a peach pit. He sat half buried in a large wing chair with a rug over his lap even though the day was warm. It was a large sunny room with long white curtains. About half a dozen old people were reading newspapers or just looking out the window. Ted Davis wore a green turtleneck sweater and was completely bald. Betsy had told Charlie that Davis was eighty-seven. He seemed silent and suspicious but when he learned that Charlie came from Saratoga he cheered up.

"That's where I should be heading right now," he said, leaning forward and gripping Charlie's hand with his own bird-like claw. "I worked in the colors room for twenty years and I rode as a jock as well. Ask me about any of those old guys. Steve Brooks, Eddie Arcaro. My last season in the colors room was when Shoe won the Travers on Damascus in sixty-seven. Over twenty-five hundred silks I had to take care of. You kept moving from the time of the first race and you didn't stop. It's easy now. All those silks are nylon and you just toss 'em in the wash. But then they were the real thing and had to be dry-cleaned. I started out riding in 1918 and rode in the Belmont Stakes when Man o' War beat Donnacona by twenty lengths and me by thirty. I rode for Woody Stephens during the war. I rode for Jacob Hirsch and I rode for Mr. Fitz."

"Blake Moss knew a lot about horse racing," said Charlie.

Ted Davis nodded energetically. "He sure did. He couldn't wait for Saratoga to start up."

Charlie sat in a chair beside Ted Davis and Betsy stood behind him. Briefly, Charlie explained that Blake Moss had had a heart attack on Sunday night. Of course he had no idea what Davis's response might be. Maybe shock, maybe grief, maybe nothing. What surprised Charlie was that Davis reacted with suspicion.

"He seemed all right to me."

"A heart attack can be very sudden," said Charlie.

"And he was young. Was anyone around when he died?" Davis

had a high tenor voice and he leaned toward Charlie when he spoke.

"He was alone. He had probably been dead about half an hour when I got there."

"Why were you meeting him in such a place?" asked Davis.

"We were going to get a late dinner. It seemed easier to go in one car."

"And he died of a heart attack?"

"That's what the autopsy said." Charlie wished he could talk to Davis alone. He didn't want Miss Thomas to know that Moss had been a detective because she would immediately realize that she had not been his primary interest; that, in fact, he had hunted her out because of Long Meadows. For that matter, she would probably guess that Charlie was a detective as well. Charlie had no idea why Moss wanted to gain access to Long Meadows but the poem seemed part of it, while Ted Davis's suspicion was itself suspicious.

"Blake told me that you'd written a poem he liked," said Charlie.

Davis's suspicion changed to embarrassment. "I enjoy writing poetry. It's like a puzzle. And it's about the only thing I can do that doesn't upset my stomach or make my body ache. I'm just a beginner though."

"I'd like to see the poem," said Charlie.

Again there was a quick look of suspicion. "You read poetry?"

"Well, it's one of the last things that Blake told me about so I'm curious."

"It's a very good poem," said Betsy Thomas. "It came in second in our contest."

"I'll go get it," said Davis. "It's in my room upstairs." He got up slowly. Davis was about five feet tall and slightly stooped. Charlie watched him limp off toward the corridor.

"I sometimes think," said Betsy Thomas, "that if people like Ted had discovered poetry earlier, their whole lives might have been different."

"How long have you worked here?" asked Charlie.

Betsy sat down on a chair next to Charlie. "I've been here two years. It's a wonderful place. The residents are so bright and eager. Every day has been enjoyable."

"And Mr. Vinner, what's he like?"

"Warm, generous, he's been a wonderful man to work for."

Again Charlie wondered what Moss had been investigating. He was struck that Long Meadows was not on Moss's current list of cases. Had he not had time to record it or was there something secret about it? And he wondered again what sort of work Moss had had for him. Somehow Charlie suspected it concerned the ex-jockey and colors man. Was it only coincidence that linked them both to Saratoga? Surely there were local detectives who Moss could have hired.

Ted Davis returned several minutes later. "I'm not quick like I used to be. I got banged up in the gate in forty-six and all those pains have come back to haunt me." He held out a piece of paper. "Here's the poem." He pronounced it as a one syllable word: pome.

Charlie took his reading glasses from his jacket pocket and put them on.

The Loss of Janice Mitchell

Her hair, her eyes, the way she wore her clothes, her smile,
her gentle manner—all proclaimed she was our friend,
the one who cared for us, the one who'd walk a mile
to make us laugh, and who our age could never offend.

But now the youngest and the best has met her end.
What happened that night, and did she really fall? What shall
we think of how she died and who did she offend?
So what, it's done, she's gone: how awful we all feel.

Charlie was silent for a moment. "It's very moving," he said at last.

"Hexameters," said Davis.

"Pardon me?"

"It's written in iambic hexameter. You know, 'That, like a wounded snake, drags its slow length along?' That's Pope."

Charlie didn't know what Davis was talking about. "What do you mean by the end here? Did she really know something?"

Davis gave Charlie a quick look. "Maybe."

"That's ridiculous," interrupted Betsy Thomas. "Her death was an accident. You know that perfectly well, Ted Davis. You should be ashamed of yourself."

Charlie was struck by her indignation. She had gotten to her feet and was standing by Davis's chair.

"She'd been down those stairs a thousand times," said Davis. "And something had been bothering her, something she didn't want to talk about."

Miss Thomas almost sparkled with anger. "Nonsense. It was dark and she was in a hurry. I've nearly slipped there myself."

Davis turned back to Charlie. " 'So what, it's done, she's gone,' " he quoted. "You know, I used to have another last line, but Betsy asked me to change it. It went: " 'What caused the accident, what does her death conceal?' "

He was talking quietly but even so Charlie felt that several other people in the room were listening. "Are you suggesting she was murdered?" Charlie tried to keep his tone completely flat so as not to make Betsy Thomas suspicious.

"It's strange, that's all."

"Did Blake Moss know both endings?"

"Yes, I told him the other one."

"And what did he say?"

"He was interested, really interested, and now he's dead as well."

"Mr. Davis," said Miss Thomas in a furious whisper, "what you're saying could hurt Long Meadows. Janice Mitchell slipped and fell."

"Nobody saw it happen."

"But that doesn't mean she was pushed." Betsy Thomas was still standing. There was nothing suspicious or guilty about her anger. She seemed genuinely indignant.

"Had she worked here long?" asked Charlie.

"About a year," said Davis. "Just long enough to get in trouble with someone."

"Mr. Davis, stop that!" said Betsy Thomas. She stepped forward until she stood between Charlie and the ex-jockey. "Since you seem unable to control yourself, I think we'd better leave you and your imagination to yourselves."

Charlie didn't want to go, but he didn't see how he could stay without rousing suspicion. He stood up, then nodded toward the *Racing Form*. "I take it you still follow the races?"

Davis dug under the blanket and pulled out a Sony Walkman. "I'm going to hear every minute of Saratoga right in this chair."

"You got any good advice for the Schuylerville Stakes?"

"Dipsi-Doodle. Right now he's five to one."

"I've got ten bucks on him," said Charlie, suddenly grinning.

"Make it a hundred," said Davis. "I wish we could go up there together, sip gin and tonics, and watch our winners come home."

"My sentiments exactly," said Charlie, reaching out to shake Davis's hand.

Moments later, as Charlie was walking down the hall with Betsy Thomas, she took his arm and began whispering at him with a sort of urgent hiss. "I hope you realize why he told you all that foolishness. He's bored, they're all bored. They sit and have nothing to do and they make up stories. I spend all my time trying to think up things to amuse them, but they're still bored. Nothing does any good. It's a kind of craziness."

"He didn't seem crazy," said Charlie.

"Boredom makes them crazy. They think too much. I've worked in many retirement communities and this is the nicest. Mr. Vinner is very gentle, very kind. That Ted Davis is just lucky that he's not stuck in a dingy room somewhere."

As they approached the main entrance, Miss Thomas pointed toward a well dressed, middle-aged man who was striding briskly through the front door. "There's Mr. Vinner now. Would you like to meet him?"

"I'd be happy to," said Charlie. He was struck by how cheerful the man seemed, how good-humored.

Betsy hurried forward to intercept him. "Mr. Vinner, could you give me a moment? I'd like you to meet someone."

She introduced Charlie as a friend of Blake Moss. Blake was dead, she told Vinner. He had died of a heart attack on Sunday night. Vinner's smile faded. "Oh, no," he said, "what a shame. How sad for you, Betsy." He put his arm around Betsy Thomas and again her eyes filled with tears. Vinner was a handsome man with thick silver gray hair. He had a wide face and thick glasses with black frames which magnified his blue eyes, making them seem particularly sympathetic. Keeping his arm around Betsy Thomas, he hugged her to him.

"Mr. Bradshaw just told me about it this morning," said Betsy. "And we've been talking to Ted Davis as well. Blake especially liked him."

"And he liked Blake," said Vinner. "We all did. This is a terrible thing."

They stood by the door. Charlie kept nodding his head and looking down at the carpet. He wished there was some way to talk to Ted Davis again.

"Did you work with Blake?" asked Vinner.

"No," said Charlie, "he was just a friend. We were supposed to have dinner on Sunday night." Charlie wondered if Vinner knew that Moss was a private detective.

"Death is a terrible leveler," said Vinner. "It takes the good with the bad. It shocks us all. We had an awful death here just a month ago. A very popular nurse fell down the back stairs. All our guests have been upset about it."

"Ted Davis showed Mr. Bradshaw his poem," said Miss Thomas.

"Then you know about it. Ted was especially hurt. He and Janice were very close." Vinner became silent again and shook his head. "And now we've had a nurse's aide resign as well," he told Miss Thomas after a moment. "Agnes Gustines has left to have a baby. She was supposed to stay until September but changed her mind. We're going to be even more short-handed until her replacement arrives."

Charlie thought this a good moment to leave. He shook hands with both Vinner and Miss Thomas. It was clear that the woman had a kind of crush on Vinner. Presumably Vinner also knew of the ex-jockey's suspicions. If so, they didn't seem to bother him. As Charlie walked to his car, he looked back. Betsy Thomas stood by the door and when she saw him turn, she waved. Glancing toward the morning room, Charlie saw Ted Davis standing by the window, watching him go. Charlie started to wave, then decided against it.

He eased his Renault into gear and drove out of the lot. The morning was sunny and warm with a slight breeze carrying the smells of freshly cut grass. The grounds of Long Meadows were immaculate. Old people sat on benches and walked along the paths. From the front, the building was a three-story white Victorian with a cupola on top. Two new white clapboard additions extended from the back. Charlie turned south on Loudon Road. On his left behind a row of pines was the green expanse of Wolferts Roost Country Club. Two balding red-faced men in a red golf cart bounced sedately across the grass, their golf bags jostling in the back. Charlie glanced in his mirror. When he turned, he had noticed a blue Chevrolet Nova follow him out of the parking lot. The car was now about thirty yards behind him. Charlie turned left on Northern Boulevard by Albany Memorial Hospital. The Chevrolet turned as well. Charlie wondered if his job was making him too suspicious. In any case, he turned right on Shaker Road to see what would happen. Nothing happened. The Chevrolet kept going straight.

An hour later Charlie was in the office of Lieutenant Bob Boland of the Albany Police Department. They had known each other for some years and that spring had fished the Battenkill for trout between Arlington and Greenwich. Charlie didn't much like fishing and had caught nothing but a bad cold, but he liked Boland. He was a tall man of Charlie's age, almost bald and with a big beer belly. As Charlie told him about the deaths of Blake Moss and Janice Mitchell, he took some notes but otherwise he listened without interruption.

"This Lieutenant Melchuk is in charge of the case in Cohoes," said Charlie, "or what case there is. I expect he's about to give up on it. I mean, maybe it's nothing at all. Maybe this Ted Davis is just bored like the woman says. But I think Moss was suspicious and I promise you that Moss wouldn't move an inch unless he had the hope of getting money from some place."

"Unlike you, right?" said Boland, grinning.

"No, I'm done with it. I don't have the access and I don't have a client. But I have a feeling that Moss wanted me to get into Long Meadows and maybe get to know this Ted Davis. Davis spent his whole life around the track and he's suspicious of anyone who didn't. My being from Saratoga was a plus. It meant he'd talk to me."

"But you don't know what Moss was working on."

"I've no idea. Maybe he wasn't working on anything. But he did make that comment about poetry and he had to be talking about Davis's poem, or at least it seems that way."

Boland rubbed the top of his bald head as if polishing it. "You got lots of possibilities but no proof."

"That's why I'm giving it to you. Just to wash my hands of it."

"We'll look into the nurse's death and run a check on Long Meadows. And I'll talk to Melchuk, but unless we have some motive or evidence that those deaths were other than natural or accidental, there's not much to be done."

"Perhaps I'll look around some more," said Charlie.

"And who's paying you?"

"I'll write it off as a gift," said Charlie. "You know, a charitable contribution."

That evening Charlie was again in the bar of the Bentley with Victor. He had returned to his office around noon to find his answering machine full of messages concerning an insurance fraud case he was working on. As a result, he had spent the afternoon searching for a green Porsche that supposedly had been burned but actually was sold. As he drove back and forth across Saratoga Charlie was painfully aware that this was the first day of racing and he wasn't at the track. Occasionally he would hear the crowd or the bugler calling the horses to post. Then, late in the afternoon, he stopped at the news and tobacco shop across from the Bentley and learned that Dipsi-Doodle had indeed won the Schuylerville Stakes at odds of six to one. It occurred to Charlie that if he had put a hundred bucks on the horse he could have had his roof fixed and maybe even have gone on vacation.

"What'd Dipsi-Doodle look like?" Charlie asked the clerk.

"A horse, man. You know, four hooves, a tail, a mane. Probably she was brown."

Charlie continued his researches into the disappeared Porsche but he felt dissatisfied. Additionally, the memory of Long Meadows kept returning to him and he kept thinking of Ted Davis listening to the races on his Walkman. When he saw Victor that evening, Charlie was still brooding about the jockey and the dead nurse.

"It could be," he said, "that the nurse was killed because she knew something she shouldn't. And it could be that Moss discovered what she knew. Would he go to the police or would he try blackmail? He might easily try blackmail, don't you think?"

Victor had been cutting his fingernails with the scissors of a Swiss Army knife, giving the operation all the care normally given to the production of great works of art. "Could, could, could," he said. "Will you cut this shit? You're just guessing and you're digging yourself a nasty hole. Now I got a real crime. Who robbed Mrs. Bigalow. Why don't you work on that for a while? It would make your old mother happy."

"I'm supposed to be good at guess work," said Charlie.

"If you're so hot, why don't you figure out what Peterson wants."

"What do you mean?"

"He's called twice looking for you. And he called yesterday as well. Remember? He said it had to do with that artists' colony. Well, you're the artist of speculation. Maybe they need you to speculate about something."

"Ridiculous," said Charlie.

But when Charlie got home around ten, he heard his phone ringing. He hurriedly unlocked his front door, then dashed for the phone. It was Chief Peterson.

"Where the hell you been?"

"Down in Albany."

"Well, I got a job for you. Be in your office at nine."

"What kind of job?" Charlie was out of breath and he tilted the phone up so he wouldn't breathe heavily into Peterson's ear.

"An artist, I know a guy who wants to hire an artist."

"What kind of artist?"

"Maybe a painter, maybe a composer, maybe a poet."

"But I'm none of those things."

Peterson laughed and Charlie again moved the phone from his ear. "We'll see," said Peterson. "Just make sure you're in your office."

4

As Commissioner of Public Safety for Saratoga Springs, Harvey L. Peterson liked to keep his laughter private. After all, he was a serious man. But sometimes he couldn't help himself and now, as he stood in Charlie Bradshaw's office on Phila Street, he bent forward clutching his stomach and let forth one barking guffaw after another. As noises Charlie felt they resembled the backfires of ill-tuned automobiles. He glanced apologetically at the third man in his office, Arlo Webster, who was the director of the Phoenix Colony. Webster was a tall handsome fellow in his early forties. He wore glasses with thin tortoiseshell frames and moved like a dancer; as if his body were no more than a silk scarf, thought Charlie.

Peterson wiped away the tears with the back of his hand. "You can dye your hair pink," he said, gasping, "and wear a pink velvet suit. Isn't that what poets wear?" Here he began guffawing again and staggered across the room, until he half fell against the safe, which was empty except for Charlie's .38. "And you can carry a lily and wear black patent leather shoes that squeak." Again came the great humorous explosions. Or perhaps, thought Charlie, they were the noises that a human-sized frog might make.

"I only suggested that Mr. Bradshaw pose as a poet," said Webster, "because that would require the least evidence of expertise. It would be far easier to pretend to be a poet than to pretend to be a painter or composer."

"What about a novelist?" asked Charlie. He knew nothing about poetry, but at least he had read some novels. And, too, there seemed to be quite a lot of poetry around right at the moment.

"The novelists tend to stay in their studios and put in long hours," said Webster, "and one can always hear them typing. The poets also put in long hours but they wander around. And being a poet would probably give you greater access to Alexander Luft. After all, poetry is his subject."

"You'll have to get a quill," said Peterson, trying to crank up his laughter again, "and probably a beret." He was still leaning against Charlie's safe while Webster had the visitor's chair.

"What sort of person is Luft?" asked Charlie. Although there were times when he missed being a policeman, the smallest exposure to Peterson, his boss for ten years, was enough to scatter such feelings.

"He's very sure of himself," said Webster, "and he seems very cold. Although perhaps we are observing him under less than ideal circumstances."

In the two weeks that Luft had been at the Colony, the windshield of his Mazda had been smashed and his room had been vandalized twice. On the first occasion, his four published books of criticism had been turned into confetti and sprinkled across the floor. The second time, blood had been poured over his computer and a foot looking very much like a human foot had been left on the keyboard. The foot now stood on Charlie's desk like an offensive paperweight. It was made of pink plastic and spotted with blood: sheep's blood.

"The difficulty is that the Colony's endowment has been decreased by necessary repairs to the mansion," explained Webster, "and we are now more dependent on grants, gifts, and an annual fund-raising drive. It is the high seriousness of the work done at the Phoenix Colony which gives us the credibility to apply for these grants and raise the necessary funds to continue. These actions against Mr. Luft damage that credibility. So far they have been kept out of the papers, but if they continue, we could be in serious trouble."

"What about security?" asked Charlie. "Do you have guards?"

Webster uncrossed his legs and leaned forward. He wore a khaki suit that seemed specially tailored for his long body. As he spoke, he took off his glasses and polished them on his tie. "During the summer there is a guard at the gate. He knows the guests and doesn't bother them. A week ago, I hired two more. Unfortunately, the atmosphere at the Colony must be kept calm, even serene. The Colony is where artists come to write or paint or compose. We can't have security guards running all over the place. One guest has left already. She had the room next to Luft. You should have heard him scream on Sunday night. Believe me, that foot and the blood seemed quite authentic. This woman took one look them and packed her bags."

"How many guests are at the Phoenix Colony?" asked Charlie. He reached out and touched a toe of the foot; the plastic was cold and smooth. Peterson had wandered behind him and was now studying a framed portrait of Jesse James.

"There are thirty at the moment, plus a dozen people living on the grounds—the foreman and some of the grounds crew."

"And any of them could have done this?"

"Theoretically. The thing is that half the guests left at the end of the month and fifteen more arrived on Monday. I had hoped that these incidents might cease with the departure of those guests on Friday. Sunday's incident dispelled that hope."

"Are the buildings locked?" asked Charlie.

"Yes, but the keys are nearby and everyone knows where they're kept. For a while, I convinced myself that these acts were being committed by someone coming in from the outside, but that seems unlikely. It is also unlikely that it's being done by one of the staff. Consequently, it must be another guest."

"One of the fifteen left over from July," said Charlie.

"Thirteen, actually."

"Maybe it's two people," suggested Peterson, "someone who left and one of the new guests."

"That seems hard to credit," said Webster. "The Phoenix Colony has been an artists' colony since 1905. There has never been anything like this. People come to the Colony to work. Many of the greatest artists of the twentieth century have stayed there: Stravinsky, Faulkner, Skoyles. It is hard enough to think that one guest might be doing this, let alone two."

"How does Luft get along with the other guests?" asked Charlie.

"Not particularly well, but there have been extenuating circumstances. Yet even when he came he struck me as distant. Along with being a critic, he is also a reviewer and some of his reviews, especially of poets, have been extremely harsh."

"So you have guests who already might have a grudge against him?"

"We have six poets staying with us, including three left over from July. I haven't asked them about Luft. But he has also reviewed fiction and written art reviews as well. If the person carrying out these attacks is doing it in revenge for a bad review, then the field of suspects becomes rather expansive."

"The Phoenix Colony takes critics as well as artists?" asked Charlie. He didn't see how he could pretend to be a poet. Although he knew that Peterson had been mocking him, he found himself wondering whether he should buy a beret. But where could he get a beret in Saratoga?

"Not normally, but Luft is writing a critical biography of Wallace Stevens and we have admitted quite a few biographers in the past. He is also a powerful man who sits on many boards and committees. If he had not done very reputable work, we would never have considered accepting him, no matter how many boards he sat on. But given that reputable work it would have been difficult and perhaps even foolhardy to turn him down."

"How much longer is he supposed to stay at the Colony?" asked Charlie. The name Wallace Stevens rang no bells. He considered asking, but thought better of it. He took at quick look at Peterson who was standing by the window. Charlie guessed he didn't know who Wallace Stevens was, either.

"Luft is supposed to stay for four more weeks."

"So I would be expected to stay until the end of August?" asked Charlie. The prospect dismayed him. How could he go to the track? How could he see Janey Burris? On the other hand, he would be making two hundred a day plus expenses. But what about Blake Moss? He had little faith in the efficiency of the Cohoes police. Yet he wasn't being paid for that and he couldn't afford the time. Then he saw Blake Moss as he had looked in the scarlet merry-go-round wagon drawn by a pair of purple race horses. And again he heard the music.

"We are hoping you will discover the culprit quite soon," said Webster. "The important thing is that no one must know you're a private detective."

"You might even write some poems," said Peterson. "You know, roses are red, violets are blue. . . ."

"You'll have the room right next to Luft's," continued Webster. "He works there during the day, so I should think that would be a period when you needn't be so vigilant. There are also a lot of the staff around during the day. The difficult times are evenings."

"What about meal times?" asked Charlie.

"He eats breakfast in the dining room, then usually has lunch in his studio. The guests all receive lunch baskets. During breakfast and dinner one of the staff watches his room. In the evening the guests tend to sit around and talk. Sometimes there is music. There are Ping-Pong tables and a pool table in the barn. And of course many guests go into the performing arts center to see a concert or the ballet. What bothers me is that these attacks have been getting worse. That's why I asked Chief Peterson about a private detective."

"And I really have to pretend I'm a poet?" asked Charlie.

"That would seem easiest. Do you know anything about poetry?"

Charlie guessed he could recite all of "The Ballad of Jesse James," but that was the extent of his knowledge. "Not a bit."

"We always take some guests who don't have a national reputation but show a great deal of promise. You'll have to be one of those. And you'll have to be from some place other than Saratoga."

"What about Boston," said Charlie, thinking of the Red Sox.

"Too many of our guests come from that area."

"Detroit? I was there last year for a week."

"Perhaps a suburb. Royal Oak or Livonia."

"Livonia it is," said Charlie. "When do you want me there?"

"Come around four-thirty. It would be best to arrive by cab. Have a suitcase, a typewriter, some books. We always have a waiting list and I'll say that you are replacing the woman who left on Monday. I'll talk to you more when you get there. I'm sure you'll be fine."

"You have just time enough to dye your hair pink," said Peterson, "and maybe to write a couple of sonnets."

Charlie wondered if Wallace Stevens had written sonnets. Then he wondered what a sonnet was. Actually a man named Will Stevens had been deputy marshal of Longview, Texas, in the 1890's; and when Bill Dalton's gang had robbed the First National Bank of Longview, Will Stevens had shot down one of the gang members, an outlaw named Jim Wallace. Maybe, thought Charlie, he could write a poem about Jim Wallace and Will Stevens.

Shortly after Peterson and Arlo Webster had left, Charlie took his bag with his bathing suit and towel from the file cabinet, locked his office and set off across Congress Park to the YMCA in order to swim his daily mile. It was a warm sunny day and the town was jammed with people who had come for the track. The traffic on Broadway was bumper to bumper and tourists were swilling spring water as fast as they could get it down their throats.

Charlie had mixed feelings about Saratoga in August. On one hand, he loved the track; on the other hand, he hated the crowds. Wherever he went, he had to wait in line. The town tripled in size and the Northway from Albany was packed with cars. The only peaceful time was from about one to five-thirty when the races were going on. Then, after the ninth race, the town again swarmed with people eating, drinking, buying souvenirs, and honking their horns up and down Broadway. The merchants all raised their prices and nothing was easygoing anymore. Even the pool was crowded and Charlie had to contend with dozens of strange swimmers so that he felt like a salmon trying to make it upstream.

The locker room was crowded as well. The floor was covered with water and only the lockers with busted doors were still available. Charlie found one that would take a lock and hurriedly put on his suit: a black Speedo that let him imagine he was fast. His belly was the same size as yesterday: too big. Where had he gotten this thing? Sometimes it seemed that he was its creature, rather than the other way around, as if his belly made all the important decisions in his life.

Grabbing his towel and goggles, Charlie headed for the shower room. It was late. He would barely have time to swim his seventy-two lengths and this would make him anxious for the entire hour. As he was showering, somebody spoke to him.

"Charlie, I think you should reorder your priorities."

Even though Charlie was blinded by the water in his eyes, he knew that the speaker was his cousin Jack, who was several years his senior and who owned a successful hardware store in downtown Saratoga. Jack often came to the Y to pump iron, as he called it.

Charlie turned off the water and wiped his face. "What makes you think so, Jack?" It occurred to him that his cousin had been giving him advice for half a century.

"My brothers and I are worried about the Bentley. We don't believe that Victor Plotz is an efficient hotel detective. He spends too much time in the bar talking to female guests. That robbery has badly damaged the hotel's reputation. My brothers and I were discussing the matter. We feel you should move into the hotel for the rest of the season. Another robbery would be disastrous."

It had always surprised Charlie how groups of men could stand around naked in a shower room and talk as easily as if they were standing on a street corner. Even he, who often felt uncomfortable with his body, hardly thought of it except as an intellectual problem. Yet here was his cousin, naked, over-sized, and pink, shampoo in his hair and soap bubbles dribbling down his chest, acting as if he had never worn clothes in his life.

"I'm afraid I can't do it," said Charlie, who believed that with his cousins dishonesty was the best policy. "I've just signed a contract with the Navy to investigate certain irregularities at the locks along the Hudson River between Albany and Glens Falls. It's a national security issue." As he uttered this lie, Charlie realized why he'd been so quick to agree about moving into the Phoenix Colony. It allowed him to stay away from the Bentley. Giving his cousin a wink, Charlie patted his soapy shoulder and headed for the pool.

"It's your mother we're worried about," said Jack, "and you should be worried too. After all, you're her only child."

Charlie winced in an attempt to imitate the expression Jesse James must have made when he was shot in the back by that dirty little coward Bob Ford. Then he opened the door and breathed deeply, letting himself be soothed by the smell of chlorine.

It depressed Charlie how every year his swimming got slower. He had never been fast, but each year his mile took about a minute longer. It was palpable evidence of the dissolution of his body. As he walked back to his office through the park after his swim he was hardly aware of the sun or the warm breeze or the ducks in the pond. Instead, he kept imagining himself at eighty dragging his sponge-like flesh back and forth across the pool for half the day, then letting an ambulance take him home.

Reaching Phila Street he was distracted from his thoughts by the sight of a blue Chevrolet Nova parked outside his building. The car was empty and Charlie walked around it several times, looking through the windows. He himself always had junk on the floor of his car: candy and chewing gum wrappers, an old program from Saratoga Raceway, maybe a copy of *True West* magazine, old Kleenex. The inside of the Chevrolet Nova was immaculate, as if the car were driven by remote control and no one ever sat behind the wheel. Impressed, Charlie shifted his backpack from one shoulder to the other, then opened the door to his building and began climbing the stairs. A man was waiting by his office door.

"Is that your blue Nova outside?" asked Charlie, sorting through his keys.

"I guess it is," said the man. "Did you see me yesterday?" He was about fifty and totally bald with a torpedo-shaped head. Sweat was pouring down his face and he kept wiping it away with a large green handkerchief.

"I guess I did," said Charlie, unlocking the door. He passed through it, then held it open for the other man, who entered uncertainly, as if expecting a trick.

"You knew Blake Moss, right?" asked the man. He wore khaki pants and a white short-sleeved shirt soaked with sweat. Charlie thought of it as a mild day. At most, maybe eighty. Certainly not as hot as it had been. The man looked as if someone had tried to drown him.

"I knew him a little. I also found his body. What were you doing at Long Meadows?"

As they walked through the anteroom into Charlie's office, the man gave Charlie a card which identified him as Joseph Stompanella of the Northeast Mutual Insurance Company. "I been upset ever since I read that Moss had died," said Stompanella. "I never knew he was a sick man. I never would have hired him."

"What was he doing for you?" asked Charlie. Although he spoke calmly, he felt particularly alert, even excited, for it seemed that some questions were about to be answered.

"Don't you have a.c.?" asked Stompanella, mopping his face and looking around.

"Just this fan," said Charlie. He took a small fan from a box behind the file cabinet, plugged it in and set it on the desk. It made a whirring noise. Stompanella adjusted it so that it pointed at the visitor's chair, then he sat down.

"I should of been born an Eskimo," he said. "Anything over seventy destroys me."

Charlie waited.

"Moss told me he wanted to hire you," Stompanella said, wiping his face again. "He wanted someone to get inside Long Meadows and see what was what. Trouble is, I couldn't decide whether Moss was being legit or if he was cheating me in some way. Now I think maybe he knew he was sick and he wanted you in there so he could get some rest."

"What was he doing for you?" Charlie repeated. He took his red towel and swimming suit from his bag and hung them on a chair near the window so they would catch the sun.

"Northeast Mutual kept him on a retainer to do work for us between Utica and Springfield, Burlington and Poughkeepsie. Sometimes he worked, sometimes he just sent us bills. Since we were paying him anyway I told him to check into this Long Meadows place. They've had a lot of claims. Theft, a garage that burned, broken windows, a couple of accident suits. Moss figured it was just make-work and didn't want to do it. Then all of a sudden he got interested and said he needed help, that he needed to hire you."

"What had he found?" asked Charlie.

"Beats me. I mean, he died. But I was sort of skeptical. I figured you were his buddy and he wanted to spread the gravy around. Why you instead of someone else?"

Charlie thought of Ted Davis, the retired colors man. "I think he wanted someone from Saratoga. In any case, we weren't friends."

"Did he tell you what he wanted you to do?" asked Stompanella.

"No. He said he had some work for me and that it concerned poetry. That was all."

"Poetry?"

"He'd been to a poetry reading at Long Meadows. A guy, an ex-jockey, read a poem about a nurse falling down the stairs and getting killed. The jockey wasn't convinced it was an accident. I think Moss wanted me to get in there and talk to the jockey."

"So if you hadn't talked to Moss and hadn't started working, what were you doing at Long Meadows?"

"I went to learn more about that poetry reading."

"Who was paying you?"

"Nobody. It was a sort of courtesy call."

Stompanella wrinkled his nose. "But Moss was already dead. So why bother?"

"But how'd he die?"

"I thought he had a heart attack brought on by insulin shock."

"Maybe."

"You mean somebody might have killed him?"

"I don't know," said Charlie. "I just wanted to learn more."

"Who did the autopsy?"

"The medical school."

"You know," said Stompanella, "this coroner system's a joke. Albany County's got four elected coroners and they're all funeral directors. So who does the autopsies? Either the medical school where students can end up doing the work, or they ship the stiff to some private pathologist. You could give them a body with the head blown off and they'd say he died of flat feet." Stompanella wiped his face with his handkerchief.

"So what were you doing at Long Meadows?" asked Charlie.

"I wanted to take a look at the place. Then you came out and I followed you."

"How'd you recognize me?"

"I ran a check on you when Moss said he wanted to hire you."

"So what are you going to do now?" asked Charlie.

Stompanella leaned forward toward the fan until his face was only a few inches from it. The force of air blew the droplets of sweat off his forehead like liquid shrapnel. "I guess I'll ask you to find out more about Long Meadows, although I don't like it. I mean, I'm not sure that any of this concerns Northeast Mutual."

"Why don't you go to the police?" asked Charlie.

"With what? A bunch of suspicions? You know the cops, they got all the tact of a Mack truck. They'll talk to Rolf Vinner and that'll be it. He'll deny everything and in the meantime he'll know that Northeast Mutual has questions about him."

Charlie knew he should say no. He had just agreed to go to the Phoenix Colony as a poet and had no time to go back to Albany. On the other hand, Webster had said he wouldn't be so busy during the day and maybe he could hire Eddie Gillespie to do some work, and then didn't Blake Moss's case deal with poetry as well?

"Maybe I can look into it for you," said Charlie.

"Just take a peek," said Stompanella. "Basically, we want to know that Moss's death was perfectly natural and had nothing to do with Long Meadows."

"And the poetry?"

"Screw the poetry. What does poetry have to do with an insurance company? Absolutely zilch."

*　　*　　*

Alexander Luft reached out and pushed a boiled potato across his plate with one pale index finger on which the nail had been heavily chewed. "What does it mean, Mr. Fletcher, to say that 'be' should be the 'finale' of 'seem?' "

Charlie sipped his milk. Fletcher was his middle name and at the Phoenix Colony he would be known as Charles Fletcher. He had first suggested C. Bradshaw Fletcher, since that seemed more poetical, but Arlo Webster had convinced him he was mistaken. Charlie had arrived in a rush at five-thirty and, after talking briefly to Webster, he spent half an hour in his room studying an anthology of modern poetry which he'd picked up at Bookworks a short time before. In it he learned that Wallace Stevens had been vice president of the Hartford Accident and Indemnity Company. An insurance man, think of that.

Luft cleared his throat. "Mr. Fletcher, your fellow artists are waiting for your reply."

"I suppose it means that you've got to keep your eyes peeled, you can't let yourself be fooled by appearances. Like the guy says, 'Let the light fix its beam' or whatever."

Luft relaxed back into his chair and smiled around at the other four people at the table. "Whatever, indeed, Mr. Fletcher. I can see you are a born critic, although a trifle straightforward. And what's this business about the horny toes protruding?"

Charlie tried to remember the line. Luft had recited Wallace Stevens's poem, "The Emperor of Ice-Cream," to the people at the table and then proceeded to grill them on it, although a man and woman at the far end kept sneaking off into their own personal conversation about the ballet, despite Luft's irritated looks. But even though Luft was addressing them all, Charlie felt that his questions were aimed mostly at him, since he was the only "poet" at the table. The other six poets at the Colony had chosen not to sit with Mr. Luft that evening. Or probably any evening, thought Charlie.

"It's the same thing," said Charlie. "He's saying we should look at those horny toes instead of all the phony makeup on her face, that reality is better than fake appearances."

"Not bad, Mr. Fletcher, but how could we grant you tenure when your answers ooze from you as slowly as treacle?"

Charlie seemed to remember that tenure had something to do with teaching. "I don't teach," he said. "Remember," Webster had told him, "don't say you are an academic. Most of these guests are academics and that's where they'll trip you up."

"And what do you do?" asked a young woman next to him. She had introduced herself and said she was a painter, but Charlie had already forgotten her name.

"I work for an advertising firm in Detroit," said Charlie.

"That's how he learned to be a poet," said Luft, "writing jingles to entice the bourgeoisie to buy those articles which he has convinced them will improve their lives. Am I correct, Mr. Fletcher?"

"You certainly are, Mr. Luft." It impressed Charlie that Luft was able to make it seem that he was familiar with the poet Charles Fletcher, whereas obviously the name was completely new to him.

"Poets like Mr. Fletcher often begin as primitives and autodidacts," said Luft, "but the textural demands of their writing can be so stringent that occasionally they gain a sophistication that raises them above their peers. I look forward to hearing some of your new work at one of our little evenings, Mr. Fletcher."

On the outside, Charlie smiled and indicated that nothing would give him more pleasure. On the inside, he wished he could run away. Why had he ever agreed to come to the Phoenix Colony? He needed a manuscript of poems, he needed something to write about, otherwise it would be obvious to everyone that he was a fraud.

Luft turned to the composer beside him and began discussing the formal qualities of poetry as compared to the formal qualities of music. Both, he said, began with counting, which had begun with the presence of fingers and toes. Even the word iamb derived from a word meaning "to limp," while dactyl referred to finger bones.

Charlie took a bite of meat which had turned cold on his plate. He felt a pain in his stomach and told himself to relax. No one was staring at him. The others at the table were either talking or eating. All in all five tables were arranged around the large Tudor dining room and thirty guests plus Arlo Webster and his young wife were finishing their meal of pot roast, boiled potatoes, and vegetables from the Colony gardens. The walls were paneled with dark wood and the room had high dark ceilings and mullioned windows looking out on the small lake, where an older man with a red cap was fishing from an aluminum boat. Charlie envied him, then he sighed to himself and took another drink of milk.

The problem was with how he had spent his afternoon. Instead of perfecting his disguise as a poet, Charlie had rushed down to Albany, just, as he had told himself, to get a better picture of things. First he had driven to Rolf Vinner's house on Pleasantview, south of Western Avenue. It was a modest turn-of-the-century house, well kept up but with a small yard and a Toyota Camry parked in the driveway. A marmalade cat was sunning itself on the front steps. The lawn mower was battered and rusty. The flower garden was minimal. The house had about two years before it needed repainting again—a cream colored paint with dark brown trim. Charlie had looked at it for about ten minutes, then he telephoned Eddie Gillespie in Saratoga and told him to learn whatever he could about Rolf Vinner without letting anyone know he was snooping around. Gillespie was a young man who often did work for Charlie when he wasn't tending bar at the Bentley or working as a guard at the Racing Museum. Recently, as he explained it, he had been laid off from both jobs. People made him nervous and the museum and bar had been crowded lately. When Eddie got nervous, he drank, then he got nervous because he was drinking and he drank some more.

"He went on a fuckin' binge," Victor had said, "and he can't come back to the bar till October first when everybody else has gone home."

After talking to Gillespie, Charlie telephoned Lieutenant Melchuk in Cohoes. Although Melchuk had learned nothing new, he had assigned another man to the case.

"This guy Boland called me from Albany," said Melchuk. "He said you'd been bending his ear about Blake Moss and some rest home. I talked to the coroner and told him that nobody's happy with this heart attack stuff. Anyway, we got another autopsy scheduled for tomorrow morning. Some honcho at the medical school's going to do it himself. If Moss still turns out to be a heart case, well, they won't be too happy with me over there. And you know what? I'm not going to be too happy with you."

Charlie had then driven over to police headquarters to see Lieutenant Boland. He, too, had been skeptical. "This nurse, Janice Mitchell, she was always running. She'd go down those stairs a mile a minute. We got lots of people who said that. I mean her death still looks like an accident."

"What about Rolf Vinner?" Charlie had asked.

"The rest home's in pretty good shape. Everybody gets paid. There're no big debts. Vinner probably takes home about sixty-seventy K a year. He's a private kind of guy but nobody has anything bad to say about him. He'd been to medical school but didn't finish, got into hospital administration instead. Then about five years ago he took over Long Meadows. He's got a wife but no kids. His wife's active in the Catholic church. As for your little jockey friend, they say he's got a lot of tall stories."

Boland seemed to be making a joke and Charlie smiled dutifully. "Did you let Vinner know you were investigating him?"

"No. When the nurse fell, a plainclothesman was over there asking some questions. I sent him back yesterday saying that he'd lost his notes and had to confirm a couple of things. Everyone was perfectly friendly."

Charlie felt he had reached a dead end. He even regretted hiring Eddie Gillespie but at least Northeast Mutual was paying the bill. By four o'clock Charlie had driven back to his cottage on Saratoga Lake to pack a bag and prepare himself for the Phoenix Colony. Everything had been rushed and he had even forgotten to pack his .38.

When he had come downstairs for dinner, the guests had just been entering the dining room. Arlo Webster had introduced him to several: a painter named Frank from Texas, a woman filmmaker, and, of course, Alexander Luft. Charlie had followed Luft to his table. Luft was a big man, and even though the room was warm he wore a heavy three-piece blue suit and a tie. Many of the other guests wore shorts and T-shirts. Luft's long gray hair had been recently brushed and when he talked he kept touching and rearranging it, until Charlie decided that the hair was one of Luft's major vanities

Then Luft had recited the Stevens poem and begun grilling them about it. Just what did it mean to be the emperor of ice cream? Charlie had felt his mind empty of thoughts the way a sink can empty of water. He hoped that Luft was now done with his questions and that this part of his trial was finished. Luft had continued to discuss music with the wispy man beside him who was wearing a T-shirt with a portrait of Beethoven on the front.

Dessert, however, was ice cream and when Charlie came back to his seat after returning his dishes, Luft was holding up a large spoonful of chocolate ice cream and contemplating it.

"Well, Mr. Fletcher, have you had any further thoughts about the emperor of this particular commodity?"

"Not really," said Charlie, who noticed a painter at the end of the table rolling his eyes.

"And what would you say the poem is about?"

"Maybe it's about things that seem to be and things that really are," Charlie suggested. He ate some ice cream. He had chosen strawberry and a little dribbled onto his chin. He wiped it away with his napkin.

"Are you saying it is about appearance and reality?" asked Luft.

"I suppose I am," said Charlie. "He's saying that what is is more important than what seems to be."

"So you seem to be a poet," said Luft, pushing back his hair, "but in fact you might be something else."

It occurred to Charlie that Webster might have told Luft that he was a private detective. But Webster had said he definitely did not intend to tell anybody. In that case, did Luft know something or was he just being pushy?

"On the contrary," said Charlie, taking another bite of ice cream, "I seem to be an ad man, but I'm actually a poet."

"So this is the true horny toe that sits before us?" asked Luft.

"You bet," said Charlie, again wiping ice cream from his chin.

5

Charlie sighted down his cue, calculating the angle which would send the five ball into the side pocket. He was not a good pool player, was never relaxed enough, and now hadn't played for several years. Giving the cue ball a poke, Charlie straightened up, then watched with surprise as the ball dropped into the intended pocket.

"Hot damn," said Frank McGinnis, the painter whom Charlie had met at dinner. He and Frank were playing doubles in eight ball against two poets: Harry Rostov, who had been at the Colony since July first, and Willis Cassidy, who had arrived on Monday. Across the big room of the renovated barn Alexander Luft was playing Ping-Pong. He was an aggressive player and loved to slam the ball across the net and then shout "Ha!" when his opponent failed to return it. He was now playing with the wispy composer and both men were sweating. Luft had taken off his suit coat but still wore his vest buttoned tightly across his white shirt. The six men had come over to the barn about ten minutes earlier in search of something to do. Charlie was there to keep an eye on Luft, without, of course, letting the critic realize his intention. Outside the wind was blowing crazily, and a branch kept banging against the roof. It was about nine o'clock Thursday evening. Earlier a dozen people had gone to the ballet. Charlie imagined the wind whipping across the stage at the performing arts center and knocking the ballerinas off their tippy-toes like ten pins.

Charlie circled the table and decided that the seven ball in the end pocket was his best chance even though the positioning was all wrong; the cue ball was frozen to the cushion and he had to contort his wrist in order to get at it. As he aimed he heard Luft's deep voice boom out, "First I will deconstruct you, then I will demolish you!" Charlie took his shot and the seven ball caromed off the cushion at least ten inches from the pocket.

"At least you hit it," said Frank.

Charlie walked over to join Harry Rostov as Cassidy took his turn. Rostov was a burly black-bearded man in his thirties. His mustache completely covered his mouth and when he spoke he hardly moved his lips, so Charlie kept being confused about whether Rostov was really speaking or if it was someone else. He wore black leather pants to protect him, as he said, from the mosquitoes, and a collarless white canvas shirt that resembled a painter's smock. He was a dramatic looking fellow and he smoked little black cigars that had a smell reminiscent of a pulp mill.

Rostov grinned at Charlie and his eyes narrowed to amused slits. "So Windy was giving you hard time at dinner?"

"Windy?"

"Windy Luft. He produces enough hot air to heat a small house."

"He was talking about a poem," said Charlie.

"Lecturing would be more like it," said Rostov. "Windy doesn't simply talk. He's in the business of edification."

"You don't like him?" asked Charlie. They leaned back against the wall and watched Cassidy take aim at the two ball. Beyond the pool table, Luft and the composer battled back and forth. Luft seemed to be winning by about ten points.

"Not particularly. If he wasn't a critic and wasn't into power, I could just ignore him. I mean, I'm not a quarrelsome kind of guy. When someone says something stupid, I can just walk away. But Luft can get me a grant or he can turn me down. He can give my book a good review or he can trash it. So I find myself saying to myself,

Go on, suck up to him, offer to shine his shoes. Then I find myself saying to myself, Just kick his ass, just insult him so you never have to think about him ever again."

"That's pretty complicated," said Charlie.

"Do you think so? My awareness of him interferes with my writing. I mean, I want him to like my work. But that very desire pisses the hell out of me."

"I gather he's had some trouble here," said Charlie.

"Yeah, the blood and stuff. Actually, that surprised me. I can see hating the man, but pouring blood over his computer is a trifle psycho."

"Were you around when it happened?"

Rostov lit another of his little black cigars. "There were a bunch of us sitting in the lounge. Luft had been holding forth about something or other, then went back to his room. Suddenly he started screaming, not in that deep bass voice of his but a high squealing scream. You know, in a place like the Colony, a huge mansion with dark corners and mysterious attics, there've always been stories about ghosts and strange things seen in the night. Well, when Luft started screaming my blood, as they say, ran cold. We rushed to his room. I don't know who got there first. That bloody foot on his computer, I thought it was the real thing. One of the painters realized it was fake. Maybe the color was off. But it was still scary. The young woman who had the room next to Luft, she refused even to spend the night. A cab showed up fifteen minutes later and took her downtown. The next day she packed her bags and went back to Manhattan."

"You have any idea who might have done it?" asked Charlie. He tried to keep the amazement alive in his voice and not sound too much like a detective or policeman.

"I've thought about it, of course. There was that other incident as well. Somebody tore up his books and sprinkled the bits around his room. Then someone smashed the windshield of his car. There's a lot of suspicion here right now and the people who came on Monday are just learning about it. Nobody's happy and everybody is wondering who's responsible. In many ways, I'm a prime suspect. Hang on, I've got to take my shot."

Rostov hoisted his cue and moved to the table. His leather pants creaked as he walked. Across the room, Luft and the composer were starting another game. Luft had a funny way of serving, a peculiar back hand twist that sent the ball in a lazy curve over the table. The composer kept hitting it into the net. "Ha!" said Luft.

Rostov tried to sink the six ball in the side pocket and missed. Then it was Charlie's turn again. He slowed his breathing and told himself to relax. Why worry, he told himself, why fret? The nine ball was a straight shot into the corner pocket and gave him no trouble. The seven, however, still wouldn't go. Not only did Charlie miss, but he came within a hair of scratching.

Across the room, Luft began shouting at the composer. "You have to improve your game. Do you think it is a pleasure to play with someone whom I can so easily demolish?" Great sweat stains had appeared at his armpits, but he still hadn't unbuttoned his vest.

Charlie rejoined Rostov as Cassidy prepared to take his shot. "Why did you say you were a prime suspect?" he asked.

Rostov tugged at his black beard, winding the tip into a point. "I guess I'm assuming that these things were done by someone staying here, and I'm assuming they were done by one person. There were only fourteen people around on Sunday, plus Luft. And maybe we can scratch that lady painter who panicked. That's thirteen. Each of these things, the confetti, the windshield, the blood would take about ten seconds, but you'd have to have the opportunity. Most nights are like tonight. You come out of dinner. You sit around in the hall for a bit, then you either come over here or you play cards or read or work, or maybe you go into town. That night four people went into a movie, some sat around and some, like tonight, came over here. Only four or five went off by themselves, meaning they had the opportunity. I was one of those four or five. So was Frank. I'm not sure who the others were. Maybe Lucy Feinstein, she's a novelist. Maybe Hercel Potter, he's a poet. Or maybe Bobrowski, that guy that Windy is whipping at Ping-Pong."

Charlie wondered if being beaten at Ping-Pong could anger someone enough to pour blood over a computer. At the moment the wispy composer looked furious, but it was a big step between anger and flinging blood around. "Possibly one of the others slipped off to go to the bathroom or make a phone call," suggested Charlie.

"Maybe, but we're talking about three different occasions. Each time some people were around and some were in town or by themselves, but each time it was different people. My shot again."

They had got to the end of the game. Rostov sunk the two ball and had only the eight ball left. He called it in the end pocket.

"You'll never make it," said Frank in a high squeaky voice. "You're too nervous, your hand is shaking, and you're frightened by success."

But Rostov made the shot and the eight ball dropped where it was supposed to.

"Let's change teams," suggested Cassidy.

Luft and Bobrowski had just finished as well. Luft began slapping his paddle loudly against his palm. "I need fresh talent," he said. "Bobrowski's just a beginner."

There was a certain amount of conversation about who would play with whom. Charlie offered to play Ping-Pong. Luft looked at him skeptically. He was taller than Charlie by about six inches and used his size in a bullying fashion, by standing too close to whomever he was talking to.

"We'll volley for serve," said Luft.

"I need to warm up first."

"No warming up," said Luft. "I don't have the patience. Either we play or we don't play."

"You're the boss," said Charlie. He tossed the ball across the table so that Luft could begin the volley. In high school Charlie had played a lot of Ping-Pong, and when he worked at Lorelei Stables, there had been Ping-Pong tables for the grooms and hot walkers. Then last winter Victor Plotz had put a Ping-Pong table in the basement of the Bentley. Consequently, although Charlie was not a great player, he knew a few tricks.

Luft lightly hit the ball back and Charlie returned it. The ball had to cross the net three times before the volley became serious. Charlie again returned it, this time a little harder. Luft hit it with one of his crazy spins. Charlie tapped the ball and it barely cleared the net. Luft lunged forward to return the sinking ball and Charlie hit it hard to the corner of the table. Luft managed to hit the ball but it careened across the room.

"Your serve," said Luft. He stood without moving and Charlie realized he was meant to get the ball. Rostov picked it up and tossed it to him.

Charlie had a fast serve that barely crossed the net. It took Luft by surprise and he returned it too hard, missing the table. "One to zero," he said.

The game proceeded. Charlie won four of his five serves, then lost four when Luft was serving. Then Charlie won three of his next five serves and soon he was behind twelve to eight. Luft wore the smug expression of a man who believes he has figured out his opponent and sees his road as downhill for the rest of the way. He stood back about two feet from the table and rarely moved. Charlie, on the other hand, was running all over the place.

"So what do you know about poetry?" asked Luft, serving one of his nasty soft slices.

Charlie tapped the ball gently but it still went into the net. Various lines drifted through his mind and he tried to determine their suitability: "A thing of beauty is a joy forever," "Only God can make a tree," "The highwayman came riding, riding . . ." "I don't know art but I know what I like." Luft served again. This time Charlie got it back, but missed on the return.

"Fourteen to eight," said Luft. "And the poetry, Mr. Fletcher?"

"My body makes the poetry," said Charlie, returning Luft's serve. "It sort of explodes it outward and then I try to make the parts fit." Luft hit the ball back, but too high and Charlie returned it hard. "Fourteen to nine," said Luft, serving again.

Charlie hit the ball back to Luft's left side. "Afterward, I try to get the poem published," said Charlie. Luft returned the ball and Charlie hit it back. "I'm like an employment office," continued Charlie, "and my poems are the guys who wander in off the street and need work. I find them places where I hope they'll be happy."

Luft hit the ball but it went into the net. "Fourteen to ten," said Luft, serving again.

"What's necessary," said Charlie, "is to keep the blue collar and white collar elements separate, since their impulses are completely opposite." They volleyed back and forth and again Luft missed the return.

"Fourteen to eleven. Your serve, Mr. Fletcher. What do you call the blue collar element?" Luft had narrowed his eyes and stared at Charlie as if suspecting a deception.

It occurred to Charlie that Luft had no idea what he was talking about—as Charlie himself had no idea what he was talking about—but Luft wouldn't admit it and, instead, he pretended to understand. This pretense, or the concentration required to bring it off, was weakening Luft's game.

"The blue collar element," said Charlie, serving, "is the non-unionized creative impulse." He watched Luft hit the ball over toward the pool table. "Twelve fourteen," he said.

Rostov tossed back the ball and Charlie got ready to serve. "By keeping the intellectual wages low," he said, "and by turning the screws on the disenfranchised creative impulse . . ." Here Charlie served, ". . . I am able to break the backs of the iambs and force them to do my bidding. Thirteen fourteen, Mr. Luft."

Luft tossed back the ball. "But how does that help you to write?" he asked.

"I divide and conquer," said Charlie, serving again. "My conscious mind cracks the whip and discovers low-paying jobs for the wetbacks of my imagination."

Luft again hit the ball off the table.

"Will you stop hitting the ball over here," called Rostov. "We got our own game." He tossed it back to Charlie.

"Fourteen all, Mr. Luft," said Charlie, serving. "Justice has no place in creativity. The sweat shop, the coal mine, the seamstress with her scarred fingers: the job of the conscious mind is to make those blue collar workers bleed and from their howls of pain, my poetry is born." During this exchange, Luft had returned the ball twice before sending Charlie a high pop-up which Charlie was able to slam across the table just as he pronounced the word "born."

"Fifteen fourteen, Mr. Luft," said Charlie.

"And what are the subjects of your poems," said Luft as he retrieved the ball from a corner and tossed it back. He had grown quieter and had unbuttoned his vest.

"At the moment," said Charlie, getting ready to serve, "I am composing a sequence of poems about the Bill Doolin gang."

"Who?" asked Luft, returning the ball badly.

"He was a bank robber and train robber in the Southwest who was shot down by Marshall Heck Thomas in 1896."

"What makes that a suitable subject?" asked Luft, returning the ball a little harder.

"Partly the poetic names of his gang members," said Charlie. "Dynamite Dick Clifton, Crescent Sam Yountis, Bitter Creek Newcomb, Tulsa Jack Blake, Little Dick West, Red Buck Weightman. They were all ex-cowboys."

Again Luft missed. "Fourteen sixteen, my serve, Mr. Fletcher. Those names may create a certain ambiance but what makes it a suitable subject for poetry?" Luft served and Charlie returned the ball.

"The love interest," said Charlie. "Bill Doolin had a wife who he was crazy about and who he kept going back to."

As the game continued Charlie described how Doolin kept returning to his wife, the Reverend Ellsworth's daughter, and how Marshalls Bill Tilghman and Heck Thomas had a motto when they couldn't find a particular outlaw: "Seek the woman," because even the worst crook always came back to his wife or girlfriend; how Tilghman and Thomas had Indian scouts keep a round-the-clock watch on Reverend Ellsworth's home, and how in August, 1896, Bill Doolin appeared and began packing up a wagon so that he and his wife and child could escape to Mexico. Then Heck Thomas showed up with his posse and there was a gun fight. Later Thomas wrote, "I got the shotgun to work and the fight was over." Doolin's body was riddled with twenty-one buckshots. Afterward Mrs. Doolin wrote a poem about her husband which she sold with copies of his picture for twenty-five cents each. Doolin was buried in Summit View Cemetery in Guthrie, Oklahoma, and instead of a gravestone a rusty buggy axle was driven into the dirt above his coffin.

Charlie won the Ping-Pong game twenty-one to sixteen.

"I'd like to see these Bill Doolin poems of yours, Mr. Fletcher," said Luft as they walked back to the mansion.

"I need to finish them first, that's all," said Charlie, and as he uttered this preposterous statement he experienced a rush of anxiety.

Later, around midnight, Charlie was on the phone to Janey Burris. "This is a funny place," he said. "I'm not sure I can bring it off."

"Why not. They're just people, aren't they?"

The phone booth was in the downstairs hall of the mansion. Charlie listened to Janey breathe and felt reassured about the existence of the outside world.

"The people are okay. It's just that I can't grill them and I can't follow them around all the time. But the worst thing is that I've got to write some poems about Bill Doolin."

"Who?"

"An old-time bank robber. It's a pickle I've got myself into. I'm supposed to be here as a poet and so I've got to produce some poems. You know, I was reading these poems in this anthology I bought and they don't even rhyme."

"That should make them easier to write."

"Maybe."

"Can I come out and see you?"

"When?"

"Right now. The kids are asleep."

Charlie felt his pulse speed up. "No, it wouldn't work. They've got guards all over the grounds and I'm supposed to be watching Luft. It would be terrible if something happened while we were in bed together."

Janey made a disappointed noise. "It was just an idea. Did you get hold of Eddie Gillespie earlier?"

"Yeah, I sent him down to Albany. So far he's been doing just what the police were doing. Talking to the guy who runs that carnival and questioning the owners of the surrounding stores."

"Is there anything I can do?"

"What do you mean?"

"I've got some free time right now. I could ask questions just as well as Eddie and I wouldn't charge a penny more."

"At the moment I'm pretty well covered."

"And you're sure I can't sneak out there?"

Charlie wished he could say yes. He felt lonely and he wished he could sleep in his own bed and have his own pillow. "Not tonight," he said.

A few minutes later Charlie started back upstairs to his room. He wasn't wearing shoes and his feet were silent on the floor. From somewhere he could hear the faint clatter of a typewriter. Hurrying through the hall, he glanced at the big fireplace. Beneath the mantelpiece was a multicolored mosaic of a phoenix rising from the flames. Light glittered on the small tiles. Then Charlie hurried up the staircase. Surrounding him were dark paintings with historical subjects, ragged tapestries, thick purple drapes, fading flowered wallpaper, Tiffany lampshades, heavy furniture. Only a few lights were lit and the dark corners were mysterious and menacing. Charlie could well imagine why people thought they had seen ghosts. Even he, a non-believer, kept thinking there was something hovering just beyond the corner of his eye.

In the upstairs hall, lamps shone dimly on several tables covered with magazines. The wind was still strong and somewhere a shutter was rattling. He glanced through one of the magazines. It contained mostly poetry. Charlie read one.

> *A man eats a chicken every day for lunch,*
> *and each day the ghost of another chicken*
> *joins the crowd in the dining room. If he could*
> *only see them! Hundreds and hundreds of spiritual*
> *chickens, sitting on chairs, tables, covering*
> *the floor, jammed shoulder to shoulder. At last*
> *there is no more space and one of the chickens*
> *is popped back across the spiritual plain to the earthly.*

The man is in the process of picking his teeth.
Suddenly there's a chicken at the end of the table,
strutting back and forth, not looking at the man
but knowing he is there, as is the way with chickens.

The poem continued in that vein. Charlie wondered what made it a poem. Couldn't he write something like that about Bill Doolin? He could write it in prose, make it sort of crazy, then break it into lines. Charlie felt a little better. Continuing to his room, he paused by his door and listened. There was no noise except for the banging of a shutter. Alexander Luft's room was to the right of his own and a light shone from under the door.

Charlie opened his own door and went inside. His windows were open and the long curtains blew into the room. He went to close them. Both his windows and Luft's looked out on the big lawn that ran down to the lake. Luft had the bigger room and Charlie could see the shapes of Luft's four windows projected brightly onto the grass below. Across that projection moved Luft or, presumably, the shadow of Luft. He was pacing. The shadow moved back and forth across the shadow of the windows. Because of the distortion, the shape looked hardly human, just a great gorilla body projected onto the grass. And the only noise was the wind rushing through the trees.

Charlie closed his curtains and walked to his desk. On it was a chart which he had begun earlier giving the times of the various depredations against Luft, the names of the people who had been in the vicinity and what they were doing. By each person's name was a little box. Charlie sat down at the desk and began filling in more of the boxes—who had gone to the movies, who had gone to the ballet, who had been playing Ping-Pong. It was past two o'clock before he finally got to bed.

At the Bentley Hotel that Thursday night there occurred an unfortunate series of events. These began around nine-thirty when Victor Plotz took a break from his prowling of the upstairs halls to go down to the bar for a bit of refreshment. The building was quiet except for the infernal wind. Many of the guests were either at the ballet or at the harness track. In two hours of pacing the halls, Victor had only seen three elderly ladies on their way back from dinner and a red-haired kid of about eight who had shot him with a squirt gun. There were now alarms on the two emergency exits, and that left the service exit in the back and the front door as the only other ways out of the hotel. Both were being watched.

In the bar Victor discovered that the hotel had just received several boxes of fresh raspberries. Although he was generally scornful of what he thought of as lady drinks, he was very partial to raspberry daiquiris. He took a table by the door so he could keep a sharp eye on the lobby—there was Raoul fiddling with his mustache, there was the bellboy yawning—then he asked the waitress to bring him a raspberry daiquiri. He liked this waitress—her name was Roxanne— she was sleek and about thirty and had legs so pretty that Victor thought of them as stems.

After she brought him the drink, he chatted her up a little. Although he normally stayed away from women under forty, Roxanne had a mature look.

"Can I buy you one of these?" asked Victor.

"I'm not supposed to drink while working."

Victor sat looking up at Roxanne. She was a tall dark-haired woman with sharply pointed breasts and Victor wondered what they looked like au naturel. "I can square it with your boss. There's no one around anyway."

It was true. The bar was empty except for a middle-aged couple holding hands by the fireplace.

"Actually, I'm allergic to raspberries," said Roxanne.

"I could tell you about my bullet wounds and the various exciting escapades of my life," said Victor, with a winning smile.

Roxanne's face remained blank. "I've got to wash the glasses."

It was as Roxanne was walking away that the first unfortunate event occurred. Maybe Victor was staring too hard at her legs or maybe he was thinking he should stick to older women or maybe he was wondering once again about the mystery of her pointed breasts. Whatever the case, he bumped his nearly full glass and spilled the raspberry daiquiri down the front of his gray suit.

"For crying out loud," said Victor, jumping to his feet and trying to wipe away the mess with a small paper napkin.

Roxanne hurried back. The bartender burst out laughing. Even the couple holding hands turned to look. There was a moment when Roxanne was wiping the bar towel across Victor's stomach when he thought that only a few seconds before he had imagined being touched by her in almost such a way. Of course he had to change his clothes.

Luckily he had some spare clothes in his office, which was along the hall between the front desk and the kitchen. As he passed through the lobby, he saw Raoul look at him sharply from behind the desk. Raoul didn't speak but he raised his eyebrows so expressively that it seemed like a polysyllabic gesture. The bellboy guffawed.

As Victor changed into another gray suit, he flicked on the TV and wished he could stay in his office long enough to see the rest of the Mets game. They were beating the Cardinals five to four but it was only the seventh inning and anything could happen. Victor watched Gary Carter hit about eight foul balls before at last striking out. Then he hurried back to the lobby.

There was no time now for another daiquiri. It was exactly ten o'clock and soon some of the guests would be returning from the ballet. Victor climbed the broad staircase to the second floor and once more began patrolling the halls.

This he did diligently until about eleven. Guests returned. There was a lot of happy chatter. Then there came those who had been at the harness races: on the whole, a glummer lot. The bar filled up. There was a lot of activity in the halls and people went to and from the ice machine. Waiters passed carrying plates with silver covers. Laughter rippled from behind closed doors.

Then, suddenly, while Victor was up on the third floor, a door slammed open and a middle-aged man ran into the hall with his shirt half unbuttoned. Seeing Victor, he shouted at him, "We've been robbed. Someone's been in our room."

Victor experienced a pain in his stomach. He hurried to the man, trying to get him back into his room before he made a scene.

The man grabbed Victor's arm and shook it impatiently. He was bald and his cheeks were bright red. "Goddammit, we've been robbed!"

Doors began opening.

"Let's go back inside," said Victor. "I'm the hotel detective. We'll call the police. Just what was stolen?" By tugging at the man, Victor got him inside and closed the door. A woman was sitting on the bed crying.

"They took my pearl necklace," she said.

"And a poem," shouted the man, stamping his foot, "they left a goddamn poem."

Victor read the poem as he telephoned the police.

> *I love the world's big spenders*
> *And their casual concern about cash;*
> *I love how they leave*
> *Their jewelry lying about,*
> *And their pride which I turn into hash.*

6

Charlie pulled the newspaper closer to his face and squinted through his reading glasses as if they were playing some trick. But they weren't. The headline repeated its dreadful information. The Bentley had been robbed again.

"Oh, no," said Charlie.

Immediately, several people, including Alexander Luft, turned to him to say, "Shhhh." They were having breakfast and all were sitting at the silent table. Charlie had broken the cardinal rule. He had made a noise.

"Poor Victor," said Charlie, hardly hearing them.

"Shhhh," came the noise again. This time louder. There were four other people at the table. Across from Charlie, Luft was reading a book with a French title. He glared at Charlie over the spine.

The headline on the front page of the *Saratogian* read ROBBER POET STRIKES AGAIN. Someone had broken into the room of Mr. and Mrs. Robert Sesnick while they were at the ballet and had stolen jewelry valued at five thousand dollars. Although the hotel employed a private detective neither he nor anyone else had seen the robber. The poem was set off in a special box with a black border.

> *I love the world's big spenders*
> *And their casual concern about cash;*

I love how they leave
Their jewelry lying about,
And their pride which I turn into hash.

"This is terrible," said Charlie.

Alexander Luft made a growling noise in his throat. "Mr. Fletcher. I realize this is your first morning at the Phoenix Colony, but rules must be respected."

Charlie showed him the poem. "What do you make of that?"

Luft glanced at it. "Doggerel with alliterative pretensions. I cannot see that it is worth an outbreak." He returned to his Grape Nuts.

Charlie watched him chew. Despite the early hour, Luft was dressed in a dark three piece suit and a red tie. His long gray hair had been carefully brushed and shone in the morning light. Charlie knew he should stay at the Colony until Luft was safely tucked in his room and had begun his day's intellectual labor. On the other hand, he could imagine how his cousins, the police, and even his mother must be reacting: Victor had let them down.

Charlie pushed back his chair. "Excuse me," he said, "I've got to rush."

"Shhhh!" said Alexander Luft.

One of Victor Plotz's qualities that Charlie especially admired was his ability to maintain a defiant good humor in the face of hard times. This morning, however, Victor was decidedly depressed. He and Charlie sat in his small office near the kitchen which was littered with newspapers describing the robbery. The room smelled strongly of bacon and Charlie guessed he would carry that smell in his clothes throughout the day.

"The Sesnicks didn't actually blame me," said Victor, wadding up the front page of the *Saratogian* with a loud crinkling noise, "but on the other hand they've already packed up their bags and moved to the Holiday Inn."

"How could anybody blame you?" asked Charlie.

Victor leaned forward with his elbows on his desk. He appeared to have slept on his hair in an unfortunate manner because some parts were squashed to his skull and other parts were sticking up at various violent angles. "Oh, Charlie, you'd be surprised. I have already heard from your cousin James, and your cousins Robert and Jack have asked if they could talk to me later. And Peterson was none too polite. Your mother hasn't actually accused me of anything but I can tell she isn't happy. The real culprit of this whole fiasco, unfortunately, was a raspberry daiquiri."

"A daiquiri?" asked Charlie.

"I let myself be tempted by fresh raspberries." Victor explained about the raspberry daiquiri and how he had spilled it all over himself. "And then there was Gary Carter fouling off these pitches like there was no tomorrow."

"So how long were you away from the lobby altogether?"

"No more than ten minutes, I swear."

"Ten?"

"Maybe fifteen."

They talked more about the robbery. Both agreed that it had to be a coincidence. Certainly there had been robberies in some of the other hotels and motels that month. Saratoga in August attracted thieves; it was a fact of life. The problem was that none of these other thieves had left poems.

"Why poems?" said Victor. "What's the point of it?"

"Maybe just to brag," said Charlie.

"But why bother?" said Victor. "He's already got the jewels."

As Charlie was leaving the hotel a few minutes later, he ran into his mother in the lobby. In fact, she appeared to be waiting for him. Mabel Bradshaw had worked as a waitress for most of her adult life and her body, in those years, had assumed the shape of a professional waitress, the sort of waitress that works at diners and short order joints: that is, she had grown lean and sinewy and quick on her feet. But once she became the owner of a grand hotel, her whole being changed. Now she was a large woman with bright red hair who wore billowy gowns. She was big and substantial and given to expansive gestures and there was no trace of the woman who had spent much of her life slinging hash.

This morning Mabel Bradshaw was wearing a light green taffeta gown that surrounded her as heavy foliage surrounds a tree. She had on a lot of makeup of an orange hue but beneath it could be discerned a kind face and a very worried one.

"Charlie," she said, embracing her son.

He tried to embrace her back but became entangled in the taffeta. "I've just been talking to Victor," he said.

Mabel Bradshaw shook her head as if Victor's very name caused her physical discomfort. "Won't you come and stay at the hotel? Victor needs your help."

Charlie disengaged himself. "I can't. I shouldn't be here even now." Beyond his mother he could see the hotel's revolving door leading out to Broadway where it was a bright sunny day and the street was full of cars.

"There've been cancellations, Charlie. This is terrible for us."

"I'm staying out at the Phoenix Colony. I've got a job there and there are other cases too." He rattled off several examples. "And a fellow I know was murdered in Albany. Really, I don't even have time to go swimming. You can hire more people here. It's just coincidence that you were robbed again. Victor's efficient. I'm sure it'll be all right from now on." As Charlie talked he continued to move slowly toward the door. Several people were standing at the front desk and he saw Raoul glance toward him and look away. From the dining room came the sound of silverware against plates.

"We make more than half our money in August," said Mabel. "These robberies could hurt us. There are bills to pay, salaries to pay. Your cousins want you here."

"No," said Charlie, almost at the door. The word "Escape" loomed before him like a divine message. "I'll try to help but I'm stuck on these other jobs. You have no idea how hard I'm working."

Only a few hours later Charlie was squirting suntan lotion into his palm and rubbing it on his chest. Then he lay back on the chaise longue. The sun was bright and he decided he needed new sunglasses. As he dangled his hand over the side, he touched the basket containing the last of his lunch and he remembered it contained a Freihofer fruit cookie. He pondered whether he should eat it now or save it for a late afternoon snack.

"A critic," said Frank McGinnis, sipping a diet Pepsi on the chaise longue next to Charlie, "is like a eunuch who feels obliged to describe the nature of sex. The fact that he has never experienced it is the very reason for his fascination. That is what is so amusing about these deconstructionist critics who claim to be artists. They are like eunuchs in drag and their falsies keep slipping."

Charlie opened one eye and squinted into the sunlight. There in the pool in front of him was Alexander Luft doing the breaststroke. He seemed able to continue it forever. He wore a red bathing cap to protect his hair and his nose was covered with cold cream. It was shortly after one o'clock and about half a dozen of the Colony's guests were having lunch around the pool.

"But aren't reviews necessary?" asked Charlie.

"Sure," said Frank. "A good review is a description of a particular work and that description leads us to decide whether to read it or see it or whatever. But most critics scorn reviews. They see themselves in the business of judging and evaluating."

"Isn't that important?" Charlie glanced over at Frank. He was a thin man in his mid-forties with a belly so flat that Charlie guessed he could set up a checkerboard on top of it. He was from Houston and spoke with a slight drawl.

"The best criticism is written by artists and it's about the only criticism that survives the life of the writer. The critics who aren't artists produce a lot and they pump each other up and get excited and they may have lots of power but their words are like smoke and a little time blows it away. Basically, they're a nuisance."

"And you think that's true of Alexander Luft?" asked Charlie.

"Sure. It would be one thing if he championed poetry and encouraged people to read it, but his judgments about poetry do a lot of harm. A critic like Luft doesn't praise poetry that has any degree of clarity. He needs an obscure poetry, a poetry which he thinks needs to be interpreted, a poetry which, in fact, needs him. Consequently, he dismisses clarity as a virtue. He dislikes the linear. He dislikes direct statement. He dislikes a compelling emotional content. He dislikes the idea that the poet should be or might be the reader's representative. He even dislikes the idea that the poet may be trying to communicate to the reader. Luft wants to be the middle man. He wants the communication to come through him. He's like a realtor or broker. He wants to insert himself between the buyer and seller."

"You sound like you hate him," said Charlie, wondering if Frank should be one of his prime suspects.

"I do hate him. He collects power and makes trouble. On the other hand, he is also absurd. He's like someone standing outside a restaurant looking through the window. He sees people eating and he stops other people on the street and explains what the food tastes like. But he's got it all wrong. He's never tasted it himself."

"Has he ever written about your work?" asked Charlie.

"He gave me a bad review once in *Arts News*."

"Would you have poured blood over his computer?"

"That's too melodramatic. I can imagine getting in a fight with him. I suppose I can even imagine shooting him. But the blood, well, it seems hokey somehow. Also it makes a disturbance here at the Colony. It frightened a perfectly good painter and drove her away. The blood's too sick. I may be angry, but I'm not sick."

"Do you have any idea who might have done it?" asked Charlie.

Frank McGinnis glanced over at Charlie. He had a long freckled face and a square chin. "Are you really a poet?" he asked.

"You bet," said Charlie, trying to give an honest smile.

Frank turned to watch Luft doing his slow breaststroke. Luft kept his arms and legs submerged and his eyes were focused straight ahead as if he were reading something. "All artists have some eccentricity. Their interior lives are overdeveloped and it makes them odd. Still, I can't imagine anyone here pouring blood over Luft's computer. All along I've assumed that someone snuck in from outside."

"What about the guards at the gate?"

"We're not walled in. There're lots of paths through the woods and all the buildings are accessible. I mean, if someone from town wanted to sneak in here, he wouldn't have much trouble. Maybe it

was even someone from the city. Luft teaches in New York, right?
There must be people there who hate him."

Charlie leaned back in his chair. He would have to look at those
paths. The racetrack was about a mile through the woods and the
stables in the backstretch were even closer. As if in response to his
thoughts he heard the bugler calling the horses to the post for the first
race: a small faraway tootling. It was just one-twenty. Why wasn't he
there instead of here? Rostov and several other guests from the
Colony had gone over to the track and had invited Charlie to come
with them. He had been tempted but he also knew that some friend or
acquaintance would come up to speak to him, and then everyone
would realize he wasn't a poet but a private detective. Still, he hated
not being there. In his imagination, he saw the horses being led from
the paddock to the track for the post parade. Some would be walking
calmly, some would be nervous and trotting sideways and pulling at
their bridles, and often at least one would break into a gallop as if the
race were *to* the gate and not *from* the gate, while his jockey stood up
in the stirrups and tried to calm him.

Although Charlie had a studio out in the woods, he let it be known
that he preferred to write his poetry in his room. There was a large
desk, a comfortable chair, a wonderful view of the lake and, just a
few feet through the wall, Alexander Luft was busily doing whatever
critics do when they put their mind to it. The pictures on Charlie's
walls showed tranquil farm scenes and the brass bed was covered
with a white summer weight spread. Twice a week, he was told,
someone would come to make it for him. As a creative environment
it was perfect and Charlie regretted he was not a real artist so he could
put the room to better use.

That Friday afternoon all of Charlie's creative energies were
directed at making a chart with names, dates, and potential suspects.
The blood had been poured over Luft's computer on Sunday evening
sometime between eight o'clock, when Luft was last in his room, and
ten-thirty, when he discovered it. The previous incident had also
occurred in the evening. Someone had entered Luft's room between
eight-thirty and eleven on Tuesday the twenty-sixth and scattered bits

of paper all over. The bits had turned out to be the shredded remains of Luft's four critical books which had been swiped from the Phoenix Colony library. Although there was a lock on Luft's door it was primitive and could be opened with a skeleton key.

The first incident had been the smashing of the windshield of Luft's Mazda. Luft had discovered it, or rather someone had pointed it out to him, on the morning of Saturday the twenty-second. He had not driven the car since the previous day and presumably the windshield could have been smashed at any time over a sixteen-hour period. Anyone could have broken the windshield because everyone had had the opportunity.

But the two evening depredations had taken place within shorter periods and on each occasion some people had been at the ballet or the movies. Of the thirteen possible suspects, only eight had been at the colony when all three depredations had occurred. Of course, there was also the chance that someone had slipped out of the ballet or movie and driven back—presumably about half an hour would be needed—but Charlie decided to follow that idea only as a last resort.

The other part of Charlie's chart dealt with the sum of his researches to date: just who had been where. He had talked to six guests and had disqualified the four who had been out on both nights. Of the thirteen possible suspects, he had just three left to talk to: a novelist, Lucy Feinstein; a poet, Hercel Potter, and the composer, Matthew Bobrowski. Charlie's assumption was that the depredations had been carried out by one person acting alone. He knew he had no proof of this and that Luft's tormentors might include two or more artists working together. Perhaps all the poets had ganged up to give Luft a nervous breakdown.

Right after lunch Charlie had called Chief Peterson and asked him to contact Luft's colleagues in New York to see if any could think of someone who might hate Luft enough to follow him to Saratoga. He also asked Peterson to run checks on the people working at the Phoenix Colony. He hadn't been very eager and had made more jokes about Charlie in the role of poet—had he been stealing feathers from pigeons for new quills—but at last he had promised "to put someone on it."

Charlie had also walked back into the grounds, investigating the various trails, and had discovered that it would not be difficult for someone who knew the area to come over from the track or from Union Avenue, avoiding the main gate altogether. It was not a reassuring discovery. He then talked to Webster and suggested that one of the new security guards should patrol the woods just in case. The question was, just how crazy was this mysterious attacker, and again Frank McGinnis's distinction came back to him: just because someone might hate Luft didn't mean that person would pour blood over his computer—the distinction being between more or less healthy hate and wacky hate.

Charlie got up from the desk and walked across to the mirror. He was still wearing his bathing suit because he had gotten a sunburn at lunch from not putting on suntan lotion soon enough. His chest was bright pink and hurt. He had very little hair on his chest and what there was was gray or blond. Glancing at his face, he again felt that faint surprise to see that he was older than he expected. Then he raised his eyebrows at himself. He had large blue eyes which he considered thoughtful. His thinning gray hair stood up in peaks and he patted it down. He had tried swimming his laps in the pool but it was too short, only about thirty-five feet, and it seemed that he had spent most of his time turning.

Charlie sighed and returned to the desk where he picked up a yellow legal-sized pad. He had one chore that was stumping him at every turn. Scratching his ear, he bit the end of his felt-tip pen. After a moment, he began to write.

> *Bill Doolin was a desperate man,*
> *A desperate man was he,*
> *He robbed the Sante Fe train in Cimmaron,*
> *He robbed it in 1893.*

Charlie sighed again, crumpled the paper into a ball and tossed it into the waste basket. Then he got to his feet again. He had to telephone Lieutenant Melchuk in Cohoes and learn the result of the second autopsy on Blake Moss.

*   *   *

Melchuk made a noise over the phone which sounded as if he were eating a very moist slice of pizza, sort of a chewing and sucking noise.

"Well, yes, the guy at the medical school found a trace of thiopental. Of course, that wouldn't kill him, but it's suspicious."

"So what's thio-whatever?" asked Charlie.

"It's what they shoot into you before you have an operation, then they tell you to count to ten."

"I never made it past two," said Charlie.

"That's the point."

"Doesn't it have to go into a vein?" asked Charlie. "Wouldn't it leave a mark?"

"Sure, but Moss was diabetic and he had lots of little holes. They even mainline insulin sometimes. Your friend Boland thinks that someone whacked Moss on the head or just held a gun on him, then gave him the shot."

"And then what?" asked Charlie.

"After that it's simple. You could put a plastic bag over his head, maybe toss in a piece of dry ice just for luck. The result would look more or less like a heart attack."

"So he was murdered," said Charlie.

"I don't want to rush into things. I mean, all we have is a trace of thiopental and obviously there's no verdict but, yes, it would seem that Moss was killed by a party or parties unknown."

"Murder," said Charlie.

"Right. I guess we should be grateful to you for insisting and making a pest of yourself. . . ."

Charlie listened for a note of gratitude but heard none. "And who turned on the merry-go-round?"

"There's no clear answer there either. At first, we figured Moss did it as a way of attracting attention and getting help, but the thiopental makes that unlikely. More likely the murderer did it to make it seem that Moss had time enough to try to summon help. I mean, with a heart attack he might have had a couple of minutes."

"So what do you plan to do?"

"I put another man on it."

"Are you going to investigate that retirement place?"

Again came the pizza noise. "There's nothing to say that Long Meadows is involved. Moss was working on lots of cases. Besides that, he was a gambler and owed a ton of money. We'll have to check all this stuff. It could take a long time."

"What about the poetry?"

Melchuk responded a trifle peevishly. "You know there was a horse running in Saratoga on Wednesday called Shakespeare's Dream and another yesterday called Black Sonnet? They've both been running at Belmont as well. Who's to say that's not what Moss was talking about? I mean, I've got to check them. We've got a small department and this is going to take all our resources."

"What does Boland say?" asked Charlie. The phone booth in the downstairs hall at the Phoenix Colony was no more than a renovated broom closet. With the door closed, the temperature was approaching one hundred and Charlie was sweating.

"He's putting a man on it too. I mean, he should, shouldn't he? I'm sick of these out of town guys coming to Cohoes to get themselves killed."

Charlie thought of several wise cracks, then decided against them. He had to learn not to alienate policemen. He sympathized with Melchuk. Good policework was like chewing mouthfuls of gristle. "I'll keep in touch," he said.

Breaking the connection, Charlie called Lieutenant Boland, then had to wait five minutes because Boland was on another line. He had his yellow pad with him and he wrote:

> *Bill Doolin was no Jesse,*
> *No Dalton Gang or Wild Bunch,*
> *He was just an Oklahombre*
> *Who . . .*

What rhymed with Bunch? Punch? Hunch? Charlie wrote down "Who was morally out to lunch." Then Lieutenant Boland picked up the phone.

"Sure, we've been over to Long Meadows. I've talked to Betsy Thomas and Vinner several times. I can't see anything in it. There's nothing suspicious over there. They all seemed shocked to learn that Moss was a private detective."

"The nurse who fell . . ." began Charlie.

"What's the motive? Moss had lots of cases. . . ."

"That's what Melchuk said."

"But it's true," said Boland. "And look at the gambling. Moss knew all sorts of shady types."

"Someone like that would have just shot him," said Charlie.

"Sure, I tend to agree with you. But give me a motive."

"I don't have one at the moment."

"But you're going to find one, right?"

Charlie could almost see Boland's smile. He liked Boland and understood his problem. He lacked the manpower, just like Melchuk. "Maybe so," said Charlie.

During the next twenty minutes, Charlie tried to track down Eddie Gillespie. First he called his answering service and was told that Eddie's beeper was not responding. Then he called a dozen other places but no one had seen him. He imagined Eddie in an air-conditioned movie drinking Jack Daniels from a hip flask. Before leaving the phone booth, Charlie reread his poem, then sighed and crumpled up the yellow sheet of paper.

At dinner that night Charlie nearly gave himself away. He was at a table with Alexander Luft, Frank McGinnis, the novelist Lucy Feinstein, the composer Bobrowski, and a new fellow named Gordon Patterson who was writing a biography of James Thurber.

"The only story I remember about Thurber," said Lucy Feinstein, "was he once said that his hardest job was to convince his wife he was working when he was looking out the window."

They were eating roast chicken and Charlie was finding it difficult to cut it apart with his knife and fork and not pick it up with his fingers. "That's just like a private detective," he said without thinking.

"How do you mean?" asked Frank.

Charlie realized his mistake. "They do most of their work in their heads, or at least that's what they do in books."

"And do you read many mystery novels, Mr. Fletcher?" asked Luft, disapprovingly.

As a matter of fact, Charlie hardly had read any unless he included the Hardy Boys and Nancy Drew mysteries he read as a child. The only names he could recall were Dashiell Chandler and Raymond Hammett, and he felt something was wrong with them.

"I love Dorothy Sayers," said Lucy Feinstein.

"So do I," said Charlie, "so do I."

Alexander Luft heaved himself up in his chair and glared at Charlie, who was sitting directly across from him. "How can you engage in such foolish pursuits, Mr. Fletcher? As a poet you must develop a consciousness of the past. You must contain within you the whole of literature from Homer to the present. You are the Grecian urn in which the culture's wine is preserved. It is this historical sense that makes a writer."

"I thought emotion made an artist," said Frank, holding a chicken drumstick and shaking it at Luft.

"You painters love to splash about in fecal matter," said Luft, "and perhaps that clouds your perceptions. The emotion of art is impersonal. Poetry is not a freeing of emotion but an escape from it. A keen sense of the past offers suitable alternatives to emotion. It offers a range of subjects to set against the I-am-unhappy poems which constitute the unfortunate hallmark of so many of your contemporaries. That was why I was so interested, Mr. Fletcher, when you spoke of your Bill Doolin poems. The American West as a subject has slipped into unnecessary disfavor. It is uniquely American and demands a uniquely American idiom. You will of course present your work to the rest of us in the near future and I hope the Doolin poems will be among the poems you choose to read."

After dinner, when Luft had gone off to play Ping-Pong with Bobrowski, Charlie sought out the poet Hercel Potter in the magazine room on the second floor of the mansion. Earlier, Charlie had glanced through Potter's book of poems in the library and was pleased that he could understand them even though they didn't rhyme. The poems dealt with Impressionist painters: Monet, Pissarro, Renoir. Charlie asked Potter if he was doing more poems about painting, but it turned out that his new work was a long narrative poem about Attila the Hun.

"I try to argue," said Potter, "that Attila was the last truly vibrant male figure in Western history."

"I thought Attila had a pretty bad reputation," said Charlie, dredging up scattered memories from high school history.

"Yes, that's the standard feminist view. After sixteen hundred years it's time for a reassessment, don't you think?"

"I guess so," said Charlie. "Luft should be happy about your historical approach. Did he review your last book?" He was sitting on the other end of the couch from Potter, who was a tall thin man with a droopy brown mustache. Charlie guessed he was about forty. He had a round gold earring and he fiddled with it as he spoke.

"He reviewed it in the *Times*. Liked it, as a matter of fact. His praise was worth a second printing to me."

"So you're not one of the people he's torn to pieces?"

"Not at all. He's always been good to me, but I don't know why." Potter closed the magazine he had been reading and put it on the seat beside him. "I like to think he recognizes my secret qualities, but he has also demolished some poets of whom I think very highly and so I see Luft's criticism as like the weather: sometimes it rains on parched fields and sometimes there's a drought."

"Does Luft have some particular theory that he pushes?"

"Not really. He calls himself 'an aesthetic critic,' meaning he believes each work of art should be judged on its own terms, rather than how it matches up with a certain set of extraliterary principles: Marxism, feminism, post-structuralism, and the like. It is this apparent open-mindedness that leads editors to seek out his articles. Also he is energetic and enjoys exercising his power."

"Do you like him?"

"No, he's a bully and he's been mean to friends of mine, but I don't mind his being at the Colony. I just avoid him, that's all."

Charlie went on to ask about the various depredations. Potter had been nearby when Luft's car window was smashed. He had been working in his studio in the woods when the confetti was thrown around Luft's room. He had been one of the group with Luft on the night when the bloody foot was found on his computer. Meaning, thought Charlie, that he had opportunity on all three occasions.

"Why are you so interested in this?" asked Potter, again tugging at his earring.

Charlie wondered if Attila had worn an earring. Hadn't Attila been some kind of pirate and all around bad guy? Perhaps Potter's allegience to Attila needed looking into. "I hope to publish my first book in not too long," said Charlie, "and I don't want to do anything to make Luft mad. I guess that makes me think of him."

"If that's the case," said Potter, "then you should stop writing right now. Thinking about Luft and his likes and dislikes will only damage your work. In that way, he has destroyed dozens of poets. In fact, there's hardly been a poet he has praised who has turned out well. I promise you, if you write for any reason outside of yourself, then you will certainly fail. That's one of Luft's worst influences. He gets inside a poet's head and tampers with the intuitions, with the creative impulse."

"Would you have poured blood on his computer?" asked Charlie.

"No, but if he leaves here, I'll be perfectly happy."

"What would Attila have done with someone like Alexander Luft?"

"Butchered him, most likely. Attila didn't fool around." Potter grinned and his gold earring flickered in the lamplight.

That night, after first squaring it with Arlo Webster and the security guards, Charlie snuck Janey Burris up to his room. Janey brought a bottle of Spanish champagne and some cheese and crackers and they had a picnic on the floor. They spoke in whispers and the only light came from the bathroom.

"So you spent the whole evening playing Ping-Pong with that man?" asked Janey.

"Only part of the evening. He beat me six games."

"Couldn't you cheat?" Janey poured more wine into Charlie's

toothbrush glass. She was wearing shorts and a dark T-shirt, and Charlie kept wanting to touch her.

"No, I managed to distract him by talking about my Bill Doolin poems, but the subject gave me such anxiety that I lost the next games anyway."

"Poor Charlie," she said, handing him the glass. "At least you're getting paid for it."

Charlie drank some wine. "I keep thinking I should be down in Albany or helping Victor at the hotel."

"What does Eddie Gillespie say?"

"Well, he's been hard to reach. Earlier he said that wherever he goes he finds the police have been there before him."

"Always a bridesmaid, never a bride. Do you want me to go down to that retirement community? I bet I could wangle my way in."

Charlie gave Janey a cracker with a piece of cheese. The mansion was completely silent, although every now and then he could hear a bump or footstep from Luft's room. "There's no motive, not even the trace of one. If there were, then maybe I'd take you up on it. I told Eddie to learn more about Betsy Thomas. Maybe something will turn up."

"What are you doing about your mother?"

"Nothing. I'm just staying away from it. It's funny about the poems though. I can't figure them out. I keep thinking of those poems that Black Bart used to leave."

He told her more about Black Bart and how his robberies had supported his rich life in San Francisco where he had gone to the opera and carried a gold-topped cane. His last robbery had been near Copperopolis in the fall of 1883. As he rode away, he had been winged in the hand by a young man who had hitched a ride with the stage to go deer hunting. Black Bart wrapped his hand with a handkerchief which he later discarded. It was an expensive silk handkerchief with a laundry mark. The Wells Fargo detectives took it to ninety laundries before they found one in San Francisco that could identify the handkerchief as belonging to C.E. Bolton. When they arrested him, Bolton admitted he was Black Bart but grew angry when they called him an outlaw. "I am a gentleman," he insisted.

"What were his poems like?" asked Janey.

"They weren't very good. One went:

> *Here I lay me down to sleep*
> *To wait the coming morrow,*
> *Perhaps success, perhaps defeat*
> *And ever lasting sorrow,*
> *Yet come what will, I'll try it once,*
> *My conditions can't be worse,*
> *And if there's money in that box,*
> *'Tis money in my purse.*

"What would Alexander Luft think of that?"

"He'd call it doggerel." Charlie got to his feet, then held out his hand to help Janey up. "Let me show you something."

Charlie led her to the window. Out on the grass they could see the lights cast by Luft's windows, while across those four bright squares moved a black shadow, back and forth, back and forth.

"That's Alexander Luft," said Charlie. "He paces every night."

7

Charlie drew his Renault Encore to a stop in the parking lot at Long Meadows, trying to park on a flat place because his emergency brake was broken. It was late Saturday morning and the day was warm and sunny. Lots of robins were harvesting worms. Across Loudon Road at Wolferts Roost Country Club battalions of golf carts were chugging across the fairway. And at Long Meadows too there was a lot of activity, most of it quite slow, as the elderly moved along the landscaped paths either unassisted or with the help of aluminum walkers. Looking at them, it occurred to Charlie that they all wanted to go some place, escape back into the worlds they had left, to resume careers, lives where the future held more than one alternative.

Charlie had come to see Ted Davis, the ex-jockey and colors man. He wanted to find out what Blake Moss had been looking for at Long Meadows and he wanted to know why Davis had responded to the news of Moss's heart attack with suspicion. And how would he respond to the news that Moss had been murdered?

Charlie had also wanted to avoid Betsy Thomas or Rolf Vinner, to talk to Davis without being interrupted. He had left Saratoga about nine-thirty, just after Alexander Luft and several others had driven off to Glens Falls where they intended to visit a small art museum called the Hyde Collection. Arlo Webster told Charlie that he would have someone watch Luft's room. Driving down to Albany, Charlie had had the sense that he had just escaped from jail.

Charlie found Ted Davis sitting on a bench beneath a giant oak studying the *Racing Form*. He was wearing a red turtleneck and his scrawny neck and bald head poked up from the collar in a way that made him resemble a baby vulture. He looked up at Charlie coming across the lawn. "How're you doing, Saratoga?" he said.

"I wasn't sure you would remember me." Charlie sat down beside him on the bench.

"I don't remember names, but I never forget a face or a horse. Did you make a bundle on Dipsi-Doodle?"

"A very small one," said Charlie. That morning he had at last reached Eddie Gillespie at home and asked him to pick up his winnings from Pinkie Schwartz. Gillespie had been happy to do it for twenty percent. As for where he had been yesterday, Gillespie had only said, "I met a girl."

"You been going to a lot of races?" asked Davis.

Charlie handed him his card. "Not as many as I'd like."

"Charles F. Bradshaw," said Davis, squinting at the card. "You're a private detective?"

"That's what it says on my license. It turns out that Blake Moss was murdered. I want to hear more of what you were talking to him about."

Davis put down the *Racing Form*. His face brightened and he seemed excited, almost happy. "You think he was murdered because of something here?"

"The police say he had lots of cases. They say there's no motive here. But I keep coming back to that poem. Just what did you tell him?"

Davis scratched his chin. His hands sticking from the long sleeves of the turtleneck looked like hooks covered with pale skin. "You know, I never wanted to come here," he said. "I got two sons and they each got wives. They got houses and they got kids. I stayed with them each for a while but it didn't work out. I mean, they didn't want it to work out. So I came here. These places are dangerous, you know that? There're germs and you figure it's a one-way street and that makes you negative about your future. I seen people come in here, get pessimistic, and just waste away. Sometimes they get shipped out, sometimes they die at Long Meadows. This is no charity place. Everybody pays. And when somebody dies, they say he had a heart attack or a stroke. After all, he was old. He was supposed to die and it's no surprise. But what happens to his money?"

"Are you saying that somebody steals from the people here?"

"Some of them have no sense of their own finances. They get confused easily. When a person comes here he turns over all his assets to Long Meadows and the place takes care of him. If he was billed twice or three times for something, he wouldn't even know. And think about some guy or some old dame who doesn't have any close family. Much of their money could be taken from them and then they might suddenly die. Who's going to say anything?"

"Who would do this?" asked Charlie.

Ted Davis grinned, showing his pink gums. "They think old people don't know anything. They think an old person dies, well, it's bound to be a natural death. But there was a man here and he began to think someone was stealing from him and he started talking about it and all of a sudden he has a heart attack and dies."

"Did that really happen?" asked Charlie, lowering his voice.

"His name was Russell Weisberg and he died in the first week of June. He'd been suspicious. He couldn't prove anything but he was angry. He was a widower with no children. He loved to play golf. He told me that his money had been disappearing, that somebody had been taking it. He said it was being done in the office. He started making a fuss about it, then he died."

"Did he tell Janice Mitchell about it?" asked Charlie.

"That's right. Of course she just thought he was being paranoid. Then, after he died, she started looking around for herself."

"So what exactly did you tell Blake Moss?"

"I said that someone was stealing from the people here and when they got suspicious or didn't have anything left, then they conveniently died."

"What did he say?"

"He was skeptical but not as skeptical as you might have thought. He asked me if I could get proof."

"Why, haven't you gone to the police?"

"They wouldn't believe me and I'm not sure it's even true. Maybe it's just an idea I've got. It's just suspicious, that's all."

"Could you get me proof?"

"I could try."

"Why Mr. Davis," came a woman's voice from behind them, "I didn't realize that you had a visitor."

Charlie and Ted Davis turned to see Betsy Thomas walking toward them across the lawn. She had been smiling but when she recognized Charlie her expression became disapproving.

"Guests are supposed to register at the front desk, Mr. Bradshaw."

Charlie got to his feet. "I ran into Ted as I was coming across from the parking lot, so I thought I'd say hello." Betsy Thomas wore a light blue dress that nearly reached her ankles and had a little ruffle at the neck. She looked like someone dressed as a grandmother in a play.

"And why did you come?"

"I hoped to find you here," said Charlie. "I wanted to tell you about Blake Moss."

Betsy Thomas looked momentarily surprised, then she recovered herself. "I've already talked to the police about Mr. Moss. He was murdered. They also told me he was a private detective. That means he was lying to me. I can only assume that he had tricked his way into my acquaintance because of something here at Long Meadows. And he wasn't the only person who has been lying to me."

"What do you mean?" asked Charlie.

"You are a private detective as well, Mr. Bradshaw."

"That's true. I lied to you," said Charlie. He stood facing Miss Thomas while Ted Davis sat on the bench between them. "But it is also true that I found Moss's body. There was something that interested him at Long Meadows and I wanted to find out what it was."

"No, Mr. Bradshaw, it's absurd to think that Mr. Moss's death was connected with anything here. If there's a problem at Long Meadows, it can be dealt with by the police or the licensing board, not by private detectives. I have already told Mr. Vinner that Mr. Moss was a private detective. And actually he was the one who suggested that you might be a private detective as well. And here you are working on poor Ted Davis, getting him to tell you all sorts of outlandish stories. I promise you, Mr. Bradshaw, that if any of Ted's crazy allegations appear in the papers, Long Meadow's lawyers will hold you directly responsible."

"I was just saying hello to Mr. Davis," said Charlie.

"I certainly hope so. And now you can say good-bye. You're a trespasser here, Mr. Bradshaw. Blake Moss tricked me and you tricked me as well. I don't like being tricked. Shall I walk you to your car, or can you find your way yourself?"

"I think I can make it myself," said Charlie. "I'm sorry if your feelings were hurt."

"Just leave, Mr. Bradshaw."

"Okay, okay. See you, Ted."

Ted Davis gave Charlie a crooked little grin and again picked up his *Racing Form*. Walking away, Charlie heard Betsy Thomas speaking angrily to the ex-jockey, but he couldn't make out the words.

As Charlie reached his car, he saw Rolf Vinner talking to another man on the side veranda. Vinner wore a blue blazer and gray slacks. He was laughing and he clapped his hand down on the other man's shoulder. Then the two began walking back toward a small garage or shed where four blue golf carts were parked. Vinner was tall and well built. He seemed comfortable with himself and he moved his arms to accent his words when he spoke. Before entering the shed, Vinner glanced back toward the parking lot. The sunlight reflected off his glasses, making his eyes resemble little headlights. Charlie stepped behind his car, although at this distance he didn't think Vinner could recognize him.

Alexander Luft climbed down from Frank McGinnis's Ford van and slammed the door. The window was open and Luft called through it. "Always a pleasure, Mr. McGinnis. Thank you for asking me."

"Any time, Alex."

Luft's smile tightened. He disliked nicknames. Still, he gave what he thought of as a friendly wave as Frank drove down the hill. Luft turned toward the library, which occupied a small stone building about two hundred yards from the mansion. Readings were sometimes given there, as well as piano recitals. The other day Luft had noticed a biography of William Carlos Williams and he wanted to look up several dates dealing with Williams's friendship with Wallace Stevens.

Alexander Luft and Frank, as well as the two poets, Hercel Potter and Harry Rostov, had been to the Hyde Collection in Glens Falls, the private art museum of a long-dead capitalist. Luft had especially liked the Botticelli "Annunciation," but he felt the Turner was overrated. As for the Picasso and Matisse, Luft had little use for twentieth century painting. He thought back nostalgically to those days when the arts were supported not by government committees but by a few wealthy human beings with taste. There was no one of that ilk around today. Good work had to go begging, to be pawed over by assistant professors with chapbooks from vanity presses. Or even worse: to be judged by graduate students.

Alexander Luft sighed as he climbed the steps of the library. At least the trip to Glens Falls had been relatively painless. On the way up he had silenced the two poets with a few slighting references to their work while mentioning a foundation with which he was intimately acquainted. Rostov was certainly someone who would have been wiser to seek his profession in the trades. And while Hercel Potter was a little better, he would always be a minor poet, a trifler. Just what was this nonsense about Attila the Hun? The fact that these men had been admitted to the Phoenix Colony was humorous at best. As for Frank McGinnis, Luft again thought of how far painters could go without being able to intellectualize their creativity. The majority, of course, were no more than decorators or finely tuned colorists. But where were the Cezannes, the van Goghs? These days the triflers were in the ascendant. And Luft shuddered to think of the success they might achieve were he not around to keep them at bay.

Luft found the biography of Williams, glanced through it, then decided to sign it out. Tucking the book under his arm, he left the library and proceeded along the driveway to the mansion. There were mosquitos about and he slapped one. On the way back from Glens Falls, he had pretended to sleep. He knew that McGinnis and the others were going out of their way to be nice to him because of what had happened at the Colony. They were suspects and Luft was amused by that. They were so nervous about possibly offending him that they were always hovering nearby, trying to do him a good turn. He wished they would leave him alone. If they were true artists, they would put their attention first and foremost on their own work.

Luft unlocked the back door to the mansion, then checked the mail table. He found his telephone bill forwarded from New York and a witty postcard from his chairman containing some sort of word play on derringer, derring-do, derriere, and Derrida. Luft couldn't make sense of it. Walking through the downstairs hall, he paused by the kitchen door and sniffed. It smelled like roast chicken for dinner. Then he ascended the rear staircase. No one was about, but from somewhere he could hear typing. His feet were silent on the carpeting. Luft had three weeks left at the Colony and he had great plans for his work during that time. It made him happy just to think of it.

He reached for the key to his room. It was now midafternoon and he had been gone about five hours. Fumbling with the lock, he opened the door and stepped inside.

He was first aware that something was blocking the light from the window. Then he saw a figure hanging by a rope from the ceiling fixture. It was a man dressed in one of Luft's dark suits, with Luft's own gray hair and glasses wedged down over his nose. In fact, it was obviously meant to be Luft himself hanging by his neck, turning slowly in the breeze from the open window.

But of course it wasn't really a man. It was some sort of inflatable doll—Luft remembered they were called love dolls and this was the male version, with a gray wig and the glasses taped to its inflatable plastic head and wearing Luft's good dark suit. And the love doll, so disguised, turned and turned with its expression of idiotic eagerness. Its eyes behind the glasses were pop-eyed. Its mouth was an opaque plastic hole.

Luft considered how to respond. His first thought had been to scream, but he rejected that as melodramatic. There was nothing frightening about the doll, but it was impressive, even unnerving. Summoning up a great weight of indignation, he stormed out into the hall. He thought again about how quiet everything was. Well, that was about to change. "Arlo Webster!" he bellowed, "I've had just about enough of this! You have no right to torment me! I'll close this place. I'll teach you to play with me!"

Doors started opening. The first person to appear was that middle-aged poet with a pug nose who claimed to be writing outlaw poems and who he kept beating at Ping-Pong. Luft was surprised by just how fast he could run and how attentive his eyes were. After seeing that Luft was all right, Fletcher stepped into the room and stopped. Luft could hear his sudden intake of breath. But then there were noises from all over and feet could be heard on the stairs and here came Arlo Webster, running fast and looking frightened.

Charlie watched Alexander Luft scraping his bowl for the last spoonful of chocolate ice cream. Then Luft stuck the spoon in his mouth, licked it carefully, and leaned back in his chair with a comfortable groaning noise. Charlie was impressed by his appetite. He himself had been able to eat little. He felt distracted and guilty about the most current depredation: a depredation which must have occurred either that morning or in the midafternoon. Before going to Glens Falls, Luft had spent about a half hour in the mail room reading *The New York Times*. In fact, Frank McGinnis had picked him up there. During that same period, Charlie had been talking with Arlo Webster. Then both Charlie and Luft had left on their separate journeys and Webster had seen to it that someone kept an eye on Luft's room. But possibly the doll had been hung after Charlie had returned, even after Luft had returned and was in the library. But wouldn't Charlie have heard something?

Presumably it had occurred sometime between nine and nine-thirty or between two-thirty and three. Charlie was struck by the gall of this latest prank since the intruder must have been in Luft's room for as long as ten minutes and might have been surprised at any time. As for who had done it, Charlie had no idea. In the morning there was a certain amount of wandering around before people headed for their studios and settled down to work. In some ways it seemed that nobody could have done it and that anybody could have done it. Certainly that was impossible, but as Charlie worked on his chart later that afternoon he had been unable to exclude any of his seven or eight suspects. It was unlikely that Frank had done it, or Hercel Potter, or Rostov, but they all had had a few loose minutes within that morning half hour. As for the afternoon, people were supposed to be in their studios but that didn't mean someone hadn't been sneaking about. Charlie felt thoroughly perplexed.

Glancing around the dining room, it seemed to Charlie that Luft was the only person unaffected by the incident. Usually at dinner there was a lot of conversation. After all, these people had been penned up all day with only their own creative impulses and dinner-time was their social unleashing. Yet tonight they were quiet. The guests who had been at the Colony for all four incidents looked depressed, while the new guests looked uncertain and confused. Several hadn't come to dinner, saying they would eat in town. Charlie suspected that most had already come to the conclusion that the prankster was not someone from outside but one of their own number. This was not a comfortable thought.

As for Arlo Webster, he seemed the most upset. So far, all word of the incidents had been kept from the newspapers. But if they continued, they were bound to become public. Certainly the guests themselves would tell their friends and families, and these people would tell others and in no time everyone would know. And how would that effect the grants, the fund-raising drives, that flow of money which was necessary if the Phoenix Colony were to continue?

Alexander Luft pushed back his chair and stood up. "Well, Mr. Fletcher, can I impose upon you to give me a little exercise at the Ping-Pong table?" Even though it was warm, he wore a dark suit with a vest and a tie. It was, Charlie realized, the same suit that had been on the love doll. Luft's gray hair was shiny and smooth. The color of gunpowder, Charlie thought.

Charlie stood up as well. "I'd be happy to." He glanced over at

Arlo Webster and caught his eye. Luft's room was being watched.

As Charlie followed Luft out of the dining room, he was aware of everyone's attention. No one stared, but there were a lot of quick looks. He noticed Harry Rostov and was struck by the anxiety in his face. For the briefest second Charlie wondered if it were guilt, but he didn't seem to be nervous about himself; rather, his concern seemed to be for the Colony and the difficulty of writing with the knowledge that one of their number, someone they had talked to and eaten with and joked with, was crazy and dangerous.

As Charlie and Alexander Luft walked up the driveway toward the barn, Charlie asked, "What do you think about what happened today? Did it scare you?"

"I am a very stubborn man, Mr. Fletcher." Luft paused to slap a mosquito. "When someone tries to push me in one direction, I invariably go in the other. Someone at the Phoenix Colony is trying to torment me. I refuse to be tormented."

They resumed walking again. The orange light from the setting sun cut through the pine trees. "Why should anyone want to torment you?" asked Charlie.

"Come, come, Mr. Fletcher, don't be such an innocent. My major work is in criticism. I see it as my duty to make sense of the confused mass of writing which is published each year. In order to make sense of it, I must judge it. In order to judge it, I must offend someone. That is no pleasure for me. On the other hand, look at all those reviews and articles which make no judgment, which merely describe. What use are they to anyone? Absolutely none."

"So you think somebody here has it in for you?"

"Obviously. Either I have offended them directly or I have offended somebody close to them. The artistic community is relatively small, Mr. Fletcher. I am sure that everyone at the Colony could summon up a complaint against me."

"There's quite a difference between complaining and doing all this stuff," said Charlie. "That dummy looked pretty realistic."

"Artists tend to be unstable," said Luft. "They live in their imaginations, even bad artists. Their imagination is a constant filter. Look at yourself, for instance: if you are a typical artist, you do not experience or perceive reality directly; rather, you perceive it through your imagination. You abstract experience through your imagination and then you deal with that abstraction."

"How is that different from what you do?" asked Charlie. He didn't know what he himself actually did; or rather, he always assumed it was thinking and logic and plain common sense.

"I take it as my duty to see what exists, without emotion, without lies, without hyperbole."

"Did you ever try writing poetry?" asked Charlie.

Alexander Luft made a laughing noise. "I have too much respect for myself to attempt it. I do not like to do what I cannot do well."

They entered the barn and Alexander Luft went immediately to the Ping-Pong table and began to adjust the net. He liked to play on the far side away from the pool table and the door, and he liked always to use a particular red paddle which, as far as Charlie could see, was no different from the green one.

As Charlie took his paddle he thought again of how much energy and emotion these people invested on an area of human endeavor about which, until this week, he had known nothing. He was more comfortable with people like Ted Davis; and if it had been necessary to infiltrate some place, Charlie was sorry that it couldn't have been Long Meadows. He was struck, however, by a certain similarity between the institutions, how both existed as shelters from the normal rush of the world. That perhaps was also true of the Bentley. All offered protection against the world and into each place the world had roughly intruded.

Charlie had talked to Eddie Gillespie that afternoon and asked him to learn what he could about Ted Davis. He had also asked him to look into the death of Russell Weisberg during the early part of June. Gillespie was happy to have new tasks. His investigations into the lives of Betsy Thomas and Rolf Vinner had turned up nothing and this led him to doubt himself and his abilities.

"It makes me think bad about myself, Charlie," he had said, "and then I think maybe a little drink will cheer me up and then I take another. You don't want that, do you?"

"Of course not, Eddie," Charlie had said.

Charlie had also told Eddie to get in touch with Maximum Tubbs and ask him to come out to the Phoenix Colony sometime that evening, to tell him that Charlie wanted to talk to him. Tubbs had been active in Saratoga as a gambler for at least sixty years and Charlie hoped that Tubbs would remember Ted Davis and be able to tell him something about the ex-jockey. Charlie had left word with security and when Tubbs showed up, one of the guards would bring him to the barn.

"You serve, Mr. Fletcher," said Alexander Luft. "I believe you could use the advantage."

"Let's volley," said Charlie.

They volleyed and Charlie lost. It occurred to him that each evening he was playing a little worse even though his basic skills were improving. Luft hit a slow, curving serve with plenty of backspin. Charlie managed to return it but hit it too high. Luft slammed it back and Charlie could do no more than watch the ball zoom past him.

"One to nothing, Mr. Fletcher."

As they played, Frank and Hercel Potter and several others showed up to shoot pool. Charlie wished he could be playing pool as well. Then he again reminded himself that his job was to observe Alexander Luft, not to care whether he won or lost at Ping-Pong.

"Four to one, Mr. Fletcher. Your serve."

Charlie served quickly.

"Let, Mr. Fletcher. Try it again."

Charlie served again, hitting the ball a little higher and Luft slammed it back.

"One to five, Mr. Fletcher. I appreciate your giving me the opportunity to practice my skills upon you. What you lack as a player, you make up by being a good sport."

"As a poet," said Charlie, picking up the ball, "I try not to let the world affect me too much." Here he served. "Otherwise it distracts me from the truer world of the imagination."

Luft missed the return and looked irritated with himself.

"Two to five," said Charlie, again picking up the ball. He thought of his conversations with Potter and Rostov and borrowed a little of their language. "I find that to be a poet is to construct from my imagination a larger world which I can set over the real world much in the way that a tea cosy covers a teapot. Three to five, Mr. Luft."

"And how do your outlaw poems fit into that particular schema, Mr. Fletcher?"

Charlie tossed up the ball and caught it. "In the same way that the outlaw is outside the society," he said, preparing to serve, "so is my imagined world outside the real world. And my imagination attacks reality much in the same way that Bill Doolin robbed banks—with an equal mix of violence and good humor. Four to five, Mr. Luft."

Luft gave Charlie the ball.

"Your ideas excite me, Mr. Fletcher. And it is with eagerness that I look forward to hearing your outlaw poems. Perhaps there will be an occasion next week. . . ." Charlie served and Luft slammed back the ball. "Four to six, Mr. Fletcher. My serve."

Alexander Luft won the game and the next game as well. But Charlie felt he was coming closer. Not perhaps in his score—after all he had lost each game by ten points—but in his search for a ploy that might weaken Luft's concentration. A third game Charlie lost by fifteen points, despite his attempts to discuss nude women, baseball and the best places in Saratoga to eat pancakes. It was with relief, therefore, that at the end of the game he noticed Maximum Tubbs watching from the doorway.

A few minutes later, Charlie was walking with Tubbs back toward the mansion.

"He's got you running ragged, doesn't he?" said Tubbs.

"It's just a game," said Charlie.

Maximum Tubbs took a handkerchief from the breast pocket of his light gray linen suit and dabbed a corner of his mouth. He was a small dapper man in his late seventies, and Charlie felt he only needed a black ebony cane to complete the elegance of his costume. "Nothing's a game or maybe everything is," said Tubbs. "He knows you're afraid of him and he anticipates you too easily. Try serving at his testicles. That'll take him by surprise."

Charlie paused. "Is that fair?"

"You want to win, don't you? Do what he doesn't expect, take h
mind off the game, startle him."

They resumed walking again. The only light came from the ba
door of the mansion about fifty feet away and it made Tubbs linen s
shine.

"You ever come across a jockey by the name of Ted Davis"
asked Charlie. He described Davis, said how he had later worked
the colors room and was now living in a retirement community
Albany.

"I wondered what had happened to him," said Tubbs. "I guess
first saw him race around 1930. I knew him a little. He was a gre
storyteller. He had a way of describing a horse race that had you
the edge of your seat even though the race was long over and you
already lost your ten bucks."

"Did you ever see him after he quit the colors room?"

"Nah, he never came back up to Saratoga as far as I knew. But
didn't really quit that job. He was eased out of it."

"How come?"

"He used to be one of these guys who'd give you a thousa
reasons why Oswald didn't kill Kennedy. And it got into the rest
his life as well. He thought certain people were trying to hurt him ar
that the racing association wanted him fired. Well, that's a kind
self-fulfilling prophecy. He got so many people irritated at him wi
all this talk that they retired him."

"So he was paranoid?"

"Nothing that extreme. He just thought people were out to g
him."

Around midnight that Saturday, Victor was sitting on a bench up
the third floor hallway of the Bentley massaging his calves, first th
left, then the right. He figured he'd walked a dozen miles—all with
the hotel, one corridor after another. He guessed he was losi
weight and he disliked that. He disliked anything tampering with h
waistline.

Down on the second floor Rico Medioli was also patrolling ar

Jack Krause was either up on the fourth or fifth. Shep Herman was stationed in the lobby and old Jimmy Hoblock was watching the back. It seemed to Victor that not even a cockroach could get into the hotel unnoticed.

As he thought that satisfying thought, he heard the elevator doors slide open and he glanced to his left to see a tall red-haired woman step into the hall. She was dressed in an orange satin jumpsuit and wore a pair of very steep high heels. Around her neck was a string of bright red beads. Victor could feel his various interest glands perking up: he liked her size, he liked her taste in clothes. Maybe the woman was in her late thirties or early forties. She was wearing dark glasses and a great drooping purple hat and Victor couldn't be sure of her age. Her bosom was large and aggressive.

She walked toward Victor, apparently not seeing him, but when she drew even with him, she turned, pursed her orange lips, and blew him a kiss.

"Va, va, voom," said Victor.

The woman kept walking. Victor was impressed by her height, but maybe that was just her shoes. But she was also quite broad-shouldered for a woman. Victor was struck that he had not seen her before and he guessed she was a special visitor on a romantic mission. Still, it was possible that she was a hooker and Victor had promised Raoul that he would keep hookers out of the hotel even though he had a certain sympathy for those simple foot soldiers of the heart.

Victor got to his feet. His legs felt stiff and it hurt to move them. "Excuse me, miss," he said. The woman was now half a dozen yards down the hall.

Instead of answering, the woman began to walk faster, wobbling on her high heels as if she weren't entirely used to them. It struck Victor that she had pretty big feet for a woman.

"Miss," Victor repeated. He took a few steps after her.

All of a sudden the woman jumped forward to the door of the stairway, threw it open, and disappeared.

"Damn," said Victor, breaking into a run.

Reaching the door, he almost tripped over the woman's shoes which lay in the middle of the landing. They were big shoes and would have fit Victor easily. Victor thought he heard footsteps above him and he started climbing. "Hey, stop!" he shouted.

A door slammed. Then another. Victor reached the fourth floor hall. At the far end, by the other stairway, he saw the woman throwing open the door. But it wasn't a woman, Victor was sure of that now. Except for the two of them the hallway was deserted. Victor started to shout, then thought better of it. He imagined the nervous guests leaping from their beds. He galloped down the hall, all his aches and pains forgotten. Where were Rico Medioli and Jack Krause? When he reached the stairway, he paused and listened. Nothing. Not a squeak. He decided to go up to the top floor.

By now he was out of breath and panting heavily. The fifth floor hall was empty. He hurried down the corridor, checked the hall to the west wing, then scrambled down the stairs to find Rico Medioli and Jack Krause. Unpleasant feelings were rising within him. He imagined scenes in the not-too-distant future in which he would be yelled at. Victor hated getting yelled at.

The next morning around ten o'clock, Charlie and Victor were walking through the rose garden at the Phoenix Colony. Victor had arrived about ten minutes earlier bearing his terrible news. Although full of sympathy, Charlie also felt ambivalent. He bent over, took a yellow rose by the stem and sniffed, then he abruptly jerked back his hand and looked at his index finger where a small drop of blood was forming. He put the finger in his mouth and sucked it. Metaphor, thought Charlie. Even surrounded by flowers he was bullied by the devices of the poet's trade. He turned back to Victor.

"Why didn't you have walkie-talkies?" he asked.

Victor had broken off a rose and was in the process of nibbling its petals. Sometimes it seemed to Charlie that Victor would eat anything, as if his friend were descended from a goat. "We're getting them now," he said. "Rico went to Radio Shack and bought 'em as soon as they opened."

It was on Charlie's lips to say that Victor should have had them earlier but he didn't care to add his two ounces of criticism to the bushels that Victor was already carrying. "And Rico had seen this girl?" asked Charlie.

"Woman," said Victor. "No, he didn't spot her. But Shep Herman saw her come in and Krause caught a glimpse of her up on the second floor. But you know Krause, he's terrified of women. He hasn't admitted it, but I think he saw this big blowzy red-haired dame waltzing toward him and he ran away. He fuckin' hid. Anyway, that was about half an hour before I saw her. The trouble is that no one saw her leave."

"And a ruby necklace was stolen?"

"Yeah, she was wearing it when she walked by me. I thought it was glass. Of course we didn't know about the theft until this morning."

"Let me see the poem," asked Charlie. They had begun walking slowly and now they stopped as Victor took a piece of paper from the breast pocket of his gray suit coat. Around them in all directions were hundreds of rose bushes with paths winding between them. The rose garden was bounded on one side by a row of pines and on the other by a long white trellis. Several stone benches were situated along the paths. Charlie took the piece of paper from Victor, took out his reading glasses, then walked to a bench and sat down. Victor sat down beside him. Charlie began to read.

> *They seek me here,*
> *They seek me there,*
> *They search but cannot find me.*
> *The police despair,*
> *So guests beware,*
> *Your gold will wine and dine me.*

"That's just a Xerox," said Victor, "the cops took the original." He paused and looked unhappily at Charlie. "That last rhyme seems forced, don't you think?"

"Do the newspapers have this?" asked Charlie.

"Tomorrow. You know, the reporters are having a ball. A guy

even called from *The New York Times*. Raoul talked to him. We guessed last night there'd be trouble, but we couldn't find anything. Then this couple starts bellowing around eight this morning. They'd been drinking pretty heavily last night. Shep Herman said they came in around nine-thirty hardly able to stand. We figure this fake broad broke into their room between eleven-thirty and twelve and robbed them while they were asleep."

"He must have been watching them," said Charlie.

"Sure. He saw them someplace at dinner. He knew they were staying at the Bentley and knew which room they had. Then he waltzes through the lobby in an orange satin jumpsuit, gets the jewels, struts his stuff right past me, and disappears, leaving behind this poem and a pair of size ten high heels. Now your cousins want me dead, Raoul calls me an incompetent, and your mother looks at me with the saddest eyes I've ever seen. And what do I do? I buy half a dozen walkie-talkies and hire a new guard. But what I really want to do is just light out. Fly down to Miami and lie on the beach."

"You wouldn't like that," said Charlie. "It's hot down there in August."

"Not half so hot as it is up here," said Victor. "And of course there've been more cancellations and people checking out."

"This burglar must have ducked into another room," said Charlie, "which suggests he has a contact within the hotel. Make up a list of the staff and people who have worked for the hotel during the past year and give it to Peterson. Maybe somebody's got a record."

"I've already done that," said Victor. "No dice."

"Is there anything similar about the rooms that were broken into?"

"No. They were different rooms in different parts of the hotel. They're not particularly near the stairways or elevators or fire escapes. I can't find a pattern anywhere except those damn poems."

"And the fact that somebody knows the Bentley pretty well," said Charlie. "How many names were on your list of people who had either worked or were working at the hotel?"

"Forty. Rico and me are beginning to check through them. You want to give us a hand? Why don't you quit this artistic shit and come back to the hotel."

"I've got a job here. This Alexander Luft, his life might be in danger." Some people were entering the rose garden over by the pines: two women with a small child. Charlie glanced at his watch. The morning was getting late.

Charlie stood up. "You'll catch this guy," he said. "You're getting closer and closer. And if you catch him your stock will go up one hundred percent. If I catch him, your stock won't budge."

"So what are you going to do?" asked Victor.

"I'm a poet. I've got to write poems."

"You? How come?"

"Because I've got to give a poetry reading, that's why," said Charlie with a certain desperation. "And if I don't have poems, they'll know I'm not a poet. Either I solve this case right away or I've got to come up with some poems."

"When do you have to read them?"

"Soon."

"And what d'you have?"

Charlie took a rumpled piece of paper out of his hip pocket and began to read.

> *Bill Doolin, Bill Doolin,*
> *You ride so fast and long,*
> *Bill Doolin, Bill Doolin,*
> *You're the subject of my song.*

"Charlie," said Victor, putting his hand on his friend's shoulder, "I don't know squat about poetry, but I think that sucks."

"I was afraid of that," said Charlie.

8

Monday it rained, a hard steady rain that drummed on the roof of the mansion and made Charlie think about horse's hooves. All the previous afternoon a west wind had carried to Charlie's ears the sounds of the track: the bugler calling the horses to the post and the roar of the crowd. About a dozen people from the Phoenix Colony had gone to the races and Charlie had been invited as well but had refused. He might be recognized and he couldn't leave Alexander Luft. For much of the afternoon he had listened to Luft working in the next room as he studied his chart and fiddled—he refused to call it writing—with his Bill Doolin poems.

> *Bill Doolin's horse pulled up lame,*
> *And so he missed the terrible game*
> *That brought down Dick and Bill,*
> *Bob and Grat that day in Coffeyville*
> *When the Dalton Gang was blown to history*
> *And Bill rode back to the Territory.*

All afternoon Charlie had been aware of races being run, races which he was unable to see. And of course the month was passing. Here it was already the second week of the meet and what had he seen? Zilch. And at dinner that night Charlie had had to listen to how

Frank had won the daily double and how Hercel Potter, who never had any luck at all, had won $437 on a trifecta by betting the birth date of William Butler Yeats. "Who?" Charlie had almost said.

But Charlie knew that his unhappiness wasn't really connected to missing a bunch of horse races. It had to do with what he was worst at, which was waiting. Here at the Phoenix Colony he was waiting for something to happen—either for the person who was tormenting Alexander Luft to tip his hand or for information to show up from some other quarter: a sudden clue or the appearance of a witness. Even with Long Meadows he was waiting. Each morning he sent Eddie Gillespie out on a series of tasks and each evening Eddie came back having learned nothing. The previous night Charlie had talked to Janey Burris on the telephone, holding the receiver pressed tightly to his mouth as if to absorb some of her warmth. He had told her about Ted Davis and ever since she had been explaining to him that she should go down to Long Meadows and get a job.

"I'm on vacation. The kids are in day camp. This is the perfect chance. Besides, I'm bored."

"There's nothing to justify it," Charlie had said. "Gillespie can't turn up anything and there's no motive. And as for Davis, well, there's a good chance it's just hot air."

"Do you think it's hot air?"

"I don't know."

"Let me go see."

"Davis said he'd get proof. I'll talk to him tomorrow and we'll decide after that."

"You want me to come out there tonight?"

"I've got too much work to do."

"You mean you know who's been tormenting that poor critic?"

"No, I've got to work on these Bill Doolin poems."

"Oh, Charlie, you're impossible! We could have played in your tub."

Monday morning at the silent table Charlie had kept his hand clamped over his mouth as he read in the *Saratogian* the story about the robbery at the Bentley on Saturday night. Even so he made some groaning noises, then had to bob his head apologetically when

Alexander Luft glared at him. The ruby necklace had been worth $15,000. Charlie was again struck by how much the thief seemed to know about the hotel and its guests. Various rude things were said about Victor both by the police and the hotel staff. The poem was set off in a little box.

> *They seek me here,*
> *They seek me there,*
> *They search but cannot find me.*
> *The police despair,*
> *So guests beware,*
> *Your gold will wine and dine me.*

Although the article was serious, it had a faintly humorous edge and Charlie could guess how much pleasure the reporters were having with the whole escapade. It was a comic event, not, of course, to anyone connected to the hotel, but to the world at large. Charlie wondered again about the poems. Black Bart had left similar poems as an act of bravado and to show the world he was not a common criminal. Possibly the same motivations lay behind the Bentley poems, but their effect was to draw tremendous attention to the hotel and Charlie began to wonder if that wasn't the point. Was it possible that the stolen jewelry was of secondary importance, that the real purpose was to hurt the Bentley? And why should someone want to hurt the hotel? Maybe out of maliciousness, maybe for revenge, maybe for some other reason.

Charlie had his lunch in the barn. The Ping-Pong table could be pulled apart and half could be tilted up to make a little wall, allowing someone, as it were, to play himself. It was still raining hard and Charlie was alone. He was trying to develop a new serve and to improve his return, but after half an hour of batting balls against the board, then crawling around on the floor to retrieve them, he gave it up. What was he doing? How had he reduced himself to writing crummy poems and playing Ping-Pong a la solo? The weather report said it would rain all day. Couldn't he go to the track? There would probably be no one from the Phoenix Colony. Couldn't he root for his winners, see horses bust their noble hearts in a dash for the finish line; couldn't he participate in the real world? Besides, with his rain hat and raincoat he would be somewhat disguised. He could get there half an hour before post time, buy a *Racing Form* and get down to serious work. As for Alexander Luft, he would check on him and then let Arlo Webster know he was going. He would make about five carefully considered bets. What was Jesse James's birthday? September 5, 1847. Surely those numbers could be turned into specific horses running in specific races. With hunches like these, he was bound to be a winner.

Charlie always bought a ticket to the clubhouse although he hardly spent any time there as he journeyed between the paddock and the track, watched the jockeys weighing in, saw the replay of each race on one of the three hundred closed-circuit TV monitors, and placed his bet at one of the five hundred and fifty-five pari-mutuel windows. But he hated being kept out of any place. So he paid the extra couple of bucks, got his hand stamped, then had to keep his hand dry just so the darn ultraviolet ink wouldn't wash away. Actually, he knew the steward who stamped his hand: Tony Geremiah, whom he had once arrested for some reason or another, maybe for fighting in a bar.

"Don't tell anyone you've seen me, Tony," said Charlie. "I'm in disguise."

"You can count on me," said Tony.

Today, because of the rain, the clubhouse and grandstand were crowded even though there were probably no more than twenty thousand people at the track. The air smelt of wet wood and pine trees and manure and mud, cigar smoke, greasy food, and wet clothing. Black umbrellas were everywhere.

Charlie arrived around one. He figured he didn't have time to make any serious judgments about the first race so he bet his age—fifty-two—on the daily double just because that was part of the tradition. The number five horse was a twenty to one shot called Nevermore. But what was two bucks? As he read about Nevermore in the *Racing Form*, it occurred to Charlie that even at the track he was unable to escape poetry. The number two horse in the second race was named Girl Fever. Not much poetry there.

Each year at the track Charlie was struck by the changes. Sometimes they were for the good, like the addition of the SAM betting machines. Sometimes they were for the bad, like jamming the grass with parked cars. This year there was a terrible change: the combining of the saddling area with the paddock. In the past, Charlie had loved the saddling area because he could get close to a horse, look it in the eyes and demand, Are you a winner or a loser? But now the saddling area was fenced off within the paddock. Some of the horses were up to forty feet away. Even when the riders mounted and the horses circled the walking ring, the fence was so crowded that it was hard to get a good look. For Charlie, getting a good look was even more important than reading the *Racing Form*. Down at Belmont people stood on a series of stone risers to one side of the walking ring and you always had a good view, but now at Saratoga it was going to be very hard. And who did these changes benefit? The owners, thought Charlie, and probably the insurance companies, who were afraid of people getting kicked. Soon it would be better to see the whole thing on TV and not bother with the track at all.

The first race was one mile and three sixteenths for maidens three years and upward. Nevermore had never come closer than a third place finish, which he'd managed down at Belmont in May. Charlie made his bet, then hurried to the rail to watch the horses being urged into the gate, which was by the one eighth of a mile pole right in front of the grandstand. It began raining harder than ever and there was even some hail. The tote board was just a gray blur.

Nevermore was the number five horse, a dark brown colt with a white blaze on his forehead and three white stockings. Charlie didn't recognize the name of the jockey or the trainer or the farm. Their colors were puce and magenta with a light green cap.

"Let's go, Nevermore!" shouted Charlie. The horse seemed to have no wish to enter the gate, or rather he wanted to enter it backward and kept rearing up and shaking his head. Nobody was happy. Everybody was sopping wet. The track was a quagmire.

"The horses are almost ready," said the announcer. The numbers stopped changing on the tote board as the pari-mutuel windows were shut down.

"Come on, Nevermore!" shouted Charlie. No more than fifty people were standing along the fence, rain beating down on their umbrellas, drenching their pants and shoes. Die-hards, thought Charlie, true enthusiasts.

Then came the bell.

"They're off," called the announcer.

Almost before Charlie could register the fact, the nine horses leapt forward out of the gate, splashed past him, and were gone in a multi-colored blur. Their hooves on the wet track made a noise like a dozen toilets being plunged at once. Mud was kicked up and Charlie even got a small hunk on the sleeve of his raincoat. He looked at it with a kind of pride, then turned back to the track where Nevermore had taken an early lead. The track was a mile and an eighth around and already the horses had disappeared by the one mile pole off to the right by Nelson Avenue. This was a quiet time as the announcer listed the order of the horses and the fans waited for developments and prepared their lungs for the last rush. The rain banged off the roof of the clubhouse, drummed on the canvas awnings. Nevermore was still first at the seven eighths pole and Charlie began bouncing on the balls of his sodden feet. He grew aware of a muttering behind him. Why hadn't he put more money on Nevermore? Never mind the double, he should have plunged to win.

By the half mile pole way off across the track Nevermore had increased his lead to three lengths. The horses were just long specks in the gray distance. The muttering grew louder and the names of individual horses began to be shouted out. More people came down to the rail. Charlie began bouncing a little higher and all his other worries disappeared. The hoof prints in front of him had filled to little lakes of muddy water, pennants flapped. At the three eighths pole Nevermore was four lengths ahead.

"He's going to make it!" shouted Charlie. "He's going to make it!"

But there is a perfectly good reason why favorites are favorites and why Nevermore was a twenty to one shot. In the home stretch everything fell apart. Nevermore was one of those horses who is brilliant at winning nine tenths of a race. And then zip, zero, nothing. He didn't even place. The horses and jockeys rushed past in a great slosh of water toward the finish line as the crowd roared and pumped up their lungs. The horses were uniformly mud-colored and the jockeys' silks were solid brown. The winner was a filly named Bright Moments. Charlie had turned away even before she crossed the finish line. Nevermore came in eighth, exhausted and frothing at the mouth.

"Why am I such a jerk?" thought Charlie. "How do I let myself get so worked up over a horse race?"

It was at that moment that Charlie saw Rolf Vinner. Of course, he didn't recognize him at first. He was only aware of seeing someone he vaguely knew and because he didn't want to be recognized he stepped back and tugged his hat down on his forehead. He realized it wasn't someone from Saratoga and he realized it wasn't someone from the Phoenix Colony. Then he found himself thinking of the old jockey, Ted Davis, and he knew it was Rolf Vinner, the man who owned Long Meadows.

He had been standing down at the rail about thirty feet from Charlie and now he was hurrying back toward the grandstand with a little smile on his face. He appeared to have a winning ticket. He wore a tan London Fog raincoat and a brown golfing cap. Although he appeared drenched, the rain didn't seem to bother him. He stared straight ahead and didn't glance in Charlie's direction.

Anyone watching Charlie would have thought that he had won as well, but in fact Charlie had stopped thinking of horses altogether. Pulling up the collar of his coat, he set off after Vinner, while making sure he stayed far enough behind so he wouldn't be noticed.

The bet on the double turned out to be Charlie's last bet of the day. For the rest of the afternoon he followed Rolf Vinner, even though his number two horse, Girl Fever, easily won the second race and usually this would have been enough for Charlie to trust a few more of his hunches. Vinner didn't bet every race, maybe he bet four of the remaining eight, but he studied each race and gave a lot of attention to the *Racing Form* and looked at the horses in the paddock. And when he bet, he went to the fifty dollar window.

Vinner seemed very calm and intense at the same time, as if all his energies were precisely focused in one direction. He didn't talk to anyone or pay attention to the people around him. He didn't eat or get himself a beer, although after the sixth race he bought a cup of coffee. He ignored the depredations of the weather. All in all he behaved like a serious handicapper and displayed little emotion during the actual running of the races. Of the five races on which he bet, including the first, he collected on three of them. It struck Charlie that it was like work. Vinner didn't particularly seem to be enjoying himself, he was doing a job. Charlie knew a number of handicappers like that. If they found themselves getting emotional, they didn't bet. Sometimes Charlie wished he could be like that as well.

It continued to rain throughout the afternoon and the track was a wreck. A number of horses were scratched. Vinner went down to the rail for each race, even the ones in which he hadn't bet. Charlie stayed back by the hot dog stand and watched. When Vinner won, his face would wear a little smile. When he lost, he showed no emotion at all. He would walk back to the grandstand or clubhouse and not even bother to wipe the water from his face.

Vinner won on the last race on an eight to one shot named Pork Belly. Charlie had stood nearby and almost bought a ticket on the same horse, but then decided not to bet, not liking to mix business and pleasure. Although Vinner collected over four hundred dollars on Pork Belly, it didn't seem to excite him. If it had been Charlie, he would have been jumping up and down and telling everyone around him about his good fortune. After the race, Vinner walked back to his red Toyota Camry, and Charlie caught a cab to the Phoenix Colony, feeling he had done a good day's work.

Before even changing his wet clothes, he called his answering service and told them to beep Eddie Gillespie. Then he waited by the booth for Eddie's call. It was about six o'clock and people were returning from their studios and getting ready for dinner.

Harry Rostov saw Charlie waiting outside the phone booth. "You look like someone tried to drown you."

"I was at the track."

"How'd you do?"

"I lost on the double. After that I studied the horses and got wet."

"Learn much?" There were raindrops caught up in Rostov's black beard and mustache and he licked them away with his tongue.

"I learned if you get emotional, don't bet. What about you?"

"I wrote a poem about critics. Maybe I'll read it when we do our little number on Sunday."

Charlie groaned. "Bill Doolin," he said. "I've got to read my Bill Doolin poems."

Eddie Gillespie called a minute later. "No, Charlie, no, no, no, I've learned nothing. All I've done is gotten sopping wet and ruined a good pair of shoes."

"I'll buy you a new pair."

"Do I get to pick them out?"

"Sure."

"What do you want now?"

"Get a picture of Vinner," said Charlie, "then look up some of Blake Moss's gambling buddies and see if they recognize him."

"How do I get a picture?"

"Pick up that brochure from Long Meadows. His picture's on the back. Do it right away, okay?"

Charlie had just time to change his clothes and get downstairs again before the dinner chimes were rung. He was one of the last into the dining room and it was only when he was seated that he realized that Alexander Luft had not come down to dinner.

At another table, Arlo Webster seemed to notice Luft's absence at the same moment. Charlie saw him call over one of the women who worked in the kitchen and ask her something. The woman shook her head. When guests planned to miss dinner, they were requested to let the kitchen know. Luft apparently had not spoken to anyone about being absent. Charlie then saw Webster asking something of the five other people at his table. As they shook their heads, Webster got to his feet and walked over to Charlie's table, walking slowly as if trying to make himself appear calm.

"Have any of you seen Alexander?" asked Webster.

Nobody had.

"Maybe he was taking a nap and overslept," said Charlie. "I'll go knock on his door."

He stood up, half expecting Webster to come with him, but Webster returned to his table, still walking slowly, as if Alexander Luft were the last of his worries.

Charlie tried to imitate Webster's calm as he left the dining room, but then broke into a run as he crossed the hall and dashed up the steps two at a time. Once upstairs, he ran to Luft's door, where he slid to a stop, took a deep breath, and tapped on one of the panels. No answer. Charlie knocked more loudly. Still no answer. Charlie tried the handle. The door was unlocked.

The first thing Charlie noticed was that papers were scattered everywhere. Then he noticed a pair of shoes, their soles pointed toward him as he came through the door. Then he realized the shoes were attached to a pair of feet, a pair of legs. Charlie ran toward them. Alexander Luft lay on the floor half covered with papers. His head was all bloody. Charlie knelt down and took his wrist, feeling for a pulse. Luft groaned and tried to roll over. The blood on his head had also streaked his face, but it was drying and the wound must have closed. Luft opened his eyes and tried to raise himself.

"My head," he whispered, then he fell back onto the carpet.

Charlie glanced around quickly, making sure no one else was in the room, then he ran out the door and down the hall. Webster must have heard his feet on the stairs because he came out of the dining room to meet him.

"Luft has been attacked," said Charlie. "I think he'll be okay but you need an ambulance and you need the police. Call Peterson himself."

"The police?" Webster's forehead wrinkled with dismay.

"There's nothing else to do, but if you get Peterson then maybe you can keep it out of the newspapers."

Charlie watched Webster hurry off toward his office, then he turned back to the stairs.

Alexander Luft was still lying on the floor, but when Charlie ran into the room, Luft groaned again. Charlie knelt down beside him and again tried to take his pulse. Luft pulled away and tried to sit up.

"There's an ambulance coming," said Charlie. The papers covered everything and it was hard to move without stepping on them. Luft wore a white shirt and the front was spotted with blood. His gray hair was disheveled and a long strand hung down over his brow. Dry streaks of blood had hardened on his forehead and cheeks. He seemed dazed and unable to focus.

"It was terrible," he said. "Someone was in my room. I came in here, everything was a mess. My manuscript. . . . Somebody must have been hiding behind the door. My head feels awful."

"Lie back down," said Charlie. He guessed that Luft could have a concussion. He might also be in shock. A broken table leg lay on the floor and Charlie suspected that Luft had been attacked with it.

The ambulance arrived a few minutes later. No siren, no hysteria, but still it caused a disturbance and when Luft was carried down the stairs on a stretcher most of the guests at the colony were there to see him go. One woman broke into loud sobs. Charlie watched them. There was no one who seemed indifferent, who didn't seem upset. Peterson arrived with two of his detectives, Ernest Tidings and Ron Novack. They were the unemotional ex-military types that Peterson favored: men with all the passion of personal computers. Both were dressed in raincoats and dark suits. They immediately began to question the guests about where they had been during the afternoon and whether anyone had seen anything unusual. Although they attempted to be tactful they were men for whom tact was a mysterious abstraction. Charlie saw Hercel Potter keep shaking his head. Rostov and Frank McGinnis were whispering together, clearly nervous and upset.

Charlie led Peterson upstairs to Luft's room. Arlo Webster followed them. Glancing back, Charlie saw Peterson gawking at the stained glass window, the carved woodwork and Tiffany lamps. He seemed quiet and deferential. Once inside Luft's room, however, Peterson toughened up.

"Okay, Charlie, where were you when this guy got attacked?"

"I expect I was downstairs on the phone. Earlier I had been at the track."

"This must be a wonderful vacation for you," said Peterson.

Webster had been picking up the papers from the floor. He stopped and spoke to Peterson somewhat impatiently. "Mr. Bradshaw had told me he was going out. I was supposed to be watching Mr. Luft."

"And were you?"

"He had been in the library, which is in another building. He left there around six. Apparently, the attacker was waiting in his room."

Peterson glanced around. He was a big man who liked to be in charge. "You didn't have anyone watching the room?" he asked.

"There was a man in the reading room. He didn't see anyone. The attacker could have come the other way, up the back stairs."

"And what were you doing at the track, Charlie, working on another case?" asked Peterson.

"That's right," said Charlie angrily. Then he remembered he had gone purely for pleasure. It was only by accident that he had seen Rolf Vinner.

"And do you have any idea who's been doing this stuff?" asked Peterson. He sat down on a straight chair by the bureau and rubbed the back of his neck.

Charlie sat down as well. "I've put together a chart but there doesn't seem to be anyone who could have done it on all four occasions. I'd appreciate hearing what Tidings and Novack find out."

"Two people, Charlie, it's got to have been done by two people. Maybe even three."

"It's hard to imagine one person doing it," said Charlie. "Let alone several."

"They're artists," said Peterson. "Artists are nuts."

Arlo Webster continued to pick up the papers and put them into a pile. Books had been thrown around as well.

"Maybe Luft will just decide to leave after this," said Charlie. "It must be doing his work a lot of harm."

"That'd make it easier for you, wouldn't it?" said Peterson, standing up again. "Plus you could chalk it up as one of your successes."

The broken table leg had traces of blood on it. Peterson put it in a plastic bag. Possibly the state police lab could do something with it.

"What about the Bentley," asked Charlie, "have you learned anything about those robberies?"

"The best thing they could do," said Peterson, "would be to dump Victor Plotz and hire some pros."

"So you haven't learned anything?"

"We got some leads."

Charlie doubted that. "What about the poems?"

"I can't figure them. They just rile everybody up. Maybe you're writing them," said Peterson, then he laughed. "After all, you're the poet."

It was nine-thirty by the time Peterson left with Tidings and Novack. People were still upset and there was a line for the telephone. A woman from Salt Lake City who carved figures from sandstone and a novelist from northern Virginia both said they didn't think they would be able to stay. There was too much tension. They couldn't concentrate on their work.

"This time I can't be a suspect," Hercel Potter told Charlie as they left the mansion for the library, where there was another phone. "I was downtown and didn't get back until dinnertime."

"Was anyone with you?" asked Charlie.

"Bobrowski and that new painter, Freddie Watts. We had a couple of beers at the Tin and Lint."

"So maybe you're doing it with somebody else," said Charlie. "Maybe two or three people are doing these things to Luft. That's what the police seem to think."

"Yeah, and Kennedy was assassinated by the Academy of American Poets."

Charlie used the phone in Arlo Webster's office. He'd had an idea about the robberies at the Bentley and he wanted to talk to Victor. He reached Raoul, who was not welcoming, then had to wait about five minutes as Victor came to the phone.

"How come Raoul doesn't like you?" asked Charlie.

"He's jealous of my good looks."

"No, really."

Victor cleared his throat. "Raoul likes things to be just right. He likes appearances. Me, I'm just the opposite. And maybe I tease him too much."

Charlie found himself thinking of the Stevens poem, "The Emperor of Ice-Cream." Perhaps Victor was a horny toe as well. "So how's the Bentley?"

"We got this place as tight as a drum." said Victor. "Not even a flea could sneak in."

"That's what you say every time."

Victor groaned. "Come on, Charlie, you sound like your mother."

Charlie decided to ignore that. "I've been thinking about those poems," he said. "What's the main effect of them?"

"They make me depressed."

"Why don't you talk to my mother and see if anyone has shown an interest in buying the hotel."

"You think she'd sell?"

"She wouldn't have dreamed of it a month ago but she might now. And that might be the very point."

"What do you mean?"

"It's not jewelry the thief's after, he's trying to damage the Bentley."

"With poetry?"

"It's powerful stuff, Victor, powerful stuff."

Charlie got back to the mansion just as a police car pulled up to the rear door with Alexander Luft. Arlo Webster hurried down the back steps to greet him and help him to his room. Luft shook him off. He was angry. A white bandage swathed his head like a turban.

"I'm not going to be pushed out of here," he was shouting. "I came here to do serious work and I intend to do it. I'm not going to be bullied."

"No one is suggesting that you leave," said Arlo Webster, holding open the back door. "We just want to make sure that you're safe."

"Then catch the person who is doing this," said Luft. "It's probably a writer." Here he glared at Charlie, who was walking behind him.

"What makes you think it's a writer?" asked Charlie. "Did you see anyone?"

"No, nothing like that. There was a reporter at the hospital. He said it was probably a writer."

"You talked to a reporter?" asked Webster.

"What do I have to hide?" asked Luft. "Aren't I being attacked and aren't you doing nothing about it?"

"We've already increased the number of security guards," said Webster, "and I'm in the process of hiring several more. You'll be perfectly safe. What did you tell the reporter?"

"I told him exactly what's been happening." Luft shook himself free of Arlo Webster and headed for the back stairs. Charlie started to follow him, but Webster stopped him.

"There's a guard upstairs." They walked along the hall toward the front rooms. When Charlie had first met Arlo Webster, he had been struck by how urbane he seemed, how sophisticated, like one of those men in a *New Yorker* ad. Now he looked frazzled and careworn and his shoulders were hunched.

"Are you making any progress?" asked Webster.

"All I know is that it can't be one person," said Charlie. "But that seems so improbable that it's hard to make sense of it."

"I'll have to call the newspaper and talk to that reporter," said Webster. "Perhaps I can get them to hold the story."

"Who would benefit if the Phoenix Colony went out of business?" asked Charlie.

"Developers, I suppose. We've got four hundred acres almost adjoining the track. The way Saratoga's growing, it could mean a fortune for somebody."

They walked past the kitchen. Although everything was locked up, a few lingering smells reminded Charlie that he had missed dinner. "Maybe there's another fake artist here," suggested Charlie, "besides me. Maybe someone came here pretending to be an artist just to damage the Colony, to try to wreck it. Luft is just the guy they happen to be picking on."

"Many of these people I know," said Webster. "Either they've been here before or I know their work. There're only about half a dozen who are new to me."

"Why don't you make a list and include their backgrounds," said Charlie, "and you might check your staff as well."

Webster looked distressed. "This is an impossible situation, Mr. Bradshaw. I hope you can make sense of it."

They had paused in the great hall, which was empty. Charlie noticed the mosaic of the phoenix on the wall over the fireplace. The light seemed to twinkle off the colored tiles. "How come this place is called the Phoenix Colony?" he asked.

"That was the name given to the mansion," said Webster. "There had been an earlier mansion but it burned around the turn of the century. This one was built on the ruins of the other, just like the phoenix rising from the flames."

"Nothing to do with Arizona?"

"Not a thing."

"It must have been a tremendous fire."

Webster tugged at his lower lip. "That's one of my greatest fears," he said.

As Charlie left Webster and climbed the stairs, he saw Frank McGinnis hurrying toward him. "You've got a phone call," he said. "I was knocking on your door."

"Thanks," said Charlie.

The call was from Eddie Gillespie. He sounded furious.

"Charlie, it's bad enough that I go around imitating the goddamn cops and talking to the same people they been talking to, but now I'm doing the same thing as Blake Moss. I'm sick of it."

"What do you mean?" asked Charlie, shutting the door of the phone booth.

"You told me to show Vinner's picture to Moss's gambling pals. I've taken it to three of them and they all say how Moss showed them the same picture and asked the same question."

"You mean Moss asked if Vinner was a gambler?"

"That's what I'm saying, isn't it?"

"And what did they say?"

"They'd never seen him before."

Charlie realized he was grinning. It seemed he was finally on the right track. He wanted to pat Eddie's coiffured head, pinch his cheeks. "Eddie, believe me, this is a good sign. Keep talking to people, talk to Pinkie Schwartz. Try to find out about dice and card games. You're looking for something fairly high class and private."

"So this isn't a bust?"

"No, no, Eddie, you're doing a great job."

After Gillespie hung up, Charlie telephoned Long Meadows. He wanted to talk to Ted Davis to see if he had learned anything. And had Davis known that Vinner bet the horses? It was getting close to ten-thirty but Charlie hoped that Davis would still be available.

A woman answered and Charlie told her who he wanted. There was a pause. "I'm afraid that Mr. Davis can't come to the phone," she said.

"Has he gone to bed already?"

Again there was a pause. "Are you a friend of his?" asked the woman.

Charlie waited. Then he realized he was squeezing the receiver so tightly that his hand hurt.

"I'm sorry to tell you this," said the woman, "but Mr. Davis passed away last night in his sleep. He had a heart attack."

9

Janey Burris crossed her legs, then tugged at the hem of her skirt so it just cut across her knee. It was a dark blue skirt and she wore it with a white blouse—a combination which she thought of as her Campfire Girl outfit. She often wore it when applying for jobs, which was why she was wearing it today.

Sitting on the other side of the desk in a brown leather swivel chair, Rolf Vinner was thumbing through Janey's resume. "You seem to have a lot of experience with the elderly," said Vinner.

"I like the work," said Janey.

In his blazer and gray slacks, with his horn-rimmed glasses and thick gray hair, Vinner didn't resemble a man so much as an institution. At least, that is what Janey thought. Most traces of idiosyncrasy and personal taste had been stripped away, leaving only the generic businessman. Even his gestures were generic, even his smile. Vinner wore a school ring with a red stone, maybe a college ring. The frames of his glasses were thick black plastic. His eyes were dark blue with yellow flecks. They stared at Janey benignly.

"Why do you want to work in Albany, Miss Burris, if you live in Saratoga?"

"My boyfriend lives in Albany. We're planning to get married. At least that's what he says."

"Would you have to take time off?"

"Maybe a day. Neither of us has money for a real honeymoon." She paused and counted to three. "To tell you the truth, he's much more eager about marriage than I am. I thought if I got a job in Albany and maybe moved here. . . ." She let her sentence trail off, then lowered her eyes.

"I see," said Vinner. His smile seemed fixed and Janey imagined him unplugging it at night and giving it a shine. "And when could you start work?" Vinner added.

"Anytime. I'm on vacation right now. I was intending to go back to personal care work if I didn't find another job. I'll just notify the agency that I've made other plans."

"How did you know we were looking for someone?"

Janey tried on a generic smile of her own. It seemed to fit. "I've had friends who worked in rest homes or nursing homes and I've done work like that myself. It seems they're always understaffed."

"That's true enough," said Vinner. "We can't pay as much as the hospitals."

"But the work is so much more rewarding," said Janey, giving the smile another try. If she got this smile down pat, she thought, maybe she'd have a future as a quiz show contestant. And what would she do with those big bucks? She'd buy Charlie a tuxedo and make him take her to the Hunt Club Ball.

"Could you start work on Thursday?" asked Vinner.

"That would be fine."

"Do you have any time right now? Let me introduce you to Mrs. Nash, she's the nurse's aide. She'll show you around and give you a sense of your duties, so on Thursday you'll know what to do."

Mrs. Nash was a large woman of about sixty who wore a white uniform that fit her so tightly that Janey imagined that when she removed it at night, Mrs. Nash would be released like Jell-O onto the floor. She had bluish-white hair which was carefully swirled and ringleted and kept in a net. All in all, Mrs. Nash communicated a sense of containment. Even her voice seemed contained and, despite her size, she spoke in a little girl's whisper.

"Pleased to meet you," she said. "I hope you'll be happy at Long Meadows." She reached out her hand.

"I hope so, too," said Janey, shaking the hand. She found the wish for happiness slightly peculiar but as an amateur private detective she was finding everything peculiar and she suspected it was one of the hazards of the job.

They were standing in Vinner's office. Outside, the morning air looked sunny and warm. An elderly man with an aluminum walker was edging his way down a garden path. Janey released Mrs. Nash's hand. Rolf Vinner was smiling as if he could smile forever.

"Let's get started," said Janey. "I've got a hair appointment at one."

Mrs. Nash took Janey on a tour of the building. Although Long Meadows housed seventy-five residents, only about ten were unable to care for themselves and most of those were Alzheimer's patients. Since Long Meadows was relatively new—just five years—the residents themselves were relatively new. It was, Mrs. Nash insisted, a total care community. When new people signed on, they turned over their assets to the corporation. Single people were given studio apartments. Couples received something a little bigger, with one or two bedrooms. When a resident became too incapacitated to take care of himself, he or she would be moved to a room in the rear right wing of the building.

"What if they don't use up their money before they die?" asked Janey as they toured the lounges and TV rooms down on the first floor. Mrs. Nash had been introducing her to everyone they met—residents and staff alike—so that Janey's smile muscles hurt.

"It's all worked out," said Mrs. Nash, "and the money left over goes to the heirs. Fortunately, the board of directors oversees that. As for me, I find even my daily reports a chore. It's the spelling. Goodness knows how people do it."

"*I* before *E*," said Janey, "except after *C*."

Charlie had told her what he knew of Long Meadows, which wasn't much. What he wanted were the names of men and women who had died in the past year who had been somewhat incapacitated and who had had no close heirs and no regular visitors: people who could have died without anybody caring or noticing. He also wanted to know about Russell Weisberg, who had died at the beginning of

June. And then there was Ted Davis and the dead nurse, Janice Mitchell.

"We're taught to be suspicious of sudden death," Charlie had said, "but at a place like Long Meadows death is built into the system. Let's say someone is taking money from some old person who is too confused to protect himself and has no close relatives. Once the person is sucked dry or becomes suspicious, who's going to call the police if he suddenly dies in his sleep? He's supposed to die in his sleep. That's what he's come to Long Meadows to do."

Mrs. Nash spent an hour showing Janey the physical plant, as she kept calling it, and introducing her to lots of old people, to the other nurse's aides and staff, as well as to the doctor who came each morning. Everyone was friendly and good-humored. The old people seemed to be treated well and with affection. Some were active and happy and engaged in various projects, a few seemed depressed, but most were occupied in one way or other. She met Betsy Thomas, who welcomed her and offered to help her find an apartment in Albany. Everyone was so cheerful that Janey began to wonder if Charlie had made a mistake.

"The place where you have to look," Charlie had said, "is in the office. Learn who died, find out about them, find the cause of death, then check their financial records. Are there lots of little expenses? Do the records look fiddled with?"

"How can I get into the office?" Janey had asked.

"You'll have keys, you'll be working at night, and no one will be suspicious. Once you find some names and we can build up a case, I'll get the police to have the bodies exhumed."

The studio apartments were large and had views of the grounds. The furniture looked comfortable. There were TVs and kitchenettes. Reproductions of Winslow Homer watercolors hung on the walls. Each room had several call buttons in case the resident needed to summon assistance.

"Residents can prepare their own meals or come down to the dining room," Mrs. Nash explained.

"Everyone seems so very much alive," said Janey, "that it must make it extra hard when someone passes away."

"We expect it, we're used to it, but it's always a shock," said Mrs. Nash.

"And didn't a nurse die as well?" asked Janey. "I read something in the papers."

"Yes, she fell down the stairs. She was a dear friend."

"How terrible."

"Janice Mitchell was always in a hurry. She was impatient. I sometimes think that by being too much in a hurry people use up their future. They crowd two moments into one moment and then of course there's nothing left. And death is here. Someone wants to watch TV or has a dentist appointment or wants to play golf, but death has other plans and taps him on the shoulder. 'Come with me,' death says, 'your time is up.' "

"How cheery," said Janey with a little shiver.

"We're cheery up until that moment," Mrs. Nash said in her little girl's voice, "or at least we try to be."

When Alexander Luft swam, he pushed his arms forward into a wedge, then swept them abruptly apart in a way that reminded Charlie of Moses dividing the Red Sea. Technically it was a version of the breaststroke but Luft made it appear somehow biblical. Or maybe it was his turban-like bandage that gave Luft a biblical cast, as if he were one of the three wise men. It struck Charlie as depressingly ironic that not only was he unable to swim his own laps, but he was forced to observe someone else doing the very thing which was denied him. He didn't dare go into the Saratoga YMCA. The two last attacks had occurred when Charlie was elsewhere, and while this did not prove that someone knew he was a private detective it meant that he had to be more careful, especially since it was certain that either today or tomorrow he would have to go down to Albany.

Eddie Gillespie was still talking to Blake Moss's gambling cronies, including the bookie, Pinkie Schwartz, and to each Moss had shown the photograph of Rolf Vinner. Although none recognized Vinner, what they remembered was Moss's certainty that Vinner was a gambler, which made Charlie think that very shortly they would get an identification. He had mentioned none of this to the police. He wanted to put together a credible case before he went to Boland and urged him to exhume the bodies of Ted Davis and maybe Russell Weisberg. And perhaps others as well. That morning he had telephoned Joseph Stompanella of the Northeast Mutual Insurance Company and told him that he was making headway and that he should gather his own evidence against Long Meadows in case Charlie had to go to the police.

"Can't you keep the police out of it?" Stompanella had asked.

"We're looking at the possibility of four murders, maybe more," Charlie said, then he listened to Stompanella breathing and muttering on the other end of the line.

"We don't like that word at Northeast Mutual. It upsets the board of directors. Let's say I put the case together, what are you going to want?"

"Northeast Mutual is going to demand that the Albany police get an exhumation order."

There was more astonished breathing. In fact, Stompanella sounded like a person whom someone had tried to drown, but who had fought valiantly and got away and had just now broken the surface into the bright blue air.

"Jesus, Bradshaw, you better be right."

If it weren't for Luft's bandage, it would be difficult for Charlie to think of depredations and murder while sitting in one of the chairs bordering the Phoenix Colony pool. It was hot and the sun beat down on his bare skin, now suitably protected by various creams. He nibbled his chicken sandwich. Next to him, Lucy Feinstein was eating from a cup of cottage cheese. She was a novelist who taught in Manhattan. Although she worked at a different university from Alexander Luft, she knew him and knew many of his colleagues. Lucy Feinstein was a small thin woman of about fifty with a mass of dark ringlets that half-concealed her bony face. She wore a black bathing suit that seemed too large and sunglasses with black frames and lots of tiny gold flecks. She was amusing and intelligent and Charlie felt comfortable with her.

"For a writer to teach," she was saying, "he or she has to love it, otherwise it chews away at you. Fortunately I love it, but I know plenty of writers who teach only because they think it gives them time to write, but they're not happy and they feel sorry for themselves and they have no respect for what they are doing. It gnaws at them. They dislike their colleagues and they either mock or envy their students. Perhaps both."

"I'd think an English department would be a perfect place for a writer," said Charlie. Several other people were also sitting around the pool eating their lunch. On Charlie's left, Hercel Potter was fussing over the crossword in *The New York Times*. Nearby on the grass Frank McGinnis was doing push-ups. He was sweating and the sun glistened on his skin. It was shortly after one o'clock.

"No, Mr. Fletcher, stick to your ad agency. Of course, I have close friends in my department, but mostly the attitude ranges from indifference to hostility. Among the most extreme post-structuralists I am simply regarded as a self-deluded throwback to the nineteenth century, but even with the traditionalists there can be friction. Writers and academics have opposite drives. A good writer is a disorderer of information while a good academic is just the opposite."

"I don't follow you," said Charlie.

Lucy Feinstein put her cup of cottage cheese back in her lunch basket, then took out a cigarette and lit it with a small gold lighter. She blew a puff of smoke out of the corner of her mouth to keep it away from Charlie. "A good writer should be pushing at the very edge of his or her craft," she continued. "He or she is looking for new ways of doing things, not just for the sake of originality but because writing itself is a process of discovery. A writer is on the side of disruption. Every page becomes a new place, a place never seen before. An academic, on the other hand, tries to order and classify and catalog and codify. Even the most radical is basically a tidier of information. The two tasks are nearly opposite but both are completely necessary to the culture."

"So they clash?" asked Charlie.

"Worse. A writer fits into an English department about as snugly as a fox into a Spartan boy's tummy."

"What about someone like Alexander Luft?" asked Charlie. "I'd think he would fit pretty well into both camps."

"I've known a few writers in his department. Windy's been very hard on them and has been effective at keeping several from getting tenure. That's surprising, considering that he used to write poetry."

"Luft was a poet?"

"I don't know if he was a poet but he wrote poetry in college. He even won one of those prizes from the Academy of American Poets and some of his poems appeared in little magazines."

"And then he stopped writing?"

"Presumably. At least I've never seen anything else. But I wonder if one would really quit. I know I couldn't. Even if I never published another thing, I'd still keep scratching away. Just out of habit I guess. Writing is how I think and see the world. I simply can't imagine not doing it."

She drew on her cigarette, then stubbed it out on the concrete beneath her chair. Her lipstick had left a red smudge on the filter. Charlie glanced away to where Alexander Luft was continuing his laps. He was struck by the fact that Luft had told him he didn't write poetry. But had he said he had never written it? Then across the still air came the bugle from the track calling the horses to the first race. Charlie stared off at the row of pines on the far side of the pool. Maybe three hundred yards further on through the woods was the fence dividing the Phoenix Colony from the backstretch.

"Is that the track?" asked Lucy Feinstein.

"They're calling the horses to the post."

Lucy smiled. "You look like a dog listening to his master's voice." Then she added quickly, "Don't be offended. I like dogs."

Charlie tried to smile, then shook his head and didn't say anything. He was surprised by the perceptiveness of her remark. He thought of the horses entering onto the track and of how much he wished he could be there.

"You know, I'm not familiar with your work," said Lucy, "and I heard several of the other poets saying they didn't know it, either. Have you been writing long?"

"Oh, yes," said Charlie, wondering if she guessed his deception. "I write things and put them in a drawer. Sometimes I send them to magazines but not often. Coming here was a big decision for me."

"We're all looking forward to hearing you read this weekend."

Charlie's stomach felt queasy. "I'm not very used to reading in public," he said.

"Oh, you'll do fine. I just hope that we'll all be around to hear you."

Two more people had left—a lady printmaker from Maine and a man from northern Virginia who wrote novels. Both had come on August first and both said that the attacks on Luft and the general suspicion were upsetting their work. Others spoke of leaving as well. Although there was little public discussion of the attacks, there had been many private discussions. People were uncertain with each other and there was no one who wasn't disturbed by what had happened. Luft's room was under constant observation and even here by the pool there was a security guard straddling a chair near the bath house picking at his fingernails and looking bored.

Charlie found himself hoping that everybody would pack up and go home. That way they couldn't hear his Bill Doolin poems. Then he felt ashamed of himself. The best way to avoid the poetry reading was to catch the people who were torturing Alexander Luft before Sunday night. The trouble was that Charlie found himself no closer to an answer. That morning he had worked on his chart and had come to the decision that the attacks were being carried out by one person at the Colony and one person who was sneaking in from outside. It simply seemed impossible that one person at the Colony was doing it by himself. He had spoken to Arlo Webster, who had agreed to hire another security guard to patrol the woods as well as to hiring another detective to check on the backgrounds of six or seven guests who Charlie thought were possible suspects. But it seemed so ridiculous. Hercel Potter was one of those guests, as was the bearded Rostov, who was right now sitting on the other side of the pool peeling an orange. Charlie couldn't believe that either man was guilty. It was not that they were incapable of violence; it was the craziness. Pouring blood on the computer and all the rest. But now something that Lucy Feinstein had said gave Charlie another idea. He began collecting the remains of his lunch and putting them in his basket. Then he got to his feet.

"Back to work?" asked Lucy.

Charlie put a hand over his eyes to shield them from the sun. To his left he noticed Alexander Luft climbing out of the pool. "I've got to work on those poems," he said.

Lucy Feinstein gave him a friendly smile. "We can't wait to hear them," she said.

Victor Plotz stood sideways before the mirror in the men's room of the bar at the Bentley attempting to study his profile. It was bumpy and aggressive. Forehead, nose, chin: all thrust themselves forward. Even his eyeballs looked fat and pushy. How then was he to keep the low profile that Charlie had suggested? Or perhaps Charlie had meant low in the sense of vulgar. Victor shoved his long tongue out from between his lips and blew a Bronx cheer, a raspberry, a noise resembling a sick motorboat departing from a dock. Then he smiled at himself and straightened his gray tie. How handsome he was, how debonair. How could he not love himself? Spinning on his heel, he headed for the door and his appointment with Mabel Bradshaw. He was going to clear up this little trouble about the robberies. He meant to get to the bottom of things.

It was approaching two o'clock as Victor passed through the lobby. He was aware of people turning to look at him. Raoul with his sly attention, Billy the bellboy, Gertrude the receptionist with her milky bosom—Victor felt their cold looks bouncing like ice cubes off the warmth of his immaculate gray suit as he headed toward the stairs and Mabel Bradshaw's suite. Certainly, he had tried to see his employer earlier but first she had been closeted with her three nephews, then she had been interviewing a new or additional detective: a blond young man with greased-back hair and a double-breasted maroon suit who was now sitting on a chair by the elevator nibbling a toothpick. The man raised one side of his mouth in a crude sneer and Victor blew him a kiss. Enemies always brought out the best in him.

"How're you doin', Rambo?" said Victor. And then he forgot him. His business was with his boss and although Victor was confident that he had a certain way with women, there was something about Mabel Bradshaw that unnerved him. She was so red—red hair, red nails, red lips, red gowns, and rouged cheeks. And then they were about the same size, maybe she was even bigger. She would look at him through eyelashes that were at least two inches long and when she batted those lashes their very movement made a breeze that pushed Victor backward, or at least that's how it seemed to him. He would fight it, he would struggle like a trooper, but it was like fighting treacle and somehow it unmanned him. But now, thanks to Charlie, he had a lead or at least a new path of inquiry.

Victor paused at Mabel Bradshaw's door at the top of the stairs and tapped out a jivey little knock, a syncopated announcement of his arrival. From inside he heard what sounded like a sigh, then a voice said, "It's open."

Victor gave the door a push and was greeted by a wave of perfume that was like a second door which he had to break down: thick and palpable and sweet like the liquor-laden desserts popular at fern bars. On the far side of the room Mabel Bradshaw was reclining on what she called her Recamier, a narrow day bed or chaise covered with a peach colored satin that clashed violently with her scarlet gown. She stared at Victor without affection.

"You've been keeping something from me," said Victor, walking briskly into the room. "How can you expect me to do my job as hotel detective when you withhold important information?"

Mabel's expression changed from dislike to uncertainty. Sitting up, she pushed strands of her red hair away from her face. Her dress made a rustling noise. "What are you talking about?" she asked. She didn't look seventy. More like a blowzy fifty.

"I'm trying to discover who is robbing the hotel. By putting together certain facts, I can only conclude that you are not telling me what I need to know. Divvy up." Victor stopped at the foot of the Recamier and folded his arms. Mabel continued to stare at him. By now she was sitting quite straight.

"I'm not keeping anything from you," she said.

Victor gave a little chuckle, then was silent for a moment as he stared back with a look which he felt combined fondness and regret. "I believe that offers have been made to buy the hotel," he said, "and that you turned them down. I need to know who made them."

Mabel's eyes widened slightly. She lowered her long lashes and heaved them up again several times. "How did you know that?" she asked.

Victor found it difficult to appear modest. To his left was a queen-sized bed with a scarlet canopy and scarlet covers. The sheets, too, were scarlet and looked like satin. "I'm a detective," he said. "It's my job to deduce things."

"There were several offers in May and June. I rejected them. They came from a lawyer, Hamilton Bryan."

"Were they too low?"

"No, they were quite respectable. I just didn't want to sell."

"And you haven't heard from Bryan since the last offer? When was that."

"About June fifteenth. How did you learn about this?"

Victor put a finger to his lips. "We have our secrets. If this Bryan contacts you again, let me know." He began backing toward the door. Once he reached it, he again raised a cautionary finger. "Don't mention this to anyone," he said. "You can't trust your closest friend." Then he was gone.

Hamilton Bryan had the face of a rich skinflint: it gave nothing away. Otherwise he was a handsome enough young fellow, or at least young in Victor's terms, meaning about forty. As for handsomeness, it was for Victor an overrated commodity since he had done pretty well without it. Bryan's face was thin and smooth and he had a little moustache and silky brown hair. As he leaned back in his swivel chair and stared at Victor across his desk he kept softly stroking his own cheek, little caresses meant to reassure himself of his own affection. He wore a tan suit and a blue bow tie. And not one of those clip-on jobbies, thought Victor.

"And do you represent Mrs. Bradshaw, Mr. Plotz?" asked Bryan. Even Bryan's voice was smooth, like the voice a Vienna Choir boy might develop after adolescence.

"Isn't that what I been telling you?" Victor had sat down without being asked, one of his more important mottos being: Always Feel at

Home. The lawyer's office had a lot of leather and dark wood and expensive rugs. An air conditioner hummed in the window.

"And so she's interested in selling the hotel after all?"

Victor discovered a speck of lint on his sleeve and dropped it in the ashtray. "Certainly she's more interested than she was," he said, "but she loves the hotel. She doesn't want it to go to just anybody."

"My clients are not just anybody, Mr. Plotz."

"Then who are they?"

"I am not at liberty to say."

Victor rubbed his hands together and looked suddenly cheerful. "It seems like we've reached a bump in the road, doesn't it?"

Hamilton Bryan didn't respond and his face remained blank.

"A regular impasse," Victor continued. "You got a buyer and maybe I have a seller, but the seller is not going to budge unless she knows who's doing the buying. Is it somebody local?"

"I'm afraid I can't tell you."

"Aren't you afraid of losing your commission?"

"My first loyalty is to my clients, Mr. Plotz."

Victor removed a red handkerchief from the breast pocket of his suit coat and blew his nose: a sound resembling the mating call of a large animal. "You tell your clients that Mabel Bradshaw wants to meet them," said Victor, "and then we can maybe go from there."

"Mr. Plotz, it's been seven weeks since Mrs. Bradshaw rejected their last offer. I am not even sure they are still interested."

"They're interested," said Victor, abruptly getting to his feet. "You just tell them what I said."

An hour later, Victor was sitting at a back table of Mother Goldberg's eating a knish. It was late afternoon and the restaurant was empty—all self-respecting people being at the track. Around him, the walls were covered with the autographed pictures of famous personalities who had once sat at these very tables. Some years before, Victor had offered the owner his own photograph but had been told there was no room to hang it. Although Victor felt that room could be found, he understood the rejection. Victor wasn't famous enough. He couldn't tap dance and he couldn't sing. Little did this fellow know! Still, Victor was magnanimous. He wouldn't bear a grudge. Besides that, he loved his knishes.

Across the table, Maximum Tubbs was shuffling a deck of cards. It was something he did very well and the pink flesh of his hands and the white of the cards combined into a blur. Occasionally he paused to sip at his glass of Vichy. He was the Vladimir Horowitz of card sharks and about the same age.

"Charlie says that the point of the robberies is not the jewels," Victor was saying, "but the poems. Not the money but the publicity. Someone wants to hurt the hotel. And he figures they want to hurt it because they want to buy it. They want to make the old lady sell."

"So who wants to buy it?" asked Tubbs.

Victor wiped a little sour cream from his lower lip. "That's what I want you to find out," he said. "This Hamilton Bryan wouldn't give me a clue. Who is this Bryan? All I could learn is that he's been in Saratoga for about two years."

"He was in Albany before coming here," said Tubbs. "That's all I know."

"Think you can find out?"

"I'm a gambler," said Tubbs, "I'm not a private detective."

Victor didn't say anything but continued to look at Tubbs expectantly.

After a moment Tubbs said, "You going to be at the hotel tonight? I'll give you a call around ten."

The difficulty with patrolling the halls of the Bentley was the number of miles chalked up in the course of an evening. Victor was tempted to buy himself one of those pedometers so he could calculate how far he'd gone, but he knew the final figures would only depress him and things were sad enough these days. What also irked him was how he had to march to Moscow and back while this new blond detective just sat in the lobby and smirked. And Victor wasn't the only one patrolling. Jack Krause and Rico Medioli were tromping along as well. Luckily the work wasn't as hard as it might have been in a jam-packed hotel. Because of the robberies, the Bentley was the only place in Saratoga with empty rooms.

A few minutes after ten the walkie-talkie at Victor's waist made a little buzzing noise and Victor shoved it up against his ear and said hello several times. He could never use the damn thing without feeling like one of Captain Midnight's lieutenants.

It was Raoul. Even over the walkie-talkie his voice sounded greasy. "You got a phone call," he said.

"Send up Jimmy Hoblock to relieve me."

A few minutes later, Victor stood behind the front desk talking to Maximum Tubbs on the telephone. Raoul stood several feet away with his back to him. His dark pin-striped suit looked like it had been put on minutes before and his dark hair was perfectly combed. Nevertheless Victor was pleased to see a few specks of dandruff on Raoul's shoulders.

"What's up?" said Victor into the phone.

"This Bryan was mostly a defense lawyer down in Albany," said Tubbs. "He's come up here to change his image. He's into investments now, taxes, real estate."

"And his clients?"

"Down there he had a lot of hoods."

"You think he's still working for them?" Victor decided that Tubbs was calling from a phone booth on the street because he could hear honking and the sound of cars roaring past.

"Could be," said Tubbs. "You know, there's always this talk of changing the laws about casino gambling, of making Saratoga like it was before Kefauver shoved his snoot into things. The Bentley wouldn't be a bad place for that. And if you had the connections, the machines, the expertise, why, when the law changed, you'd have the jump on everyone."

10

The carnival was gone; the parking lot nearly deserted. Charlie walked over to where the carnival had been but he couldn't even locate specific scratches on the blacktop. It was eerie. A fine mist was falling, not hard enough to be called rain, but every few moments Charlie wiped the drops from his forehead and face. In a far corner of the parking lot, two beat-up cars were parked side by side where some kids were sharing beers. Music drifted from them, the high squealing of guitars. Charlie turned his attention to the row of two-story buildings across the street. Everything but the Kentucky Fried Chicken was closed. It was ten o'clock Wednesday night. Charlie looked until he located the Easy Times Unisex Hair Boutique, then he began walking toward it.

He had left Eddie Gillespie in his room at the Phoenix Colony and a security guard had been sitting in the hall. Alexander Luft had expressed his intention to read a little, then go to bed early. His head still hurt and he was tired. Charlie had spoken to Arlo Webster and it seemed an airborne bomb attack couldn't get through the defenses he had left behind him. As for what Charlie was doing in Cohoes, that was relatively simple. In his quest for someone who might recognize the photograph of Rolf Vinner, Gillespie had come upon a small-time loan shark in Troy who had said, "You try that poker game in Cohoes? I told Moss I'd seen that guy there, I know I did."

The poker game turned out to be across the street from where the carnival had been, right above the Easy Times Unisex Hair Boutique.

"I'll visit that one myself," Charlie had said when Eddie called late that afternoon. All Eddie knew was that a poker game could be found there three or four nights a week.

"It may not be tonight," Eddie warned.

"I'll chance it. At least it'll give me a break from the Phoenix Colony."

There were few cars parked on Columbia Street and no lights were shining above the boutique, which was the third storefront down from the intersection. Charlie crossed the street, then walked to the corner, where there was an automotive supply store. He continued around the building to the back. Behind the boutique about ten cars were parked and there was a light over a door. The ground was muddy and Charlie kept stepping in puddles. Reaching the door, he tried the handle. It was locked. He pushed the buzzer. After a moment a voice crackled over a small speaker to the side of the door.

"What is it?"

It occurred to Charlie that he had no names. All he knew was that maybe, just maybe, there was a poker game upstairs. "I want to play cards," he said.

"Beat it," said the voice.

"Rolf Vinner sent me."

There was a pause. Charlie imagined furious muttered conversations on the floor above him. The speaker crackled again. "Beat it before you get hurt," said the voice.

Charlie found himself wondering where his revolver was. Had he left it at the Phoenix Colony or was it in his office? He had meant to bring it but other things had distracted him. Why was he becoming so forgetful? Was it just age or was there something wrong with him? He would have to start leaving himself notes. Note 1: Possibility of danger, bring revolver. Note 2: Load it.

"I think you better talk to me," said Charlie, "unless you want to be visited by a whole lot of guys in blue uniforms."

There was another pause, then a buzzer sounded. Charlie gave the door a push and it opened onto a hall. He brushed the rain from his face one more time, wiped his feet, and entered. Ahead of him rose a flight of stairs and to his right was a dark hallway. Just as he passed the hallway, he heard a noise behind him. Before he could turn, someone grabbed him and shoved him roughly up against the wall and proceeded to search him from his ankles to his ears without much concern for his feelings. Charlie didn't protest, although he disliked being touched.

"He's clean," said the man behind him.

"Bring him up," said someone at the top of the stairs.

Charlie received a push and stumbled toward the stairs. Was he really clean? He had showered yesterday. Or perhaps it meant clean as a Boy Scout is clean: clean of spirit. He felt deficient on both counts. At the top of the stairs was a dimly lit room and in the center stood a large table with six or seven men seated around it. Above the table hung a light with a green glass shade. Several men turned to look at him. They didn't seem nervous; rather, they appeared irritated by the distraction. Charlie received a push toward another doorway and passed into a little office. On a small love seat sat one of the fattest men that Charlie had ever seen. The door closed behind him.

"So what do you want, pork chop?" said the fat man.

Charlie took a step forward but was again grabbed from behind. "Stay where you are," said the man behind him.

The fat man wore a shiny brown suit which was so big that it looked like one of those mysterious tents that utility workers erect at the ends of streets. He sat with his arms spread on the back of the love seat and his legs stretched out in a V before him. His feet seemed peculiarly small and were encased in maroon patent leather shoes that sparkled in the light. It was impossible to tell his age—maybe twenty-five, maybe fifty. His face was smooth and stretched, with a mouth like the opening of a satchel and cheeks that hung down like little pink purses. His eyes were tiny: twin raisins disappearing in a sticky bun. The man occupied the whole of the love seat. On a table beside him was a large white jar and, as Charlie watched, the fat man dug his hand into it and extracted a glob of Marshmallow Fluff which he licked from his fingers with little slurping noises.

"I'm a private detective," said Charlie, taking out his license. "I want to know if a guy named Rolf Vinner plays cards here. How much he wins, loses. Here's his picture." He took the brochure from Long Meadows from his jacket pocket.

The person behind Charlie took the brochure and Charlie's license to the fat man on the love seat. It was the first time Charlie had gotten a good look at him. He was a black man in a black muscle shirt, black kung fu pants, and kung fu slippers. Although small, he looked like he spent about twenty hours a day in the weight room. His head was shaved and when he turned, Charlie saw that his two front top teeth were gold.

The fat man took the brochure and license and studied them. His hands were like loaves of bread. "Why should I tell you anything, pork chop?" he asked. "Why shouldn't I just tell Willie to break you?"

Charlie scratched his chin. He found talk like this irritating. "Because this is a murder case," he said. "An Albany private detective who was investigating Vinner got himself killed right across the street. You can either talk to me or to the police, but if you talk to the police I promise you they'll slap you in jail so fast that you'll be a skinny man by Thanksgiving."

"Hey," said Willie, "the boss don't like that kind of talk."

"Calm yourself," said the fat man, stroking Willie's arm. "Was that the fuss which occurred a week ago Sunday?"

"The very same," said Charlie.

The fat man held out Charlie's detective license and the picture of Vinner. Charlie took them. They were sticky and he tried to wipe them off on his damp raincoat.

"I'm Sweets," said the fat man. "I don't like to be threatened."

"I'm just describing the future," said Charlie. "Either you can tell me about Vinner or you can tell it to the police. I don't particularly care, but it will be faster if you tell it to me."

Sweets pouted and his whole round face collapsed into a mass of fleshy gullies and ravines. Then he sighed and stuck his hand back into the jar of Marshmallow Fluff. He licked at his fingers somewhat sadly. "It takes two considerable skills to play poker," said Sweets. "You gotta be able to count and you gotta be able to lie. Mr. Vinner, he can count but he can't lie. Oh, he tries hard enough, but whenever he lies his eyes get a little tinny look. You gotta see it to know it. But we know it and when we see it we know that a few of our bills are going to get paid, a few of our problems solved. And Mr. Vinner, he's got still another deficiency that hurts his game. That is, he don't know when to quit."

"Was Vinner here the night of that commotion across the street?" asked Charlie.

Sweets continued to lick his fingers. "He was supposed to show but he never did. In fact, he hasn't been here since."

"You know an Albany private detective by the name of Blake Moss?" Charlie described him.

"Never had the pleasure," said Sweets. Willie stood slightly behind his boss. He had taken out a knife and had begun to clean his nails. Every now and then he looked at Charlie with an expression of extreme disgust, curling his lip and making his gold teeth twinkle.

"How long has Vinner been coming here?" asked Charlie.

"About a year. He likes the atmosphere. You see, this is a very private game. We got some judges. We got some state senators. We even got a professor of English. Everything stays at the table except the money. Mr. Vinner came every Sunday night. In fact, I've been worrying about him. I was afraid he might've dropped into a hole."

"You know anything about what happened across the street?" asked Charlie.

"Only that there were a lot of police cars. I didn't see it myself. I tend to be rather sedentary because of my delicate feet." Here he lifted his head—Sweets had no neck to speak of—and looked affectionately at his feet which he turned a little to the right and a little to the left so the light glittered off the maroon patent leather. "But Willie described the incident quite faithfully. At first we were afraid of an official visit, but fortunately we were spared. A day or so later the paper informed us that some poor gentleman had had a heart attack. Murder you say?"

"I'm afraid so."

"To tell you the truth, I was struck by the coincidence of Mr.

Vinner's absence. I'd prefer to keep the police ignorant of our existence, Mr. Bradshaw. Moving is such a nuisance. It means walking and walking means pain. . . ." Here Sweets helped himself to another handful of Marshmallow Fluff.

"I'll do what I can," said Charlie.

"I can see you are a gentleman," said Sweets. "Think of us if ever you are in the mood for cards."

Twenty minutes later Charlie was back on the Northway heading toward Saratoga. The rain had stopped and the sky had cleared. Off to the northwest a quarter moon was exposing itself somewhere above Ballston Spa. Charlie wanted to see Janey and talk to her about Long Meadows, where she would start work tomorrow. And he also wanted to see her because he missed seeing her, because seeing her made his eyes feel better. In a corner of his brain a voice kept telling him to call Lieutenant Melchuk or Boland. But he was tired of giving the police evidence which they ignored. He would save it up till he could hand them the whole business. And he imagined Boland's surprise when he gave him proof of a slew of murders. But Charlie was also excited because he was getting close. He had tracked down Rolf Vinner and found a motive. The guy was a gambler. Worse, he was a loser.

Charlie wished he were making similar progress at the Phoenix Colony. During the day he had made about twenty phone calls trying to discover some old friends or acquaintances from Luft's college years and all he had learned was the phone number of someone in Seattle whom he could call tomorrow. That evening after dinner he had again played Ping-Pong with Luft and although their scores were a little closer, Charlie had lost five straight. All during the games, Luft had discussed Charlie's Bill Doolin poems which not only did something terrible to Charlie's return but messed up his serve as well. The reading was only four days away.

"I'll be sitting in the front row, Mr. Fletcher," Luft had said. "I'll be your most eager listener."

And Charlie had swung and swatted at the Ping-Pong ball as if swinging at miniscule bullets.

Throughout the day, whenever he had had a free moment, Charlie had struggled with his Bill Doolin poems. The results filled him with embarrassment.

> *Heck Thomas caught you wandering*
> *Out on a starry night.*
> *Heck Thomas caught you wandering,*
> *Did you even put up a fight?*
> *Heck says you battled hard*
> *But others say he lied*
> *That from behind a rock he fired*
> *And then you crumpled and died.*

Was this what he planned to read to a roomful of poets and other artists with the country's major poetry critic sitting in the front row? Charlie gagged at the thought.

It was eleven-thirty by the time Charlie reached Janey Burris's house near the train station. The porch light was on and Charlie could see another light burning in the kitchen. He climbed the steps and knocked on the front door. Although there was a doorbell, it was broken. Janey must have been expecting him because she opened the door right away.

"I'll never be a poet," Charlie said.

Janey hugged him. "Who wants an old poet anyway? I like you as a private detective." She was wearing jeans and a Pep Boys T-shirt. Her spiky hair made her head look pin-cushiony.

Charlie entered the hall. The house smelled of liver and onions. "I'm not so hot at that either, but at least I've managed to get some stuff on Rolf Vinner." He told her about it as they walked into the kitchen. Janey poured them each a shot of Jim Beam green and they sat down at the kitchen table. Their glasses clanked against the white enamel surface.

"Blake Moss must have known that Vinner would be coming down to that poker game. He wanted me to see him, probably so that I would believe he was a gambler. After all, this guy's the head of a Boy Scout troop. Unfortunately, Vinner got to him first."

"Why didn't he just go to the police?" asked Janey.

She had rumpled Charlie's hair and he was trying to smooth it down again. He tasted his whiskey. He liked how it sizzled at the back of his mouth.

"I think he had other plans," said Charlie. "You know, I keep being struck by the fact that Moss didn't have Long Meadows listed with his other cases. I think he was purposely hiding something. Moss was always short of money, always in debt to his bookie. He might have planned to blackmail Vinner."

"Why would Moss have thought you would help him with that?"

"Probably he would have kept the blackmail from me. But otherwise Moss was an amoral kind of guy. As long as there was money in a deal, then right and wrong didn't figure into it as long as you didn't get caught. I doubt that he could have imagined my objections. My job was simply to dig up additional information. He wanted to get someone inside Long Meadows, get someone to talk to Ted Davis and find out what was going on."

"Just like you want me to do," said Janey.

"Except that I'm being paid by an insurance company and we'll be turning the whole business over to the police."

"Have you talked to the police about Vinner's gambling?"

"Not yet."

Janey grinned. "You're a sneaky guy."

"I'm not sneaky," said Charlie with some indignation. "I'm just careful, that's all."

Janey kept grinning. "So what do you want me to do?"

Charlie sipped some whiskey. The children's drawings on the refrigerator were far better than he could do. He wondered if Janey's daughters wrote poetry as well. Maybe they could dash off a few Bill Doolin poems.

"As I say, find out who's died in the past year. There shouldn't be many because the place is pretty new. Then get their files. You're looking for a lot of expenses. Maybe the file will look tampered with. You know, White Out and erasures and Xeroxes of Xeroxes. What are your hours?"

"Twelve to twelve. Three days on and four off."

"Hopefully you'll find what we need pretty quick. Just be careful of Vinner. He's killed four people and probably more."

"And what will you be doing?"

"Writing poetry," said Charlie, beginning to feel desperate again. "That's what I should be doing right now, that and listening to Alexander Luft pace back and forth." Charlie got to his feet.

"Not so fast, Mr. Bradshaw," said Janey, giving him a little push so he sat back down and had to grab the table to keep from falling. Then she messed his hair again, making it stand straight up. "We've got a little necking to catch up on. I been studying some new holds."

Janey's office at Long Meadows completely baffled her until she realized it was meant to impress prospective residents rather than serve those who had already moved in. It looked like the den of a writer or university professor. There was a fireplace and above it was a large framed lithograph of sailing ships. There was a red Bokhara carpet in which the red and white rectangular medallions in the center oddly resembled bikers' belt buckles. The lower part of the walls was paneled with dark wood and on either side of the fireplace were floor-to-ceiling bookcases in which could be found not one single book relating to medicine or old people or aging. Instead, there were complete sets of Conrad, Dickens, Thackeray, Trollope, and Winston Churchill, as well as art books: van Gogh, Renoir, Monet. In place of a desk, there were two burgundy leather wing chairs drawn up before the fireplace. The actual clinic was located in a further room and was an efficient display of white formica and stainless steel. Each morning from eight to twelve a doctor was in residence. Patients who needed pills or some sort of minor treatment were seen by nurse's aides. If something more serious was required, then Janey was sent for. But mostly Janey's job, at least during the afternoon, seemed to be inquiring after the physical and spiritual well-being of the elderly men and women under her care. She sat by the fireplace and various people were ushered in to chat about their problems. Janey had never seen such a place.

Part of Janey's consultations dealt with the discussion of real or imagined aches and pains that could be dealt with specifically or were some of the untreatable burdens of aging. But mostly these consultations were just talk. Some old people wanted to get to know her, some were lonely, some were depressed, some were bored, some loved to chat. And so from two to six Janey chatted unless there was an emergency, which there wasn't. In the evening after dinner she was again available until eight-thirty and then she had her "rounds" which entailed making sure that everyone was getting to bed all right. At midnight she would be replaced by another nurse.

Several times in the past, Janey had worked in rest homes or nursing homes which were far more taxing. The difference at Long Meadows was its relative newness and the fact that no one had been there longer than five years. Also, Long Meadows was a kind of retirement community and its residents—there were no patients here—were relatively affluent. Certainly there were a few residents who couldn't look after themselves, but the major problem at Long Meadows was boredom, which made Betsy Thomas's job far more complicated than Janey's, what with field trips to museums and concerts and movies and organizing bridge tournaments and poetry competitions and talent nights. Janey didn't dislike Betsy Thomas but she felt somewhat antipathetic to her. Betsy was too buttoned, too zipped-up somehow. Even so, she admired the way Betsy got everybody going, the way she didn't allow the residents to dig little depressed holes for themselves, because no matter how pleasant Long Meadows might be, it was still a mortal cul de sac. Nobody left Long Meadows to go to some nicer place or, in Janey's mind, to any place at all, and even the most cheerful senior citizen was occasionally sobered by this thought.

Janey had arrived at Long Meadows at ten that morning and spent two hours getting to know the night nurse, Maria Bruce, who gave her some further notion of her duties, showed her where the medicines were kept and the schedule of who needed what pills, although that was generally taken care of by the nurse's aides. And then after lunch Janey prepared herself to talk to whoever wanted to talk. The first two old people arrived with back pains and foot pains, but what Janey realized after poking and prodding and suggesting was that their wish for conversation was greater than their wish for treatment, no matter how real that wish for treatment might be. It was with her third appointment that Janey developed the chatty manner which she employed for the rest of the day.

She was talking to an elderly man who was just recovering from a case of shingles which he said was like having his skin rubbed with sandpaper or maybe like having sandpaper instead of skin. In any case, he was glad it was going away. His name was Francis Haskins and he was portly and bald and wore a bright red necktie.

"Field trips," he was saying, "what I hated was missing the field trips. Everything was such a nuisance for me."

Janey and Haskins sat across from each other in the wing chairs. Although it was too hot for a fire, there were logs piled in the fireplace just in case. "Saratoga would be a nice place to go," said Janey. "All those horses. You might pick up some spending money."

"I'm not a betting man," said Haskins, "but there was a fellow here who talked about Saratoga all the time. He made it sound quite nice."

"Was it someone who worked here?"

"No, it was a resident. He used to be a jockey."

"And what happened to him?"

"He passed away, just last Sunday in fact."

Janey made a little sympathetic noise. She was wearing a starched white nurse's uniform and whenever she moved, it rustled. "Had he been sick?" she asked.

"No, it was quite sudden. Heart attack, I think."

"How terrible," said Janey. "Everyone here seems so healthy and vital. I wouldn't have thought there had been any deaths at all."

"Oh," said Haskins, "there've been a few."

"But surely they were people who were already sick."

"Sometimes, but there have been a number of sudden deaths as well. The old ticker gives out and there you are: cold meat." Haskins gave a little smile. He was about eighty and full of vigor.

"That's dreadful," said Janey. "Do you think they die from too much exertion, you know, out on the grounds or playing golf?"

"Mostly they died in their sleep," said Haskins. "At least Ted Davis did and so did Russell Weisberg back in June."

"And were there others as well?" asked Janey.

"There was a woman in March. I forget her name."

The conversation then drifted off to Haskins's years as a certified public accountant and how he could still add up a column of figures as quick as ever. Janey had learned, however, that people wanted to talk and that she could determine the direction of their talk quite easily. After Haskins, Janey saw a tiny woman with cataracts named Marcia Meeder who had pains in her back and carried a special cushion wherever she went. Janey thought the whirlpool bath might help and recommended special exercises which she had once learned in a Yoga class.

Marcia Meeder had never married but she had many grand-nephews and grandnieces and soon she was showing Janey their pictures.

"We go out once a week," Marcia said. "Every Sunday I go to someone's house for dinner. I'm lucky there are six of them. That way none of them gets too bored with me."

Janey asked her how she liked Long Meadows.

"I have nothing to compare it with, you know. But it seems quite pleasant. Of course it's also horrible. After all, this is the end. But I suppose at my age this is as good as it gets." She gave a bright little smile, made even brighter by her lipstick and rouge.

"I have a great aunt in Troy who had a friend who was here," said Janey. "I don't remember her name. Poor thing, she died in March."

"That must have been Agnes Lovell. I didn't think she had any friends. At least she never had any visitors. She hardly ever left her room."

"They had been friends when they were younger," said Janey. "Did she have much pain?"

"No," said Marcia Meeder, "she died in her sleep. That's how I hope to go myself."

Janey crossed her legs and her white skirt made a crinkling noise. "Does it happen often?"

Marcia Meeder held up five fingers. "In the past year, five people have died in their sleep. Then another died of cancer, another had a stroke while dancing, and two died in the hospital, although one of those was cancer as well."

"What about the nurse who fell downstairs?" asked Janey.

"She was young and it was an accident," said Marcia. "Oh, but it was terrible. She was a friend to us all." Marcia looked away toward the fireplace and her gray eyes got a little grayer.

Janey considered her own experience with death. Statistically speaking, it seemed that too many people were dying in their sleep. She wondered what their files looked like.

Charlie sat at his desk at the Phoenix Colony. His sleeves were pushed to his shoulders and his hair stood up in peaks. On the floor around him were little balls of yellow paper, the discarded sheets from a legal pad which he was getting to the end of very quickly. Through the window he could see boats on the small lake and the Green Mountains in the distance. The sky was blue, the air was warm, but Charlie was not in the mood for natural beauty. He was in the throes of poetic creation.

Bill's first bank was in Spearville, Kansas:
Eighteen grand in a bag of canvas.
Bill rode back to Indian Territory.
But Crescent Sam wasn't quite so lucky.
His horse went lame and he had to walk
While Sheriff Beeson hunted him like a hawk.
Sam stole a horse and rode to his sister's farm
Near Orlando, where he could hide, be safe from harm.
But Beeson and Heck Thomas tracked him in the night
And at the first sign of morning there was a fight.
"Throw up your hands," called Thomas, "you're under
    arrest."
Sam drew his gun and got three bullets in the chest.
He rolled on the ground; he cursed, he cried.

They took him back to Orlando where he died.
The forty-five hundred he had stolen from the till
Stopped the first bullet. There's a picture of it still.

"Absolute rubbish!" shouted Charlie, getting to his feet and wadding up the piece of paper. There was an immediate knocking on the wall. His shouting had disturbed Alexander Luft. Charlie threw the wad of paper at the sound.

"What am I doing?" he said more quietly. "How did I ever get myself into this mess?" It was Thursday afternoon. He had to read his Bill Doolin poems in approximately seventy-five hours. Glancing into the mirror, he smoothed his hair down again. His face looked haggard and careworn. At this rate he would look sixty in no time. No wonder poets hit the bottle and divorced their wives. This was hard work.

Charlie went to the door. He had to make a phone call to Seattle, his fifth attempt that afternoon to reach a fellow named Rodger Milsaps who had known Alexander Luft in graduate school. Milsaps was a professor at the University of Washington; first he had been getting his car fixed and then he was closeted with the dean. Charlie had been told he would be free around noon, which, in Seattle, was about now.

At the end of the hall was a young man in a straight chair reading a copy of *Amazing Stories*. Charlie nodded and the man winked back. He was one of the new security guards hired by the Colony, although he looked more like a college kid who had taken the job for the summer. Charlie passed him and headed down the stairs.

The phone booth was empty and Charlie slipped inside. He always grew faintly excited when phoning someone very far away, imagining his voice sliding across thousands of miles of wires, hearing another voice as if it were in the next room but knowing it was really on the other side of the country. This time he reached Rodger Milsaps quite quickly. Charlie introduced himself as William Doolin.

"Dr. Milsaps, I have been engaged by the *Connecticut Quarterly Review of Literature* to do a critical/biographical piece on Alexander

Luft and his impact on contemporary poetry. I gather you knew him as a young man?" Then Charlie waited. Was Milsaps really three thousand miles away? What was the weather like there? What were people doing? Were they happy?

"We were fairly close for a while, at least until I moved out here."

"How would you describe Professor Luft in those days?" asked Charlie, making his voice sound serious and a little Germanic.

Milsaps appeared to think for a moment. "In a word? Acquisitive, perhaps."

"How do you mean?"

"He wanted everything. He wanted to assume the cloak that T. S. Eliot had let drop, or was in the process of dropping. He wanted to combine within himself the roles of premier poet and critic. Alexander had great ambitions."

"He wrote poetry?"

"That was his passion. Later, I gather, he gave it up. I don't know. We drifted out of touch. These days I know nothing about him, apart from his articles and that he teaches in New York."

"He's doing a book on Wallace Stevens," said Charlie, "and he's staying at the Phoenix Colony in order to do it."

Milsaps made a sort of hum-hum noise. "I remember him applying to the Phoenix Colony years ago as a poet," he said. "He was very disappointed when he didn't get in. Funny to think of him there now."

Charlie was surprised. "When was that?"

"Around 1960 or sixty-one. He had some pretty good recommendations from a few writers at Harvard but it wasn't enough."

"What was his poetry like?" asked Charlie.

"Very smart, of course. His poems bristled with intelligence. Unfortunately, they were short on feeling and he had absolutely no ear. He's never had one, as a matter of fact. I remember him once arguing that rhythm is a result of metrical control, which is foolish. Meter is only one of the many elements of rhythm. But when you lack an ear, then meter is what you hang onto most."

"How come?" asked Charlie.

"Well, anybody can count but not everyone can dance. Alexander would argue and argue and all his arguments seemed logical and true but his poems still clumped along."

"How did that affect his acquisitiveness?" asked Charlie.

"I'm not sure. As I say, we drifted out of touch. Alexander had a tremendous need to be right. But even when he wrote poetry, I feel that what he was really interested in was power. He wanted people to think he was right, that he was an authority. Maybe that's just T. S. Eliot again. But more than just being right, he wanted to silence other writers. What he wanted to do with his poetry, I sometimes thought, was to make other people stop writing, as if other writers would see his genius and just quit. Not only did he want to be the best poet, he wanted to be the only poet. Actually, that was one of the reasons for our drifting apart. He didn't want argument; he wanted agreement. I just couldn't give it to him."

It seemed to Victor that the only thing that kept Alaska from truly being the land of opportunity, a haven for the hounded, the hen-pecked, and the hunted, was that it was cold. Otherwise, it was far away and that was what Victor wanted. He wanted to be three thousand miles from the Bentley. To hell with Saratoga and its glorious past. Like Garbo, he wanted to be left alone. But were there beautiful women in Alaska? He supposed as much but he didn't have any firsthand information. Perhaps the chamber of commerce or the Alaskan tourist commission could solve that sticky question for him.

At the moment Victor was sitting on the stairs of the third-floor landing of the Bentley massaging his feet. They hurt. It was eleven-thirty Thursday night and he had been walking for hours. Then, during the day, he had abused his poor legs even more as he had walked hither and yon trying to learn about Hamilton Bryan and whether any of his clients might be a possible suspect. The result had been an embarrassment of riches. In his two years in Saratoga, Bryan had been respectable, modest, and unassuming. However, during his ten years in Albany, he had defended every crook in town and at least a dozen had Mafia connections. To investigate the entire list would take months. Not only that, but these were rough fellows. It could lead to bloody noses, black eyes, and maybe a pair of concrete sneakers out in the Hudson River. Even without girls Alaska looked good.

Victor heaved himself to his feet and groaned. He hated to feel stress. It put bags under his eyes and wrinkles on his forehead. Well, in another hour he could go home and another day would lie behind him. But even as he thought that, he heard a noise. It sounded like a distant shout. Victor was hoping he had been mistaken when he heard another. Then his walkie-talkie began squawking his name—Vic, Vic, Vic—like a demented parrot.

Victor snatched the walkie-talkie from his belt. "What's going on?"

"Someone's running through the halls," shouted Rico, "he's heading up the stairs on the north side. I called but he won't stop."

By this time Victor was running down the hall to the other stairway. Even with the rug, his feet were making an awful racket. When Victor was fifteen feet from the stairs, the door was thrown open briefly to expose what appeared to be a midget wearing a black mask.

"Ha!" shouted the midget and disappeared again.

"Oh, Christ," said Victor. Reaching the stairway, he heard noise above him. He grabbed the walkie-talkie and shouted for Jack Krause who was either up on the fourth or fifth floor. Maybe it was a jockey, a bandit jockey.

"Krause, catch the little guy who's coming!" shouted Victor.

There was a bumping noise and a yell, then Krause's voice squeaked through the speaker. "I see him! He's going up to the fifth floor!"

Victor started climbing.

"Hoblock and me got the south stairwell blocked," shouted Rico through the walkie-talkie. "You sure he's up there?"

Victor had just reached the stairwell to the fourth floor when a small masked face appeared above him on the stairs. "Ha!" shouted the face, then it disappeared again, heading up to the fifth floor.

"He's here, he's here," shouted Victor into the walkie-talkie. It occurred to him that the big trouble with having a bunch of old farts guarding the Bentley was that they were slow. Victor puffed his way up to the fifth floor and stepped into the hall. At the end, Rico Medioli was running toward him like a bowling ball set loose in its alley. There was no one between them. The jockey bandit had disappeared.

"The roof!" said Victor.

The steep and narrow stairway to the roof was to the left of the elevator. Victor and Rico reached it at the same time. Just then Jack Krause and old Jimmy Hoblock appeared at the end of the hall.

"Each of you take a stairwell," shouted Victor, "and wait there!" People in bathrobes and pajamas were opening their doors and looking anxiously into the hall. Victor imagined further cancellations and complaints. He turned and began climbing the stairs to the roof. Rico was right behind him. Normally the door leading to the roof was kept locked, but Victor could see it open above him and through it he saw a quarter moon glimmering in the night sky. Victor had a pistol, a little .32 automatic, and he took it from the holster under his arm. Ducking down, he took a deep breath and burst through the doorway.

At first Victor could see nothing in the darkness. Then he saw a shape sitting perfectly composed on an air vent.

"Took you long enough," said the shape. "I guess I get another twenty bucks."

It was a kid. He had taken off his black mask and was twirling it around his finger, which was stuck through one of the eyeholes. The light from the open doorway fell across him.

"Who the hell are you?" demanded Victor, who had to restrain himself from giving the kid a poke. The boy looked about twelve.

"Maxie Shepherd," said the kid. "You sure can't run fast, can you?"

"I'm saving myself for the marathon," said Victor. "How come you're running through the hotel?" By now Rico Medioli was standing beside him. By the doorway, Victor noticed the fancy new detective, whom all day he had been calling Grease-Bag.

"Guy bet me forty bucks that I couldn't make it to the roof," said Maxie. "He gave me twenty just to try and said I'd get twenty more if I made it. So I'm wondering where's my other twenty."

"What guy?" demanded Victor.

"Just a guy on the street."

"What did he look like?"

"I don't know, just a guy." Maxie Shepherd had a quick perky voice as if he'd be happy to chat all night.

"Was he old, young, tall, short, fat, thin, bald? Come on, kid. You want to go to jail?" Victor had a bad feeling deep inside him. The sort of feeling he got when he thought he was being tricked.

"He wasn't too tall. Maybe he was in his thirties. Not too fat, not too thin. He had on a dark jacket, you know, a sports coat. You got that twenty bucks?"

"And all you were supposed to do was make it to the roof?" asked Victor.

"Yeah, that and wear this black mask."

Victor turned abruptly. "Let's get downstairs fast." He started shouting into the walkie-talkie again. "Jack, get downstairs. Someone's being robbed!"

Victor pushed past the new detective. Several guests were on the steps peeping rabbitlike out onto the roof. "Come on, come on," said Victor, "get out of the way!" Once on the fifth floor, he ran for the stairs, then bounded down them, clutching his pistol in one hand and the walkie-talkie in the other. He could hear people calling to each other. Dimly, he imagined a future full of criticism and verbal abuse.

Just as he burst through the door into the second-floor hall, he heard the screaming. A woman's voice, first just yelling, then screaming for help. Victor couldn't find the right door. Other doors were banging open and the hall was filling with people in night-gowns and dressing gowns or with their shirts off. Then he found the right door and yanked the knob. The door was locked. Victor began hammering on it. He saw Rico and Grease-Bag running toward him. Abruptly the door was flung open and Victor staggered forward.

"Help me, help me!" said a woman, grabbing his arm.

Victor looked past her. The room was dark. The window was open and there was a movement as if a shadow were just passing through it. The woman had her arms around him. Victor disentangled himself and ran toward the window, half stumbling over a pair of shoes. He had a stitch in his side and was out of breath. The window looked out on the roof of the kitchen. On the far side, Victor saw a figure just climbing over the edge. Again, above him, he was aware of the quarter moon.

"Stop!" shouted Victor. He raised his pistol and fired, although by now the figure was out of sight. The small explosion startled Victor so much that he nearly dropped his gun. He considered jumping onto the roof but the distance was about eight feet. Old bones break quick, he thought. He turned back into the room where somebody had put on the light. It was full of people. Mabel Bradshaw was comforting the woman whom Victor had shoved aside at the door. She was wearing a rather sheer nightgown and was quite pretty. It struck Victor that he had actually embraced her and he tried to summon back the experience. Then, however, he was distracted by Rico Medioli who was walking toward him or, rather, rolling, he was so round and compact. Rico was holding out a sheet of paper. Victor forgot the woman and shivered as if a bunch of geese were tromping back and forth across his grave. It was a poem.

> *I could go to Paris*
> *I could go to Rome*
> *With all my new found fortune*
> *Why should I stay at home?*
> *But stealing gives me pleasure*
> *And terror gives me joy.*
> *Why should I leave the things I love*
> *For in foreign lands to toy?*

11

Every morning Alexander Luft received two poached eggs for breakfast, each perfectly centered on half a toasted English muffin. If they were too hard or too runny, he sent them back. And every morning Alexander Luft went about eating them in exactly the same way. He took his fork and abruptly stabbed the yolk like a sailor harpooning the eye of a whale. Charlie found something awful about it, yet he couldn't help staring. It was as if all the little grudges that Luft had built up during the night were released with this miniscule gesture of violence. After he had stabbed the eggs, he looked at them with a pleased expression. Then he ate them with an appropriate mixture of speed and efficiency, all the while dabbing at his lips with a white napkin and making little sighing noises.

As Luft finished off his eggs, Charlie hardly ate anything while he watched and tried to keep his watching from being too obvious. This Friday morning as Luft took his last bite, Charlie gave a little sigh himself and turned back to the *Daily Saratogian* which was folded in a tidy rectangle next to his plate. He supposed he was growing used to chaos and disruption. In any case, the news of the most recent robbery at the Bentley brought forth hardly a murmur from his lips. Certainly not enough to disturb his fellow artists at the silent table. Still, Charlie grieved. He knew that his friend was receiving abuse from everyone around him, and he also felt sorry for his mother, whose frustration was so sharp that Charlie felt pricked by it even though he was sitting two miles away. And he wondered if his refusal to involve himself with the problems at the Bentley was not determined partly by petulance: irritation with his cousins and the suggestion that he should drop everything the moment they called. He seemed unable to plot a truly objective course in his dealings with his family. But perhaps with one's family nothing was objective.

In any case, half an hour later when Charlie was in his room wrestling once again with the difficulties of immortalizing Bill Doolin in verse, he felt almost relieved when a maid tapped on his door and told him there was a Victor Plotz downstairs who would like a few words with him. Charlie hurried out. Seated at the end of the hall within sight of Alexander Luft's door, Eddie Gillespie was polishing his nails with a battery-powered buffer. Eddie had been hired as an extra security guard and his only disappointment was that the job didn't include a uniform, since Eddie loved uniforms. Instead, he wore a blue suit that looked almost like a uniform.

As Charlie hurried past him, Eddie leaned forward and whispered the word "poetry" and then chuckled happily as if pleased to have articulated a word so neatly combining the profound and the goofy. Charlie didn't respond. Downstairs he found Victor pacing back and forth in front of the grand piano smacking his forehead with the flat of his hand.

"I heard the bad news," said Charlie.

Victor paused with his hand in the air. "I couldn't be in worse trouble if I'd shied a stone at the Ayatollah."

"Let's go outside," suggested Charlie.

They walked across the lawn to the edge of the lake. The sun was hot but there was a bench under a large willow where they sat down. Several fishermen were casting from rowboats. Charlie imagined they were men with nothing to do, who didn't have whole lists of problems in their futures, who went to bed with easy consciences and woke fully rested and not with the sudden shock of failures lying ahead.

"So you took a shot at him?" asked Charlie.

Victor struck his forehead again. "Even that was a mistake. We had a guest who was keeping his Mercedes back there. He thought it'd be safer. The bullet busted his window, knocked off his rearview mirror, and tore up the leather seat. He checked out, of course."

Charlie made a sympathetic clucking noise, then asked, "Any leads?"

"No, that kid had us all distracted. Nobody saw nothing. While we were all galloping around at the top of the hotel, the thief was busy on the second floor."

"How did he get into the room?"

"That I can't tell you. But there's one funny thing. The woman who had the room, she's an insomniac. Every night she dopes herself up. Last night she didn't. She'd had a couple of drinks and was afraid the pills and the martinis would make her OD, so she was lying there counting sheep. Suddenly there's this guy in the room. She didn't even hear him come in. She starts screaming and he jumps out the window."

"Could she describe him?"

"Thin, that's all, and he was wearing a dark suit. He threw an ashtray at her so she was trying to hide under the bed."

Charlie picked up a small willow branch and began stripping the bark from it. "Did he have time to steal anything?"

"Just her watch: a Rolex. And of course he left the poem. The thing is, this woman complains a lot about her insomnia and the fact that she dopes herself up. The maid knew it. The bellboy knew it. So you wonder who else knew it."

"Do you think it proves that someone in the hotel is working with the thief?"

"Maybe. It would explain how this guy gets into the rooms so easily even after we had the locks changed."

They were silent a moment as they watched a man in an aluminum boat reel in a fish. The man was about their age and wore a tan fisherman's vest with colorful flies attached to the front and a tan porkpie hat. The fish looked like a bass. The sun flickered off its scales as it kicked back and forth. The man unhooked it and tossed it into a big white bucket of the kind that had once held joint compound.

"You turned up anything among the employees?" asked Charlie.

"Nothing, nobody looks like an obvious burglar. The thing is that if some crook wants to buy the hotel, which seems likely, he could be giving one or more people a bundle to rob these rooms. As you say, it's not the money he's after but the bad publicity."

"And that kid?"

"Maxie Shepherd? He didn't know anything. Somebody stopped him on the street. It was dark. He didn't see much. The guy promised him forty bucks if he made it to the roof, then gave him twenty as a kind of retainer. Shit, I had to give him the other twenty myself, he was bitching so much."

"So what are you going to do now?" asked Charlie. He dabbled the point of his stick in the water, then watched the little circles. He wondered why he didn't do more fishing. No time, most likely.

"Beats me. I thought you might have some smart ideas."

"Try to narrow down the employees at the hotel who might be passing information to someone outside."

"You don't want to come down and help? It would take some of the heat off. Your mother wants to kill me and Raoul acts like I'm a speck of gristle that he's got caught between his teeth."

"I've got to stay here." Charlie explained again about watching Luft. Everything he said sounded like a poor excuse. "And I've got to write these darn poems."

"What kind of poems?"

"Poems about the outlaw Bill Doolin that I've got to read to absolutely everybody in about sixty hours."

Victor began to look hopeful. He gave Charlie a friendly nudge in the ribs. "Shit, Charlie, if you give me a hand with the hotel, I'll write the poems for you no sweat."

"You can't write poems."

"Sure I can. If that's all that's stopping you, I'll write poems that'll get you the fucking Nobel Prize."

"It would never work." Would it work? thought Charlie, is there any chance it would work?

" 'Course it would. You catch the crooks and I'll write the poems. A perfect combination. It's called a simby-something."

"Symbiosis."

"Damn straight. What we got is a bad case of the symbiosis."

The older guy in the aluminum boat had just caught another fish. It looked like his lucky day. Maybe all his days were lucky days. Good times today and better times ahead.

"I'll think about it," said Charlie.

After lunch Charlie visited Arlo Webster in his office. Although Webster was as courteous as ever, Charlie felt he was disappointed in him. Webster sat in a swivel chair with his cowboy boots up on his desk. They were soft and gray and looked expensive. Webster was a long lanky man whose every movement exuded a sort of careful fluidity. He wore a white cowboy shirt and tan Western pants. His glasses slightly enlarged his eyes, making him appear owlish.

Charlie described what he had been doing, including the fact that he had learned that Luft had once been a poet.

"I didn't realize that Alexander had ever written poetry," said Webster, "nor that he had applied here as a poet. That must have been a long time ago. We don't keep records of the people we've turned down. Do you think it means anything?"

"I don't know," said Charlie. He had never in his life felt so full of uncertainty. The new chart he had worked on for most of the morning suggested that three people would probably be required for the attacks against Luft. Either three people or a fantastic amount of luck. The only actual clue he had turned up concerned the painter Frank McGinnis. On the night that the bloody foot had been dumped on Luft's computer Frank had said he was downtown. The guard at the gate, however, swore that Frank had never left the Colony.

"If it makes any difference," said Webster, "I feel certain that Luft is a friend of the Colony. Several years ago he even offered to read submission manuscripts for us. That can be quite a chore."

"Did you let him do it?"

"No. Applicants are judged by their peers and we saw him as a critic, not a poet. But our letters to one another were quite cordial."

"Has he ever given money to the Colony?"

"No, but there are many guests who never give a cent. We don't require it of them."

"But you ask them?"

"They certainly are notified about our fund-raising drives and are invited to contribute."

Charlie thought about this. Webster's office was paneled in a light colored wood, maybe birch. Through the window was a hill of pine trees. Charlie could hear a couple of robins kicking up a racket as if there was a cat nearby.

"I don't mean to press you, Mr. Bradshaw, but do you have any indication who might be doing this?"

Charlie was tempted to lie, talk about business interests in town conspiring to take over the Phoenix Colony, then he just threw up his hands. "None at all," he said. "Or at least I don't think so. I just don't see how it could be another guest, even two guests."

"We're now employing ten extra people, not including yourself . . ."

"I know, I know. I can't tell you how bad I feel about it."

"I don't mean to criticize you," said Webster hurriedly, "but if you have any idea or plan . . . ." He paused and looked at Charlie encouragingly.

Charlie was again tempted to lie, but he shook his head instead. He had been shaking it so much that his neck hurt. "I don't know. Maybe I've got an idea. I just don't have the shape of it yet."

During the afternoon Charlie worked on a new chart. This one listed everyone at the Colony, including the staff; marked down where each had been at the time of each depredation; said who could corroborate their presence; inserted what percentage of a chance there was of the corroborator lying; considered the possibilities of two, three, four people working together—people known and unknown. Never before had Charlie felt so much in need of a computer. Along with his chart were pages of background on everyone, including the staff— including even Arlo Webster, including even the security guards: information which had been gathered by Charlie, Webster, the guards, and with the help of Chief Peterson. It ran to about forty pages. One of the gardeners had had a drunk driving conviction three years earlier, so Charlie put a little star by his name. A woman painter from Tucson had once threatened to stab her husband, so Charlie starred her name as well. Harry Rostov had once thrown a bucket of ketchup over another poet at a poetry reading in a SoHo coffeehouse. Did this show a violent and unpredictable nature? Charlie starred his name. Frank McGinnis had had a tooth knocked out in a bar fight in Odessa, Texas, in 1985. Did this indicate a significant deviationalism? Charlie starred his name. But certainly Eddie Gillespie had done far worse, as had another security guard, Franklin Atwell, whom Charlie had arrested years before for shoplifting but who was now a born again fundamentalist who carried his Bible on his rounds. Charlie starred both their names and for a moment wondered crazily whether he should star his own name as well.

He came back again to Frank McGinnis. There was still the problem of where he had been on the night of the bloody foot. Also Frank had missed dinner on the evening when Luft was attacked, although Charlie remembered seeing the painter when Luft was carried out to the ambulance. Frank said he had gone into town to eat, but that very morning the guard at the gate told Charlie that Frank had never left the grounds. Had Frank actually lied on two occasions? And where had he been the other times? The trouble was that Charlie liked Frank. After all, Jesse James's brother had been named Frank. Charlie found himself thinking that if Frank were mixed up with these attacks on Luft, he must have a good reason for it. He tried to think what those reasons might be and who else might be involved but his mind kept slipping back to Bill Doolin. Two days, he had two days to come up with some poems.

Around him on the floor were little wadded-up balls of yellow paper each containing the beginning of a Bill Doolin poem.

> *Bill Doolin he was cruel and bold*
> *He robbed the banks in days of old . . . .*

and

> *Out of the night Bill Doolin rode,*
> *Out of the night on his horse so . . . .*

and

The marshalls found the Doolin gang in Ingalls,
Drinking and fighting and seeing the damozelles.
The marshalls filled the Trilby Saloon full of holes,
The outlaws fought back to save their souls.
One by one they made it to the livery stable,
Where they kept shooting as fast as they were able.
Deputy Tom Houston was killed by Arkansas Tom,
Deputy Dick Speed fell to Bill Doolin's gun,
Deputy Lafe Shadley was blasted by Bill Dalton,
Firing from horseback as he hunted Bitter Creek Newcomb,
Wounded but triumphant, the outlaws rode from town,
Followed by Newcomb's lover, the Rose of the Cimmaron.

At dinner that night Charlie sat with Frank McGinnis and Harry Rostov, and he studied them for evidence that they might be working together against Luft. He hoped it was not so. Of all the guests at the Phoenix Colony, he felt most comfortable with these two and his few moments of pleasure had come from their games of pool. But Charlie was aware of his attraction to outlaw types. Maybe even the fact that he liked them was suspicious.

"Where do you go when you eat in town?" Charlie asked Frank.

Frank seemed surprised. "Hattie's Chicken Shack, mostly. It reminds me of Texas."

All through that Friday Charlie had also been worrying about Janey Burris, who had begun working the previous day at Long Meadows. He was half expecting a phone call, but he had heard no word from anyone. That night when she got off work she had promised to visit him and Charlie had already alerted the guards. In addition to being worried, Charlie also felt guilty. If Rolf Vinner was really a murderer, then surely it was wrong to put Janey in danger. And Charlie wondered about his tendency to involve the people he cared most about in the most perilous of escapades, as he if were somehow doing them a favor by risking their lives.

After dinner Charlie had hoped for a soothing game of pool, but Alexander Luft insisted on his presence at the Ping-Pong table.

"I need my exercise, Mr. Fletcher. All day I have been forming sentences of exceeding brilliance. My mind has had its workout but my body grows enfeebled. Help me to restore it to its natural vitality."

"Sure," said Charlie, thinking of bank shots to the corner and sinking the eight ball straight in. "My pleasure."

Charlie trailed Luft over to the barn as if Luft were leading him to jail. McGinnis and Rostov were already playing a happy game of cut throat with the composer Bobrowski and asked Charlie to join them.

"Maybe later," said Charlie, wondering if a game called "cut throat" were evidence of anything.

Luft took off his suit coat, but kept his vest tightly buttoned. "I feel aggressive tonight, Mr. Fletcher. I hope you're ready."

"Shall we volley?" asked Charlie, picking up the green paddle

"You serve, you need the advantage."

"Let's volley," said Charlie.

Luft won the volley and four out of his first five serves. Charlie had been working on a new serve and a new return but he hadn't gotten them right yet. He knew it was not simply skill that would beat Luft, it was also confidence. That night, however, Charlie felt terrible and Luft won their first game twenty-one to ten.

As Charlie began serving the second game, he tried a different tack. Even if he didn't feel confident, he could at least fake it.

"I wrote five wonderful poems today," he said, as he served.

Luft returned the ball a little high. "How fortunate for you."

"Yes," Charlie continued, "five poems that would knock your socks off."

Luft returned the ball into the net. "Are they your Bill Doolin poems?"

"They sure are," said Charlie, serving again. "How does this sound?"

> *Five thousand citizens greeted Bill Doolin*
> *In Guthrie, when Marshall Tilghman's arrest*
> *For six months ended the outlaw's foolin'*
> *But no jail could hold Bill, not even the best.*

Bill tricked the jailer and grabbed his key,
Then Bill and thirty-seven crooks broke free.

Through this recitation Charlie had scored another point and served again. Luft swung at the ball and missed.

"Three zip, Mr. Luft."

"Your language seems a trifle conventional, Mr. Fletcher, but I look forward to hearing this poem and others on Sunday night."

With these words Charlie's small run of confidence petered out and his next serve missed the table. Luft came back hard and won the next four games, beating Charlie by at least ten points each time and without ever even loosening his tie.

Janey didn't arrive at the Phoenix Colony until about one. Eddie Gillespie brought her up to Charlie's room. Charlie had been dozing, caught up in a half dream in which Bill Doolin was standing on a tree stump shaking a finger at him. Consequently, he was only partially awake when he opened the door to find Janey in her white nurse's uniform looking rather spectral.

She put a finger to her lips. "Mum's the word," she said.

Charlie stood back to let her enter, then shut the door. As he was turning, she surprised him with a kiss on the cheek.

"You have anything to drink?" she asked. "I need whiskey." She sat down on the edge of an armchair and began taking off her white shoes. Then she rubbed her feet as Charlie poured out shots of Jim Beam green. Her short black spiky hair reminded Charlie of the hedgehogs in the children's books of his youth.

"You know, Joyce, the nurse's aide down at Long Meadows, and Harold, the security guard, are having an affair," said Janey, lighting a cigarette as she balanced the glass of whiskey on her knee. "They keep slipping off to have sex which leaves me alone in the office, which is good, but also makes me horny as a coot, which is bad. Or at least it's a distraction on the job."

Charlie was still feeling pretty groggy. The idea of Janey being as horny as a coot made him feel peculiar inside and he wished he could remember what a coot was. Sipping his whiskey, he tried to pinch himself alert. "Are the files in that same office?" he asked.

"They're in an adjoining office which is kept locked, but I found the key. Would you like to come home with me tonight?"

Charlie pointed his thumb at the wall separating him from Alexander Luft. "I can't," he said.

"How about if we find some romantic music on the radio and dance cheek to cheek?" Janey blew a puff of smoke into the air away from Charlie.

"That sounds great," said Charlie, "but this doesn't seem like a good moment."

Janey sighed and stubbed out her cigarette. "I guess you're right," she said. "But you always read about people who are so swept up by sexual desire that they do it right there on the floor or, you know, like in those Emmanuelle movies. She's always being swept up. I guess I'm just not like that. I need more time."

"Me too," said Charlie, who had never seen an Emmanuelle movie.

"Anyway, nine guests at Long Meadows have died since last September and five of those died in their sleep. Two of those nine actually died in the hospital. I've looked at all their files."

"All?" said Charlie, impressed.

"I told you Joyce and Harold were having an affair. I've got to do something to keep me busy." Janey lit another cigarette. "Three of the people who died in their sleep had a lot of expenditures. They were Russell Weisberg, who died in June, Agnes Lovell . . . ."

"Wait," said Charlie, hurrying to the desk, "let me write this down."

Janey took another puff of her cigarette. "Agnes Lovell, who died in March, and Wilbur Potter, who died in January. Lovell, Potter, and Weisberg had no close family. According to their files they had been drawing a fairly large allowance in the past year, plus buying other stuff, like a television, a tape deck, expensive clothes. None of them had unusual expenses during the previous year. Of the other two people who died in their sleep, one was a man last fall who had a large family and no unusual expenses and the other was Ted Davis. I looked at some other files and while everyone had various payments and expenses there are none like Potter, Lovell, and Weisberg."

"So what does that say to you?" asked Charlie.

"I'd say someone was swiping their dough."

"Did you look at the files of anyone like them, anyone who is still alive?"

"What do you mean?"

"Well, presumably Vinner is stealing from other people right now and probably they are people of the same type: somewhat enfeebled and with no close family."

"I'm not sure who they'd be. Most likely it would be someone I haven't met, someone who stays by himself or herself. Tomorrow I'll make a special point to visit the shut-ins."

Charlie had sat down by the desk. Janey was still sitting on the arm of the big easy chair. The only light was from the desk lamp and the room was shadowy. "Do you see much of Vinner?" asked Charlie.

"He comes through now and then. He seems friendly enough but he keeps looking at me in a funny way."

"How do you mean?"

"Well, maybe it's just sexual, but often when he's around I look up and find him looking at me."

Charlie wondered about that for a moment. "I could send Eddie Gillespie down there."

"What would he do, sit in his car and comb his hair? No, I'll be all right."

"How is it down there otherwise?"

Janey started to light another cigarette, then changed her mind and put it back in the pack. She was trying to cut down. "I like it, as a matter of fact. I've always liked working with old people. They can be so brave. Of course, many get depressed but they try to fight it. I get them talking about stuff. They have whole lives that they want to talk about and they think nobody wants to hear. Well, I like to hear. Imagine having eighty or more years trailing behind you. Even the most boring ones have stories. Sometimes I wish I had a tape recorder so my kids could hear some of it. One old guy was telling me about being in the First World War in the Middle East and once he saw Lawrence of Arabia in Damascus. The place is full of history. That's what's so hateful about Vinner, if he's really doing what you say. He doesn't even see them as people. To him, they are just things to rob." Janey stuck the cigarette back in her mouth and held out her glass to Charlie. "Give me some more of this," she said. "I'm feeling cross."

"How are your kids bearing up?" asked Charlie, pouring the whiskey.

"Well enough. I spend the mornings with them, before they go to day camp, and then we get a lot of videos. Emma's pretty mature and the others do what she says." Emma was eleven. Janey's other daughters were nine and seven. "And the woman next door looks in from time to time." Janey drank some whiskey and got to her feet. Restlessly, she walked to the window and looked out. Her white uniform made a rustling noise as she moved. Charlie thought how pretty she looked. Going to the radio, she turned it on and began fiddling with the dial. One of the public stations played jazz after midnight and Janey tuned the dial to it. The muted sound of an orchestra playing "Moonlight in Vermont" drifted into the room. Janey held out her arms and turned in a slow circle.

"Come on, Charlie, let's dance."

"You mean, just us? Here?"

Janey took his hand. "That's right. Just the two of us."

"I'd feel silly."

"So what? Long Meadows is full of old people who have all sorts of things they wanted to do and all sorts of regrets that they didn't do more. They were too busy or they had no time or they thought it was silly. Well, I don't want to be like that and I want to dance so stand up."

Charlie got uncertainly to his feet. He took Janey's right hand in his left and put his other on the small of her back. Her uniform felt cool and slippery. He kept about a foot and a half between them. He guessed he hadn't danced for about fifteen years. He felt stiff and uncertain and his shoes scuffed on the rug.

Janey pulled him closer and nuzzled her face into his neck. "We need time to dance," she said, "time to do all sorts of things."

"I guess so," said Charlie, trying to relax. As they neared the window he looked out. His were the only windows to shine their light onto the lawn; theirs were the only shadows visible.

Saturday morning Charlie felt dazed from a lack of sleep. Janey hadn't left until after four and they had both drunk too much whiskey. He had walked her out to her car but he was afraid they had been noisy and he worried that Arlo Webster would come to him with complaints: drinking, dancing, and rowdy women in his room at all hours. That is not to say that Charlie hadn't had a good time, and he wondered if it was indeed possible for him to have a good time without feeling a little guilty afterward.

During the morning Charlie fooled with his chart, worked on his Bill Doolin poems, and tried to track down people who had known Luft years before. The chart depressed him because it was so complicated and took him nowhere. The poems depressed him because they were so simplistic and terrible. He brooded about Victor's offer. Could Victor really get him a few passable poems by tomorrow night? Even the word "tomorrow" filled Charlie with anxiety and he again began scribbling on his yellow pad.

One of Bill Doolin's gang members was Little Bill Raidler, a short, rodent-faced ex-college student from Pennsylvania. Although born to a wealthy family, Raidler had contracted TB and went west looking for a cure. There he fell in with the outlaws. Raidler had a great memory and when the outlaws were camped at night he would often recite poems by Keats and Wordsworth and Shakespeare while the others sat and listened. In September of 1894, Marshall Bill Tilghman trapped Raidler and brought him down with a couple of shots from his Winchester. Raidler then spent a few years in a penitentiary in Columbus, Ohio, where he became friends with another inmate, William Sydney Porter. Later, under the pen name of O. Henry, Porter wrote about Little Bill and his years with the Doolin gang.

> *What did he think, sitting under the stars*
> *Listening to Little Bill recite from Keats?*
> *Had he ever seen a Grecian urn or listened*

To the nightingale's song? What did these
Words mean to Bill Doolin, that a thing
Of beauty is a joy forever, this man who
Robbed banks and had killed so many? What did
It mean to him, the "Ode to Immortality"?

Charlie tore off the page and crumpled it up. It didn't rhyme and it seemed too serious.

It wasn't until after lunch that Charlie reached Luft's old colleague, a retired professor by the name of B. J. Bauer, at his summer place near Owl's Head, Maine. The telephone system in Owl's Head seemed rudimentary and there was a lot of static on the line.

"What did you say your name was?" Bauer shouted.

"Fletcher," said Charlie, "and I'm working on a project at the State University of New York at Albany on contemporary critics."

"And you're interested in Alexander Luft?"

"That's right. I gather you knew him."

"I don't know about that," said Bauer, with an abrupt laugh. "Windy and I were in the same department for twenty years but as for knowing him, I never got to know him a bit better than when I first met him." Bauer sounded rather elderly. His voice kept cracking and he often paused to clear his throat.

"Did he write poetry when you first met him?"

"Yes, or at least he talked about writing it."

"When did he give it up?" Charlie had shut the door of the phone booth but it was too hot and so he pushed it back open a little.

"That I can't tell you. Some time or other I realized he had stopped talking it. Maybe he never gave it up, maybe he just stopped mentioning it. But I know he was disappointed when he couldn't get his book published. What surprised me, actually, was why he wrote poetry in the first place."

"What do you mean?"

"Well, he never seemed to like it and he never seemed to read it. Poetry never seemed a pleasure to him."

"What about his criticism?" asked Charlie. "He must have read poetry for that."

Bauer cleared his throat again: a noise that reminded Charlie of distant automatic weapons' fire. "The poetry criticism came a bit later. Actually, it was something he seemed to stumble into. He was asked to write one of these big reviews for some journal. You know, a roundup of all the books of poems published in 1960. He found the task relatively easy and so he just kept it up. And of course it was useful to him as an academic to have an area in which he could publish a lot of articles. After a while, he had carved out a little niche for himself and soon he was an authority."

"Do you think he got to like poetry?" asked Charlie.

"No, I don't think he ever did. He'd talk about duty and so on but I don't think he ever enjoyed poetry. Nor did he understand it."

"What do you mean?" asked Charlie. He couldn't imagine how Luft could make a living interpreting poetry if he didn't understand it.

"Windy's idea of a poem is that it should be an obscure and verbally elaborate accumulation of words which requires him to explain it. That need for explanation is the first criterion for excellence. The second is verbal peculiarity."

"Why peculiarity?"

"Because for Windy peculiarity and originality are synonymous. But the poem doesn't need to give pleasure or touch the emotions or be beautiful. His approach to the poem is like that of a chemist approaching a new molecule. Actually, I doubt if Luft has any true sense of beauty. His favorite terms of praise are that the poem is striking and fluid. Words like beauty he finds sentimental."

"What was Luft like as a colleague?" asked Charlie.

Bauer paused again. Way in the background, Charlie could hear a dog barking. "He was not to my taste," said Bauer. "He was quick to call other colleagues stupid and once he tried to get a professor moved to another building by complaining about his body odor. And he had a long memory. There was one professor who had voted against his tenure. Years later, fifteen as a matter of fact, when the older professor was retiring, the department wanted to give him a special emeritus position but Luft fought it. They had been fairly cordial during all that time but when he tried to block the appointment

Luft used the same criticisms that this man had used against him years before, namely that Luft did not truly love literature."

"What happened?" asked Charlie.

"The man wasn't appointed."

There was an oddish note to Bauer's voice, almost a kind of hiccup. Charlie considered what Bauer was telling him and how angry he must be. "Were you that man?" asked Charlie.

"Very clever, Mr. Fletcher. You should consider a career in law enforcement."

It began raining that afternoon about four o'clock: buckets and buckets that cascaded against the windows and sent little rivers rushing down the lawn to the lake which was nearly invisible in all that wet, just a darker gray against a lighter one. The sound on the roof was deafening and the maids hurried to and fro with pots and pans to catch the sudden leaks. The thunder was continuous and a bolt of lightning struck one of the trees on the front lawn with such an explosion that Charlie, who was still wrestling with the poetic transformation of Bill Doolin, leapt in his chair, sending his pen in one direction and his yellow pad scooting off in another. That was the end of his attempts to write poetry, as if the thunderclap had been a celestial warning. By five o'clock he was on the phone to Victor.

"But they've got to be good poems," Charlie kept saying.

"Hey, Charlie, trust me," said Victor. "These poems will send electric shocks through everyone who hears them. They'll weep, they'll laugh, they'll be amazed. Charlie, their very lives will change. If they're drinkers, they'll go sober. If they're smokers, they'll kick the habit."

"Be serious now, Victor."

"Vic."

"Okay, okay, but how're you going to manage these poems?"

"There's a summer poetry workshop over at Skidmore and a couple of cuties have been coming into the bar. They'll help. But remember, Charlie, giving is a two-way street. If we knock off these poems, then you've got to catch the guy who's been robbing the hotel."

"I'll do everything I can," said Charlie, who was uncertain that he could do anything.

"That's all I ask," said Victor. "Just give me a few details about this Bill Doolin character and we'll take it from there."

So Charlie told Victor about Bill Doolin and Victor took notes. Afterward Charlie felt as if a great burden had been lifted from his shoulders. He was amazed at how light he felt. In the half hour before dinner, he ran through the rain over to the barn, tilted up the table and practiced his two new devious serves and returns until he felt positively dangerous.

At dinner Charlie didn't feel like sitting with Alexander Luft, nor did he care to grill Harry Rostov and Frank McGinnis. Instead he sat with a new poet, Ann Remington, who came from Colorado. They talked about Glenwood Springs, where Doc Holliday died of tuberculosis in 1887 at the age of thirty-six. Across the tombstone of this fierce gunfighter were written the words: "He died in bed."

Ann Remington was also reading her poems on Sunday night, along with Harry Rostov. Charlie suggested they all go downtown afterward for a soothing drink. Others wanted to come as well and so an expedition was planned. Perhaps they would go to the Bentley or to another of those fancy places.

After dinner, Charlie and Alexander Luft, as well as McGinnis, Rostov, and the composer Bobrowski gathered umbrellas and rushed through the rain and thunder to the barn. On this occasion it was Charlie who suggested Ping-Pong and, rather patronizingly, Alexander Luft had accepted.

Charlie felt lightheaded. The fact that Victor had taken over the task of the Bill Doolin poems made the future seem rosy. This time when Luft urged Charlie to serve first because he needed the advantage, Charlie agreed. The best of his new serves was a kind of slice which put backspin on the ball and let it barely slip over the top of the net. Any return that didn't hit the ball up, drove it downward. The first serve took Luft by surprise and he hit the ball off the table.

"You seem to have been studying, Mr. Fletcher. I see I will have to play full force." Luft took off his blue suit coat and laid it across a chair.

Charlie won his second serve as well, but on his third Luft hit the ball up so that it crossed the net.

"Tell me," said Charlie, returning the ball, "did you really give up being a poet or do you just not talk about it?"

Luft hit the ball high and Charlie was able to return it hard.

"What makes you think I ever wrote poetry?" asked Luft, returning the ball.

"I heard it someplace. You had a whole manuscript that you couldn't get published."

Luft hit the ball off the table. Harry Rostov picked it up and tossed it to Charlie.

"Writing poetry was an error of my youth, Mr. Fletcher, and I had the good sense to stop, unlike some."

"I don't believe you really stopped," said Charlie, serving the ball.

"Certainly I did." Luft hit the ball into the net, then retrieved it and tossed it to Charlie. "I have too much respect for myself to be a closet poet."

"I bet you work on poems every day," said Charlie, making his last serve. He was ahead, four to nothing.

"Preposterous," said Luft, slamming the ball so that it shot by Charlie's hand too fast for him to return. Again Harry Rostov tossed it back. Outside the rain beat against the windows and there was the occasional rumble of thunder.

Luft served and they volleyed back and forth. Charlie thought of his own frustration as the author of a few Bill Doolin poems. "It must have been difficult for you to fail," said Charlie, sympathetically.

"I didn't fail, Mr. Fletcher, I simply gave it up." Luft missed the return. He prepared to serve again. He was losing one to five. His repertoire included half a dozen nasty serves and he tried a fast slice that Charlie returned too high. Luft slammed it back.

Charlie kept talking to him. "But it must have hurt not to have your poems accepted. Did it make you bitter?"

"The time and the voice must be in conjunction," said Luft, serving. "Mine was not."

"So you feel your poems were ahead of your time?"

"Either that or behind it. What does it matter?" Luft sent the ball skimming across the room. "Must you insist on talking while we play?"

"It helps to pass the time," said Charlie. "Your serve, two to six."

"You think you can distract me," said Luft, serving again.

"Not necessarily. Do you think that critics are born or made?"

"I have no idea." Luft made the point and prepared to serve again. He had a way of concealing the ball when he served so that it seemed to suddenly spring from the paddle.

Charlie lunged and hit the ball back across the net. "Why do you think someone has been breaking into your room?" he asked.

"Viciousness and spite."

"And you didn't see who attacked you?"

"My back was to the person. Must you keep talking?"

"My serve, seven to three." Charlie kept saying to himself, "I'm good, I'm going to beat him." Even so, Luft took Charlie's first serve and slammed the ball so that it hit the middle of Charlie's side of the table and careened untouched past his cheek. Charlie served again. "Do you think the person who attacked you is still around?"

"Silence, Mr. Fletcher."

"I get nervous if it's too quiet," said Charlie.

He won the serve and the next as well. He was leading nine to four. "Do you think it will rain all night?" asked Charlie, serving.

"Silence, Mr. Fletcher!"

"Don't you want to take off your vest? You look a little hot."

"I am perfectly content," said Luft, sending the ball into the net. A loud crack of thunder shook the windows and the lights flickered.

"Does it worry you to think you might be attacked again?" asked Charlie, taking his last serve.

"They have guards, Mr. Fletcher. I feel quite secure."

"Are you sure you know nothing of the person who attacked you?" asked Charlie. "Maybe he had a funny smell."

"No more talking, Mr. Fletcher." He hit the ball so it kissed the very edge of the table. "My serve, five to ten."

Luft served quickly and Charlie was unable to return the ball. Luft sent his second serve skimming to the opposite side of the table and again Charlie missed. In fact, he dropped his paddle. Picking it up, Charlie told himself to stay calm.

"Why are poetry critics necessary, Mr. Luft?" asked Charlie, returning his third serve.

"Because no work can describe itself. Therefore critics are needed to describe it."

"Is that what you're going to do after you hear my poems tomorrow night?" asked Charlie. "Are you going to describe them?"

Luft sent the ball off the table and prepared to serve again. "Mr. Fletcher, please don't say another word."

"Seven to eleven, Mr. Luft."

Luft took the next two points and then it was Charlie's serve. He again tried the first of the two serves he had been practising, but Luft could now return it easily and Charlie lost the point.

"Eleven to ten, Mr. Fletcher."

Charlie's second new serve was a slice which slowly crossed the net while making a half moon shape. The serve took Luft unawares and he hit the ball off the table.

"Not bad, Mr. Fletcher."

"No talking, Mr. Luft." There was a flash of lightning followed almost immediately by thunder. Rain drummed on the roof.

Luft missed the next three serves as well but at least got the third one back over the net. Then he served, sending a shot by Charlie's paddle with such speed that Charlie hardly saw it.

"Eleven to fifteen, Mr. Fletcher." Luft prepared to serve again.

"What if I don't like your description of my poems, Mr. Luft?"

"That is simply fate, Mr. Fletcher."

"Are critics always in agreement?" Charlie returned the ball hard and Luft missed it.

"You are talking again, Mr. Fletcher. I insist on silence."

"But my question?"

"I am the critic you should listen to."

The remark unnerved Charlie—how could there only be one critic?—and Luft took his next four serves. Then it was Charlie's turn to serve. He was ahead but only by one point: sixteen to fifteen.

Charlie served a fast slice which Luft was unable to return, but then Luft slammed Charlie's next serve past his ear. Charlie remembered Maximum Tubbs's advice: hit the ball hard at Luft's testicles. Could he bring himself to do it? Luft scored another point, tying the score seventeen to seventeen.

"Maybe the person who is attacking you is really another critic," suggested Charlie, "someone who's sneaking over from Skidmore or even from Albany. Do you have enemies there?" Another burst of thunder shook the building.

"Ridiculous," said Luft, hitting the ball into the net. "My serve."

"Aren't critics competitive?" asked Charlie, putting a little spin onto his return.

"Won't you hold your tongue?" He again hit the ball into the net.

"Maybe some other critic resents your being boss critic," said Charlie, returning Luft's serve. "Are you really boss critic, Mr. Luft?"

Luft hit the ball into the net. "I must have silence, Mr. Fletcher." He picked up the ball and served it hard. Charlie tried to return it at Luft's body but missed.

"Eighteen to twenty, Mr. Fletcher. Remember, you have to win by two points." He served and again Charlie missed the ball. "Nineteen to twenty."

"Would Wallace Stevens appreciate what you are writing about him?" asked Charlie rather desperately.

"Silence, Mr. Fletcher." They volleyed back and forth but at last Charlie hit the ball into the net.

"Twenty twenty," said Luft. "Your serve."

Charlie thought again of Maximum Tubbs's advice. Instead, he went back to his first serve. The slice took Luft by surprise and he hit it into the net. "Twenty-one twenty, Mr. Fletcher. Remember, you must win by two points."

It seemed to Charlie that Luft was prepared for anything that he hit at him. Again he remembered what Maximum Tubbs had urged: a fast shot at the testicles. Charlie stepped back and served the ball hard at Luft's body but jerked his hand at the last moment.

"Let," said Luft. "Try again, Mr. Fletcher."

Charlie stared ahead desperately. He would serve the ball hard over the net right at Luft's zipper. Luft was glaring at him. His hair was mussed and he had unfastened his tie. Charlie tossed the ball then swung the paddle hard. But he couldn't do it. His hand wrenched to a halt. Even so, he made contact, a piddling little bump that barely poked the ball over the net where it dropped immediately. Luft had seen Charlie swing hard and had stepped back. When the ball turned out to be hit not hard but softly, Luft lunged forward on top of the table with a crash. He returned the ball but it was too high and Charlie whacked the ball to the corner of the table before Luft was able to regain his feet.

"My game," said Charlie, "twenty-two twenty."

"I want another," said Luft angrily.

"No," said Charlie, "my Ping-Pong playing is over."

Luft was not happy. "You think you are very clever, don't you, Mr. Fletcher."

Something told Charlie to be careful. "I just try to get by," he said. "And one winning game is enough for me, especially if it's the last one."

He glanced over at Harry Rostov, who was grinning at him. Charlie felt pretty good. Not only had he won, but he was forming an idea about how to catch the person who was perpetrating these attacks. After putting on his coat, Charlie took his umbrella and headed back to the mansion. It was still raining hard and branches had fallen, littering the driveway. Eddie Gillespie was standing on the back porch. "You got a phone call," he said. "I was just coming to get you."

"Go keep an eye on Luft, will you? He's playing Ping-Pong."

Charlie hurried down the hall to the phone booth. He assumed the call was from Janey Burris, but he was wrong. It was from her oldest daughter, Emma.

"Charlie, some man called here. He asked if you were a friend of my mommy's. I said yes. Did I do the wrong thing?"

Charlie wiped the rain from his face. He felt chilled. "Did he give his name?"

"I asked, but he wouldn't say. The person wanted to know if

mommy knew you and some other man, but I didn't recognize the other name."

"What was the name?" asked Charlie.

"It sounded like Black something."

Charlie could again hear the thunder crashing outside. "Was it Blake Moss?" he asked, feeling frightened.

"That's right. Blake Moss. He asked if mommy knew you and Blake Moss. Was it wrong to say anything?"

12

Janey Burris had lost an earring. It was big and dangling and had a small turquoise stone in a silver setting. Charlie had given her the pair for her birthday in June. If she couldn't keep a pair of earrings for more than six weeks, then what sort of person was she, anyway? She couldn't be sure when she had had it last but she was positive she had been wearing both at dinner because old Louisa Phelps had commented on how pretty they looked and when Janey had raised her fingers to touch one, she had noticed the nut was a little loose.

It was now half past nine and she was sitting in the office. Joyce and Harold were nowhere to be seen. Presumably they were holed up in one of the empty rooms tugging at each other's clothes. Just the thought of it made her miss Charlie. Janey stirred in her chair and wished she had a cigarette. She hadn't gotten to bed until nearly five that morning and then her kids had roused her at eight to ask her if she wanted pancakes. Now she'd been yawning all day.

Outside, the rain was beating at the windows and the thunder was kicking up a racket. It made her a little jumpy. The old part of the building was full of creaks and bangings. Probably she wouldn't have felt so nervous if Rolf Vinner hadn't been around. She had seen him in the downstairs hall half an hour earlier and he had given her one of his empty looks: like a fish looking at her through the walls of its tank. At the moment she had no idea where he was, only that his car was still in the lot. She began to imagine scenes from old horror movies—bloody hatchets and lopped-off limbs—and then stopped herself.

She got to her feet and poured herself a cup of coffee. But wasn't she right to be nervous? What she had learned seemed to clinch the fact that Vinner was a murderer. If he had already killed six people, why would he pause at killing her? She glanced at the phone and considered calling Charlie. But in less than three hours she would be getting off work. She would go to the Phoenix Colony, tell Charlie what she had learned, and then tomorrow or Monday Vinner would be arrested. The only danger was that something might happen to Mrs. Preston in the meantime.

Janey had first met Mrs. Preston that afternoon. The old woman had been originally from Ohio and settled in the Albany area after the death of her husband. They had had no children. Mrs. Preston was one of those old people whose age, or rather the fact of it, had cast her down into some black place: everything was over, her friends were dead, her own end was coming, her mind was failing her, everything was falling apart, and no one cared. She saw herself as slipping away like a sigh in a darkened room. Mrs. Preston rarely left her apartment and spent long hours watching the TV, although it hardly mattered if the machine were on or not. Next to her she kept a ragged sheet of paper with lists of names: her parents, her cousins and aunts and uncles, her husband, friends from college, friends from church.

"I'm forgetting them," she told Janey. "I read them over all the time, but now I often read a name and I have no idea whose it is. It's just a sound. It has no face any more."

Mrs. Preston was a small old lady with thin white hair. She wore a blue house coat with food stains on the lapels. Her apartment was messy and there was the smell of food that had gone bad. Later, when Janey spoke to one of the nurse's aides, she was told that people had tried to clean the apartment but the old woman kept kicking them out.

"She screams and screams," the aide said. "It's awful to go in there."

Janey had found two other shut-ins that day: an old man with Alzheimer's and a woman in a wheelchair. The man had no family but the woman had a daughter who visited her once a week. But it was Mrs. Preston whom Janey felt was her best chance simply because she would be easiest to rob. She had been wealthy and now she just didn't care.

"Why should I be here instead of someone else?" she kept asking Janey. "I didn't ask to be alive. What is there to look forward to? Why eat or not eat, breathe or not breathe? When my husband died, I felt released and I moved here from Columbus. But now I'd happily change places with him."

She had a halting way of talking and she kept having to stop to search for the right word.

"There're lots of things do," said Janey. "People to visit and interesting places . . . ."

"You sound just like what's her name, that Betsy woman. Why should I care about museums or movies or bridge tournaments? Those are just distractions."

"But you should make an effort," said Janey.

"Why? Whether I do something or do nothing I'll die just as soon. Why bother?"

There were no pictures on Mrs. Preston's walls, no photographs anywhere.

"What about books or magazines?" asked Janey.

"Reading hurts my eyes. Anyway, I have no wish to read about other people's happiness."

"Do you like music?"

"I hate noise. Even the sound of your voice irritates me."

When she left Mrs. Preston, Janey wrote a memo to Betsy Thomas urging her to help the old woman. There must be something that she liked. Or maybe people could just make a point of calling on her and trying to draw her out of her depression. Then Janey waited around for Rolf Vinner and the office staff to leave for the day so she could get into the smaller office and sneak a look at the records of the three people she had visited.

That opportunity hadn't come till after dinner when Joyce and Harold had slipped off to an empty room. Janey felt jumpy all over as she unlocked the door of the small office. She thought of the story of Bluebeard and of the young wife for whom all the doors were open but one. She thought of the nurse who had died in June, falling down the back stairs and hitting her head on the newel post.

Of the three people who seemed to lead isolated lives only Mrs. Preston had been having large expenses. These included an allowance of two hundred dollars a week and expenditures for a new television, a camera, and quite a few clothes. Janey had replaced the files and left the office, worried about what she had learned and wondering whether to call Charlie right away. Instead, she went down to the clinic where she spent an hour seeing several other old people who had various complaints: psoriasis, coughing, stomach pains, constipation. Although Janey was in a hurry, she was careful not to hurry them. They, after all, were her future; they were what she would some day become. Once they were gone, however, she went back to talk to Mrs. Preston whose apartment was up on the third floor near the rear of the building. On the way she saw Rolf Vinner in the downstairs hall. He had looked at her but hadn't spoken. By then it was nine o'clock.

"What would I want a camera for?" Mrs. Preston had asked.

"It must be a mistake," said Janey. "Someone said they saw you taking pictures. He must have been thinking of someone else."

"You were in here earlier, weren't you?" asked Mrs. Preston. "And you were asking strange questions then, too."

"Not so strange," said Janey, kindly. "What about that television," she asked, pointing to a small color set on the table, "is that new?"

"Of course not. I brought it from home. Are you teasing me in some way?"

Janey smiled and shook her head. "I'm just trying to see if there is anything you want, anything that would make you happy."

"The only thing that would make me happy would be to be left alone," said Mrs. Preston.

"If you need anything," said Janey, "or want me to do anything, just ring the buzzer. I'll be in the office for the rest of the evening."

Janey walked back through the building. The storm made the windows rattle and from somewhere there came a banging noise. The wind sounded as if its only desire was to get inside, to roar through the building upsetting tables and chairs, scattering people like playing cards. She met nobody in the hallways and only two people were in the lounge downstairs: two old men watching a Mets game on the TV. When she got back to the office there was still no sign of Joyce or Harold. Janey hoped they wouldn't get in trouble with Vinner. She wondered where he was. Chairs had been moved so she knew someone had been in the office since she was last there. She looked over at the glass door of the smaller office where the files were kept but the room was dark. Had he been in there?

It was around this time that Janey realized that her earring was missing. She reached up and realized it was gone. Had she dropped it in Mrs. Preston's room? Would she have heard it fall? She looked once again at the door of the small office. What if she had dropped it in there? She was tempted to look but was afraid that Vinner would catch her. And what if she had dropped the earring by the file cabinet and Vinner had found it? Would he know it was hers? But he had seen her only a half hour before. She had walked right past him and he had only been a few feet away. And her hair was short. He could have easily noticed that she was missing an earring.

Janey went to the phone and dialed the number of the pay phone at the Phoenix Colony. She wanted to tell Charlie everything she knew right away.

A woman answered after about seven rings.

"May I please speak to Charles Fletcher?"

"I'm sorry, I saw him drive off about ten minutes ago."

Janey sat back in the swivel chair and turned it thoughtfully. She was frightened but she wasn't sure that she had good reason to be frightened. Maybe her nervousness was due to the fact that she had run out of cigarettes. She sipped her cold coffee. Suddenly there was a crash of thunder and she jumped, sloshing the coffee onto her wrist. She stood up nervously, then laughed at herself and walked to the window. The branches of the big oaks and pine trees were whipping back and forth in the wind. Broken branches littered the lawn. Across the street at the golf course the flag on a putting green fluttered wildly.

There was a sudden buzzing and again Janey started, but it was only the call panel. One of the residents needed her. A small orange light shone next to number 306. Checking the directory, she saw that the room belonged to Mrs. Preston. Janey gave another laugh. It was obvious what had happened. She had dropped her earring in Mrs. Preston's room and the old woman had found it. Janey hurried to the door.

Although there was an elevator to the third floor, Janey took the front stairs. Again she didn't pass anybody. Even the two old men were gone from the lounge. The building creaked and moaned as if it were trying to root itself up from the ground and walk away.

Reaching Mrs. Preston's door, Janey paused to catch her breath, then knocked. There was no answer. Janey tried the knob. The door was open. She gave it a push, then entered quickly. The room was dark and this surprised her. "Mrs. Preston," she called. Perhaps she was in the bathroom. The door clicked shut behind her.

Perhaps she saw a shadow, perhaps there was a foreign smell, but whatever the case she instantly had the sense that someone was behind her. She leapt forward across the carpet. There was a grunt and puff of air as the person behind her leapt as well, trying to grab her but grabbing nothing.

Janey backed across the room, trying to avoid chairs and a small table. Her eyes were becoming accustomed to the dark but she could still only see a blurred shape crouching toward her.

"Who is it?" she demanded. "Mrs. Preston, are you here?"

The shape rushed at her and Janey dodged behind a chair and kicked a footstool back toward the person, making him stumble— or perhaps it was a woman. No, it was too large for a woman. The person crashed to the floor and there was the splintering of breaking wood.

"Bitch," said a voice. It was Rolf Vinner.

Janey stood against the far wall. There was no sign of Mrs. Preston. What did Vinner intend to do? Then she realized she knew the answer. Vinner wanted her dead. Even so, it seemed inconceivable, as if there had to be some simple misunderstanding. Had he killed Mrs. Preston as well? Should she scream? She had to get to the door. The room was stuffy and hot and outside the thunder was banging away harder than ever. Even if she screamed, who could hear her?

She again became aware of Vinner moving toward her—a hunched figure moving through the dark. He seemed to be holding something. Janey stepped to her left and bumped into a standing lamp. Quickly, she snatched it up with both hands. There was a slight tug as the cord ripped from the wall. Swinging the lamp over her head, she threw it in Vinner's direction, then she leapt for the door. There was a yell, then more crashing as Vinner fell against a table. Janey tugged at the doorknob. At first it stayed closed. Then she slipped the lock and yanked the door open. The light from the hall hurt her eyes and threw a jagged triangle of whiteness back over her shoulder. Vinner was just getting to his feet. There was something in his hand. Was it a syringe? His face was knotted, nearly twisted. It held such hatred that it surprised Janey and she stared at it, unable to move. Then Vinner jumped toward her and she bolted down the hall.

She turned left, toward the back of the house. Her intention was to get to the office and hope to find Joyce and Harold. If not, she would just scream and scream until every old person in the building came to rescue her. But as she ran down the hallway, she quickly realized she was running for those same back stairs that the nurse Janice Mitchell had fallen down—where, in fact, she had been killed. Janey stopped. There must be another way. She grabbed the door handle of another apartment but it was locked. Looking back she saw Vinner burst from the room and turn toward her. Again she was struck by how twisted his face appeared, how red it was. He lunged toward her and again she turned and ran.

The stairs were only about fifteen feet ahead. They were dark, just a dark hole going down, down. She had used them once during the day. They were narrow and covered with a rubber runner that was torn in places. The handrail was rickety. She again looked over her shoulder and saw that was a mistake. Vinner was much bigger and faster and he was closing rapidly. Janey hit the top of the stairs, grabbing the banister and jumping forward.

Her feet clattered on the steps. Far below her she could see a light at the second floor landing. Her foot slipped and she crashed against the side, still clutching the banister. The light from the hall above her was cut off as Vinner appeared at the top of the stairs. Janey again flung herself forward and heard Vinner's feet banging down the steps behind her and his breathing, a rushing gasp, a breathy shout. She bounded down the steps, hardly touching them. There was a bright flash of light, followed immediately by an explosion of thunder as if the building had been hit by lightning. Her foot missed a step and she fell forward. Grabbing at the banister, she spun around and began falling backward. Vinner was only a few feet behind her, a great dark shape flying down upon her. Janey tried to grab hold of something, to kick up her foot at this thing leaping toward her. She fell to her back and slid, banging from one side of the stairs to the other, her feet flying over her head, her white skirt flying up, her shoulder smacking the railing, then going head first again, toppling backward. She grabbed at the banister. She was nearly at the bottom of the stairs. Then there was a sharp pain in her head, a sudden blow. Everything stopped. Vinner seemed poised above her like a dark glove, ready to snatch her up. Then he disappeared, the stairs disappeared, and there was a great rushing noise, like a rush of wind sweeping her away.

Parts of Route 9 south of Siena College going into Loudonville were flooded and in one section two kids were paddling a red canoe. Charlie's Renault did not like rain and had been known to stop dead center in particularly large puddles. Consequently, he drove through them fast so that great wings of water leapt out from either side. It was still raining hard and his windshield wipers batted weakly at the drops. Now and then flashes of lightning illuminated the sky ahead, showing houses and trees and small shops hunkered down in the heavy weather. The thunder was a constant rumbling, as if the sky were trying to talk, to express some unhappiness. Charlie drove as rapidly as possible and was glad there were few other cars on the road.

Imposed across the flickering sky Charlie kept seeing Janey Burris and all the terrible things that might be happening to her. For some reason Rolf Vinner had become suspicious and his suspicion had caused him to telephone Janey's home. Once Vinner realized that Janey knew Charlie, then she was in danger.

Ahead of Charlie on his left behind a row of houses was the dark expanse of the golf course belonging to Wolferts Roost Country Club. In the flashes of lightning, he could see the pine trees waving wildly. The driveway to Long Meadows was about a hundred yards further up on his right. As he slowed to make the turn Charlie saw something so peculiar that for a moment he was distracted from his driving, then he had to brake abruptly and slide sideways so not to miss the turnoff: a golf cart was trundling across the highway, then it proceeded down a slight embankment toward a putting green. Charlie saw a hunched shape within it and a flash of white. He could imagine no reason for it to be there unless it formed part of a bizarre wager concerning the ability to play golf in a raging thunderstorm, and a dangerous wager as well considering the amount of lightning about. Charlie finished making the turn, then accelerated quickly toward the front door.

As Charlie got out of his car, he saw three or four golf carts parked in a small shelter near the parking lot. Presumably, the residents at Long Meadows had privileges at the country club and presumably the golf cart had come from here. As he ran through the rain toward the door, he wondered if some form of senility or Alzheimer's or dementia could lead an elderly person to decide to play golf at ten o'clock on a Saturday night in a thunderstorm.

The office at Long Meadows was just to the right of the main entrance. Charlie noticed a light on and he headed toward it. Through the glass window on the door, he saw a man talking on the telephone. Charlie opened the door just as the man hung up.

"Who the hell are you?" asked the man. He was wearing a dark brown uniform and Charlie assumed he was the security officer. He wondered if this was Harold, who had been having the affair with the nurse's aide, Charlie couldn't remember her name.

"My name's Charlie Bradshaw," said Charlie, giving the man his ID. "I'm looking for Janey Burris." He wiped the rain from his face, then noticed he had tracked mud onto the blue carpet.

"She's disappeared," said the man, "and just when we need her most, too. We got an old woman comatose up on the third floor. I just called an ambulance." Harold was about Charlie's height and gave the impression of thickness. He was in his thirties, red-faced and heavy-jawed.

"When did you last see her?"

"I don't know, around dinnertime."

"Is Vinner around?"

"I haven't seen him, either. Look, buddy, I can't just stand around yapping. We got a lot of nervous people upstairs." Harold started walking toward the door.

Charlie took hold of his arm, stopping him. "How come?" he asked.

Harold glanced down at the hand on his arm, surprised. "They say people were running in the halls and shouting and that someone fell downstairs. We had a nurse that died like that. I figure it's just the storm but it's taking all our time."

"Did you see anyone in a golf cart just now?" asked Charlie.

Harold pulled himself free and stepped away. "You crazy? In this kinda weather?" He looked at Charlie as if he thought he might need an ambulance for him too.

"Where do you keep the keys for the carts?" asked Charlie, heading for the door.

"There's a little cabinet in the shelter. They're hanging on hooks inside. What's this got to do with anything?"

But Charlie was already out in the hall. "Call the Albany police and get them out here, and tell them to contact Lieutenant Boland."

Vinner's red Toyota Camry was parked in the lot. Seeing it, Charlie turned and ran for the golf carts. His feet splashed in the puddles and it was hard to keep his balance. His .38 was in his raincoat pocket and he tugged at it, trying to keep the hammer from catching in the fabric.

Four dark blue golf carts were parked in the shelter. They were electric, had three wheels, and were steered with a tiller. Charlie found a cart at the end of the line that was fully charged. He got the key, then took his place in the front seat, which was a sort of upholstered bench. Although he had no experience with golf carts, they seemed simple enough to drive. He turned on the ignition and the cart made a humming noise. Pushing the gear shift forward, he pressed down on the accelerator and the cart bumped out of the shelter. Immediately, the rain swept down against him, filling his eyes and tugging at his raincoat. Charlie turned the tiller, then had to turn it quickly in the opposite direction when the cart veered too sharply to the right. He zigzagged across the lawn, pressing down more firmly on the accelerator. The cart was not very stable and Charlie guessed he could roll it quite easily. Once he had straightened it out, the cart hummed quickly toward the spot where Charlie had seen the other cart cross the road. Drops of rain stung his cheeks and he wished he had a hat. He saw a switch for a light and turned it on, then turned it off again, uncertain whether he would be better off with or without it.

He bounced across the road, then braked as the cart dipped down the embankment into the golf course. To his left was a house but he could see nothing ahead. Then a flash of lightning lit the path and on it Charlie saw the tracks of the other golf cart. He pressed down on the accelerator and his cart bumped along the path. How fast could the thing go? Maybe twenty. He could barely distinguish the lighter color of the path, then off to his right he saw a sand trap. And just what was Vinner doing out here? The question filled Charlie with fear. He imagined that he had Janey with him. Was she hurt? Was she dead? Charlie found himself thinking what he would do to Vinner if it turned out that he had killed Janey. Putting a bullet in him seemed too kind. But what did he plan to do with Janey?

Charlie saw something ahead of him and hit the brake. It was a little bridge over a stream. He was still going too fast when he reached it and the cart zoomed up and its front wheel left the ground. Bracing himself, Charlie held the tiller straight with both hands. There was a crash as the cart hit the path again, then it veered left onto the grass. Charlie stopped and turned the cart back to the path. He would have to use his light. But just as he touched the toggle switch, he saw a flash of red like a brake light far across the fairway. Charlie turned the cart toward it. Constantly he had to wipe the rain from his eyes in order to see.

Here the way was more dangerous. A stream wound along beside him on his left and small bushes sprang up before him. The golf course was very hilly and around him were clumps of pines and evergreens. After he had been going across the grass for about a minute, he suddenly swerved to avoid plunging down into a sand trap, then had to wrench the tiller back as the cart tilted up on two wheels. The cart skidded sideways on the wet grass and Charlie lost all sense of direction. Turning the cart again, he guessed where he had last seen the other cart and pressed his foot down on the accelerator. Right away he plunged down an embankment of another sand trap, a small one this time. Charlie accelerated across it, his wheels kicking up sand behind him. It seemed a matter of speed or surprise. Deciding that speed was most important, Charlie flicked on his light. Immediately, it reflected off something in the distance, something that might have been another golf cart. Charlie pushed the accelerator to the floor, zigzagging across the grass to avoid a bench, another sand trap, the small pines.

There was a flash of lightning, followed directly by thunder. Charlie swerved in surprise. But in the light, he had seen the other cart about three hundred yards ahead and driving off to the left. Charlie again sped up. The lightning must have struck one of the trees nearby. He remembered stories about golfers being hit by lightning. There seemed far too many stories like that. He took one hand from the tiller to wipe his face and again the cart swerved. He could see no sign of the other cart. Then, just as he was about to change direction, he saw another flash of red light.

Charlie was bouncing across the grass. It was hard to keep his place on the bench-like seat and he wished he had a seat belt. Did golf carts come with seat belts? Ahead was a dark area and he swerved just in time to avoid crashing down a little cliff. Even so the cart shot down a steep incline and Charlie had to clutch the tiller with both hands just to avoid falling off. His raincoat was buttoned up to the neck, but his clothes underneath were soaked. It was a cold night—one of those August nights that carry a taste of fall—and Charlie's fingers were stiff as they clung to the cold plastic that covered the tiller. Another flash of red showed him that the other golf cart was bearing off to the right. He could now see the glow from the other cart's headlight. He wondered if Vinner was aware of him yet. He doubted it. On the other hand, it would only be seconds before Vinner noticed Charlie's light. He flicked it off and promptly had to slow down. Everything was black except for the distant glow of Vinner's cart. There was another flash of lightning and Charlie saw a stream ahead of him. He turned left, looking for a bridge or a place to get across. Reluctantly, he flicked the light back on.

The rain had increased the size of the stream and the two or three places that looked fordable were also extremely muddy. Ahead his light reflected off a small bridge and Charlie accelerated toward it. To his right he saw the other golf cart going almost parallel with him between the trees. The rain pelting against the stream made a constant hissing noise. Charlie turned onto the bridge and as he turned his headlight swept across the fairway in a wide arc. Instantly he saw the other golf cart turn away. Charlie accelerated and shot down the other side of the bridge. He was now close enough that his light picked up the other cart's reflectors. The cart bounced and slid across the wet grass. He seemed to be gaining on Vinner, who was certainly carrying more weight. Not only was he bigger than Charlie but he presumably had Janey as well. Charlie hunched over in a way that he had seen motorcycle racers do in order to decrease wind resistance. Another flash of lightning showed that he was less than a hundred yards from the other cart. Now Vinner knew that Charlie or somebody was after him. Charlie took out his revolver, then stuck it back in his pocket again. How could he shoot when there was a chance of hitting Janey?

The golf cart was going full speed. Maybe twenty, maybe twenty-five. The ground was bumpy and rolling and Charlie had to keep himself braced on the seat with one foot pressed against the front. He kept bouncing up. It was hard to keep the tiller aimed straight, yet if he swerved at this speed he would surely tip over. He squinted into the rain and saw that he was still gaining on the other cart. Then he had to brake and swerve to avoid a juniper bush. The cart tilted up on two wheels, then crashed back down. Another flash of lightning illuminated the fairway, bright enough for Charlie to see the blue color of the other cart and to see that Vinner was not alone. Something white lay in the back. Charlie crouched down and tried to make his cart go even faster.

There was a gunshot, then another. A bullet pinged off the front of Charlie's cart, then whined away. Gradually he was gaining but what could he do against Vinner's gun? He took his own revolver from his pocket, trying to hold the cart steady with one hand. Pointing downward, he fired two shots at the ground. As if in response to the explosions, the other cart swerved to the left, then swerved right again. Charlie's cart got a little closer. He was now within thirty yards. He fired again at the dirt.

Then Vinner fired back at him. There was the sound of breaking glass and Charlie's light went out. He crouched down so he was nearly sitting in the floor. Another flash of lightning showed a line of trees in the distance. Charlie edged a little closer. He could see nothing but the shadow of Vinner's cart ahead of him. He tried to stay directly behind it. He was struck by the whiteness of what Vinner had in the back of his cart. Abruptly Vinner veered and Charlie veered as well. Then, through the shadow to his right, he saw a bench go rushing by. Another gunshot and again there was a ping and ricochet as the bullet smacked against Charlie's cart. Charlie tried to aim his revolver at one of Vinner's rear tires but he was bouncing too much. Instead he again aimed at the ground and fired. He had moved up to within ten yards.

There were lights off to their left, street lights, and Charlie could see the bushes and high grass of the rough. To their right was the stream. The carts rushed forward through the dark. The fairway seemed to be narrowing. Another gunshot. This one missed but even so Charlie began to move the tiller back and forth a little, moving from one side of Vinner's cart to the other. Charlie expected that Vinner could see very little of his own cart: just a pursuing shadow. He was aware of the fairway getting narrower and narrower. Charlie had to swerve to avoid going into the trees. He wished he knew what lay ahead. They were going too fast to stop easily. Wiping his sleeve across his face, he tried to see past Vinner's cart but there was only darkness and shadow. Charlie moved a little closer. Another gunshot and again the bullet banged off the front of Charlie's cart.

A bolt of lightning lit up the sky. Less than fifteen yards ahead Charlie saw a great dark space. At first he wondered what it was, then he slammed down on the brake. They were rushing at a cliff above a sand trap. Then Vinner saw it too and slammed on his brake, sliding sideways across the wet grass. But he was too late. His cart flew up into the darkness. Charlie's cart slid toward the brink of the trap. Vinner's single headlight zigzagged crazily across the sky. Another flash of lightning showed the cart in midair: a dark tumbling mass. Charlie leapt from his cart and rolled on the grass to the edge of the embankment. There was a crash and a scream. Charlie jumped over the side, pushing himself down through the wet sand. Ahead of him, he saw the other cart lying on its back, its rear wheels still turning, its light focused across the sand to the rough. Gripping his revolver, Charlie crouched down and ran toward the cart. He tripped over something and saw it was a shovel. Then he reached the cart. There was no sign of Janey. As for Vinner, he was half under the cart with his feet sticking out into the sand. His breathing sounded like it was being squeezed from him, more like grunts than breaths.

In the light of the headlight, Charlie saw a white shape lying about ten feet away. He ran toward it, slipping and stumbling in the wet sand. It was Janey in her nurse's uniform. He bent down beside her and touched his fingers to the artery in her neck. It was beating. Feeling her arms and legs, he tried to determine if anything was broken. Slowly, he turned her over so that she lay on her back, then he began to wipe the sand from her face. The rain kept beating down upon them. After a moment, Janey opened her eyes. First she looked frightened, then she relaxed when she saw Charlie. She smiled at him and the light from the cart's headlight shone on her face. "Charlie," she said, "did anyone ever tell you that you look cute with water dripping from your nose?"

13

Charlie and Victor were again in the rose garden. It was late Sunday morning and hot. Bees drifted from flower to flower and their buzzing blended with the sound of cars from the Northway as Saratoga filled for another day of racing. Another day, thought Charlie, which would pass without him seeing a single horse. What a terrible state of affairs. But that would change. Soon he would get this business at the Phoenix Colony straightened out. He had the beginnings of an idea, the rudiments of a plan.

"I just need to know," said Charlie, "if you're really going to have those Bill Doolin poems for me tonight."

Victor had broken off a yellow rose and he paused to sniff it. "And what time is the reading?"

"Eight o'clock. I've told you that about thirty-five times."

"Don't be so touchy. And you're reading with other people?"

"There are two others. I'll be reading third."

"So you won't really need the poems until about eight-thirty or even later."

"Victor, I'd like to look at them first."

"Vic."

"Okay, okay." It surprised Charlie that in the thirteen or so years of their acquaintance, he had never slugged this man: his best friend.

He picked up a small branch that had fallen onto the path during the storm and tossed it into the underbrush.

"And what about the other part of the deal?" asked Victor. "You know, catching my bandit poet?"

"I've already talked to Janey."

"Is she doing okay?"

"Some black-and-blue places but otherwise she's fine. You can expect her around noon. She says she needs the rest."

"And how's the other guy, Rolf Vinner?"

"He's in the hospital but I guess he'll recover. In any case, he'll be going to jail." Charlie noticed three Japanese tourists in matching blue baseball jackets on the far side of the rose garden taking pictures. First one man would pose before a particularly luxuriant bush, while another photographed. Then the second would pose, then the third, then two would pose together, until they had worked out all the combinations. Charlie started walking in the other direction hoping to avoid being asked to take a picture of all three.

"What was Vinner doing with Janey out on the golf course?" asked Victor.

"He meant to bury her in a sand trap. He could smooth over the sand again and the rain would cover the traces."

"Nice guy," said Victor. "And he'd found her earring in his office?"

"It was in his pocket."

Charlie had been at Long Meadows until well past midnight. Today Lieutenant Boland was seeing to the exhumation of the four elderly people who had died in their sleep. He had asked Charlie if he wanted to tag along, but Charlie didn't. Exhumations gave him the shivers. As for old Mrs. Preston, she was still in intensive care but was apparently going to make it. Rolf Vinner had attempted to suffocate her with a pillow but had been interrupted by Janey's arrival. Those hours had passed for Charlie in a sort of blur. His main thought had been that Janey was okay and relatively unhurt. Even during the remainder of the night back at the Phoenix Colony he kept waking up feeling glad and not knowing why and then remembering that Janey was safe.

"Did Vinner confess or anything?"

"No, but he had a notebook which listed his bets, his wins and losses, mostly losses. There were a lot of them. Now tell me what you're going to do about these poems."

Victor tugged at his tie and shot Charlie a quick look. "Well, they're not going to rhyme, that's for sure. You can't demand poems at the last minute and expect them to rhyme."

"But you're working on them?"

"I'm not doing it personally, but I'm directing the operation. I got these girls working on it. One of them's even published; she had a sonnet in her college magazine."

"Great," said Charlie gloomily. "Just get me the poems before the reading and if they're terrible, I promise you'll never catch your bandit poet. In fact, I'll help him escape."

"That's a cruel thing to say, Charlie." Victor plucked a petal from his yellow rose and nibbled it. "And how's Alexander Luft?"

"He seemed fine at breakfast. Eddie Gillespie was watching him last night. I guess everything went okay. Eddie hasn't shown up yet."

"You got any ideas about who's out to get him?"

"Not really clear ones."

"But do you have a particular person in mind?"

"I think so but it's complicated. There's a guy here, a painter, who's been lying about where he's been."

"And you think he's the guilty party?"

"Maybe, maybe not."

Victor slapped Charlie on the back so that Charlie staggered forward. "That's what I like, positive thinking. And if it's not this painter, then who is it?"

"It's too crazy," said Charlie, recovering his breath. "I think I'll keep it to myself."

After lunch Charlie was in his room at the Phoenix Colony working on a new chart. This one was based on the idea that one of the guests who had an alibi during an attack on Luft had actually managed to slip out of the ballet or whatever, sneak back to the Colony, do his dirty work, then sneak back to the ballet. Or possibly, like Frank

McGinnis, the person had never gone downtown at all, had simply lied about leaving the Colony. It was complicated but it might work. Even so, it seemed to require at least two people, perhaps three, while the passions involved were absolutely mystifying to Charlie, hatreds and desires for revenge so intense that the perpetrators would go to any extreme. Charlie couldn't fathom it.

Yet if it were true, then Frank McGinnis would seem to be part of it and Charlie expected that Harry Rostov was involved as well. At first Charlie had thought of trapping the two men. Then he decided it would be better just to confront Frank about his lies, to choose a public place with lots of people nearby and ask him directly.

Charlie also had another chart, one that concerned Luft alone and itemized all the information that Charlie had learned about him, ranging from the fact that he used to write poetry to the fact that every night he paced back and forth in front of his window. Charlie was studying this when there came a light tapping on his door.

It was Eddie Gillespie and he looked embarrassed. "Charlie," he said, "something happened last night. I didn't want to tell you. I sort of messed up."

"Why don't you come in," said Charlie as politely as possible. Actually, he felt some exasperation, but when Eddie believed that a person was angry at him he would just go silent and shake his head and stare at his shoes. Sometimes he would even shut his eyes tight and not open them again until the person went away.

Eddie was wearing his dark blue suit that looked like a uniform. He was an extremely fit young man with dark tousled hair that glistened with some perfumy stuff that he sprayed on it. His brown eyes glanced at Charlie, then seemed to scuttle off. "You're not going to yell at me?" he asked, walking slowly into the room.

"Eddie, you're my pal."

"You mean it?"

Charlie patted the back of the armchair. "Why don't you sit down and make yourself comfortable. You want a cookie? I have one left over from lunch."

"Maybe just half," said Eddie, lowering himself into the chair.

Charlie gave Eddie half of a Freihofer fruit cookie, then nibbled the other half himself as he sat on the edge of the desk trying to keep an eye on Eddie but not wanting to stare at him. The windows were open and from somewhere came the sound of a power mower.

Eddie stared at the cookie, broke off a little piece and ate it. "You see, Charlie, it's so boring sitting out in the hall doing nothing. I sit and sit and maybe I do some isometrics, maybe even some pushups, but after a couple of hours I'm ready to go crazy."

"Have you tried reading anything?"

"Reading hurts my eyes. Anyway, all these men and women who write books, they're just pushing you around with their ideas. Think this, they say, think that! Well, it makes me a little nervous."

"So what happened?" asked Charlie, as gently as possible.

Eddie finished the last of his cookie, quickly glanced at Charlie, then looked back at the floor. "Around midnight, I went downstairs. There's a refrigerator down in the hall where people keep stuff. I thought maybe I could rip off a couple of beers. Anyway, I popped a Budweiser and this girl comes out of the phone booth. She's kinda cute and she's got paint on her face. It turns out that she's not been making a call or nothing but she's afraid of bats, so right off she asks if I've seen the bat. I don't see nothing, I tell her, but I'm so bored that even a bat would cheer me up. So she says she was walking down the hall and this bat came zooming at her and she jumped inside the phone booth to escape. She's been there about ten minutes and was figuring on sleeping there until she heard me ripping off the beers. Then, as we're standing in the hall jawing, this little bat comes zooming down at us and the girl flings her arms around me. Well, you know, I tell her that maybe she'd like me to walk her back to her room and any bats that show up, well, I'll fuckin' whack them outta the air. So she takes me up on it and she's hanging onto me and I got my arm around her but we don't see any more bats. Turns out she wants to go to her studio which is back behind the garage. So I get her there sopping wet through the rain and we start up a fire and drink our beers and yak about this and that and I tell her about the exciting things I've done as a detective and what it feels like to get shot at and before you know it about an hour goes by. So I start feeling nervous and tell her I gotta get back. We shake hands and she kisses my cheek and then I split. Well, I get back to the mansion and go up to the second floor and everything is dark. Someone has turned off all the lights. So I take out my little flashlight and flick it on and there's somebody in the hall all hunched over and suspicious looking. Hey, I shout. And this guy, or maybe it's a broad, takes off like a rocket and I take off after them. The guy, let's call him a guy, pelts down the back stairs, then down the hall. I'm way behind. I get to the living room and there's no sign of him, though a door's open to the outside. I look around. Remember it's raining like crazy. I even look back upstairs but I don't see a thing. I tell the guards outside, then I go back up and turn on the lights. That's about it."

"Did you check on Luft?"

"Yeah, I knocked on his door. It took him a couple of minutes to answer it. Tell you the truth, I was ready to break it down. But he showed up all right. He said he'd been sleeping. Anyway, he was fine and hadn't heard a thing. 'Course he was pissed at me waking him up."

Charlie got up and walked to the window, then turned back again. "Could you recognize this person who ran?"

"No way. Like I don't even know if it was a man or a broad."

"And you think that maybe the person didn't go outside, maybe he went back upstairs?"

"Sure, I mean I have no idea where he went. I spent about an hour searching all over the place and one of the guys from outside helped me."

"You find anything?"

"Nothing."

"Nothing that wasn't there before."

"Yeah, I guess so."

"What do you mean, you guess so?"

Eddie pushed his hands through his hair, making it rise, then fall again. "Well, upstairs here in the hall I found a pack of matches."

"Matches?"

"Yeah. I mean maybe it was there before, maybe I just didn't see it, but I don't think so."

*   *   *

Victor Plotz didn't really like to smoke cigars—after all, they were bad for your health—but he liked chewing them. He liked rolling them back and forth across his lips and chewing on the soggy end, especially those rum-soaked ones. At the moment, he was sitting in one of the soft chairs in the lobby of the Bentley manipulating a cigar from one side of his mouth to another and keeping an eye on the new slick-looking detective—Victor had been calling him Sherlock all day—who was sitting in a straight chair next to the elevator. Sometimes the detective looked at Raoul, who was standing behind the front desk fiddling with papers, and sometimes Raoul would look at Sherlock. But neither would look at Victor. And Victor liked that. He knew that they knew he was there and he knew that the more he sucked his cigar and waggled it around in his mouth, the harder it was for these guys not to look at him. But they were troupers, they weren't going to give in, and Victor had almost come to the decision that he was going to have to light the fucker and fill the lobby with noxious fumes when Janey Burris burst through the front door with about a dozen suitcases and a poor old dilapidated cabby who was helping her lug them.

It seemed to Victor that Janey had so much color on her that she must have been wearing maybe three or four dresses instead of just one: swirls of yellow taffeta and violet and light green, and yellow stockings, and a flouncy yellow hat, maybe three or four different necklaces, and then bright bracelets and rings and two bright scarlet shoes like the kind that kid wore in the Wizard of Oz, or maybe it was the witch. Her jewelry jangled and seemed expensive although Victor knew it was fake. About ten people were in the lobby and they all stopped to stare as Janey swirled up to the front desk.

"I don't have a reservation," said Janey, "I don't believe in them, but I hear this is the one place in Saratoga with rooms available. Is that true or not?"

Victor couldn't hear what Raoul said in response, but he guessed it was yes. Raoul had a whispery way of speaking which was meant to sound intimate but only sounded sneaky. Raoul stood very straight behind the front desk in his dark suit and slicked-back hair. He looked like he was just dying for someone to ask him to dance the tango and at the first slither of violins he'd clap a flower between his teeth and off he'd go. Just seeing him made Victor want to spit.

Janey was filling out a registration card. "Don't ask me for credit cards," she said to Raoul, "I don't believe in them." She paused to dig in her over-sized purse. "Here's a Cleveland. When you run through that, I'll give you another. I want a room for a week and it better be a good one. Not too many stairs and no noise."

Raoul was staring at the thousand dollar bill as if it had kissed him. It occurred to Victor that Janey might be overdoing it. Maybe she was playing her hand a trifle heavily. But this was Saratoga in August. There was no such thing as overdoing it. Extravagant gestures were what Saratoga was all about. Raoul gave a little smile. His lips were as thin as the two strands of a stretched rubber band and his little Don Ameche mustache seemed to quiver. He caught Victor's eye and snapped his fingers. "Would you help this lady with her bags?"

So Victor and two bellboys and the dilapidated cabby wrestled Janey's dozen bags up to the second floor, but not Sherlock. He sat in his straight chair next to the elevator and he looked at Victor and he curled his lip, one of those grins expressing neither sweetness nor light. Victor tossed him his cigar and was pleased to see him jump.

"Food!" called Janey to Raoul from halfway up the stairs, "bring me champagne and caviar and Bremer wafers. I've eaten nothing since breakfast." As Janey spoke, her jewelry seemed to hop and sparkle and ring-ding together. Raoul moved faster than Victor thought quite possible. Then Victor grabbed a couple of bags and began dragging them across the lobby.

Upstairs, Janey paid off the bellboys and the cabby with ten-dollar bills. Victor was the last one out. As he started to close the door, Janey winked at him.

"Do I make a credible cheese?" she asked.

Victor didn't follow her. "Hunh?" he said.

"Charlie said I was his cheese."

"Maybe he meant squeeze," suggested Victor, "like in main squeeze."

"No, no, silly. Cheese for the trap."

*   *   *

Although meals at the Phoenix Colony were not elaborate, Sunday dinners were special. Sometimes there was roast turkey with stuffing, sometimes it was veal. This evening it was prime rib and Charlie went back for a second helping because he felt he had a full night ahead of him. For dessert there was strawberry shortcake, but as he gobbled it down Charlie wondered if he wasn't over-indulging himself. His stomach felt stretched. He was sitting with the two other poets who were going to read in less than an hour: Harry Rostov and Ann Remington.

"I eat very little before I read," said Rostov. "Maybe just a sandwich."

"And I drink only water," said Ann.

Charlie, who could barely move without grunting, said, "Eating doesn't bother me much, or not usually."

"You're a lucky man," said Rostov. "I once saw a friend blow lunch while he was reading: puked all over the podium."

"And I had a friend pass out," said Ann.

"That's not a bad idea," said Charlie. He took a deep breath in order to contain his terror. It struck him that if Victor didn't show up with the poems, he could simply fall down on the floor and pretend to be unconscious. "What do you plan to read?" Charlie asked Ann. "New stuff?" Ann was young and blond and was wearing a blue dress with a white collar that made her look about twelve years old.

"Oh, I wouldn't dare read anything new here at the Phoenix Colony. This is probably the most critical audience in the world. I'll just make selections from several of my books. That seems safe enough."

"Me, too," said Rostov. "I once knew a young poet who tried to shoot himself after a reading at Phoenix Colony during which everyone laughed at his elegies. Me, I'll read the tried and true. What about you, Charlie?"

It seemed to Charlie that fainting as a possibility looked better and better. He yearned for the comatose state. Even death couldn't be scoffed at. "Oh," he said, "I haven't quite decided."

"Some good old stuff, I hope," said Rostov.

"A little of everything," said Charlie.

"Well, I'm glad I'm going first," said Ann, "it's best to get these things over with. Going last is like peeling off a Band-Aid slowly."

"That's right," said Rostov, "the guy who goes last gets the most attention. I'm sure glad it's not me."

"I don't mind waiting," said Charlie. "I'm happy to let you guys go first." He was still holding his spoon with a little bit of strawberry on the tip. Glancing at it, he saw that he was clutching the spoon so tightly that he had bent it into a V.

Shortly after Charlie left the dining room, Arlo Webster approached him in the hall. "I'll be introducing you tonight," he said. "Are you sure you still want to go through with it?"

"They've got to think I'm a poet," said Charlie. "And we have this trip downtown afterward. Almost everyone is going. I've got a plan."

"And you have things to read."

"I think so."

Webster leaned over to Charlie and touched his shoulder. Charlie was struck by how kindly he seemed. "Look," said Webster, "if things get out of hand, just pretend you're choking and I'll stop the show."

"Out of hand?" asked Charlie.

Arlo Webster looked apologetic. "Sometimes these evenings get pretty rowdy."

Within seconds of leaving Webster, Charlie was on the phone to the Bentley trying to track down Victor Plotz.

"He must be upstairs someplace," said Raoul.

"Could you have him call me when you see him?" asked Charlie.

Raoul was not pleased. "I don't know if you know this, Charlie, but we're in the process of hunting down a burglar."

"You mean right now?" asked Charlie, wondering if it was possible that Victor had someone trapped at the Bentley even as they spoke.

"No, no, I mean in spirit," said Raoul, crossly. "Life has been very busy at the Bentley."

"Life has been busy everywhere," said Charlie.

Leaving the booth, Charlie considered driving downtown or

running out to the woods or maybe just hiding under his bed. But as he stood in the hall trying to make up his mind, Alexander Luft appeared. He looked jovial.

"Ah, there you are Mr. Fletcher. I'm only sorry that we don't have time for a little Ping-Pong before your performance. Shall I walk you over?"

Luft was wearing a dark suit and tie. Although he was smiling, he did not have a face upon which smiles looked comfortable. They came as visitors rather than tenants.

"Sure," said Charlie, cursing himself for leaving the phone booth.

"So this is the night on which the Bill Doolin poems will be unveiled," said Luft.

"I guess so," said Charlie as they walked down the hall. The reading was to be in the library.

"I can hardly wait," said Luft with a sort of booming eagerness. "To think that all these days your creative juices have been flowing just on the other side of the wall from me, just in the next room."

Charlie glanced at Luft as they left the mansion. Was he being serious? Charlie squeezed his eyes shut, then opened them again. He was a private detective, not a poet. He had to get back on the job.

"You know," said Charlie, "we're all going downtown after the reading for a drink. I hope you can come along."

"I'm not much of a drinker, Mr. Fletcher," said Luft, shaking his head.

"Maybe a Coke," suggested Charlie.

"No," said Luft, "I believe I'll stay here and try to get some work done. We critics are not like you creative types. We have to keep our noses to the grindstone every minute."

They were walking along the driveway. Ahead, Charlie could see other people making their way to the library. "Won't you be nervous at the Colony by yourself?" asked Charlie.

"Of course not. If everyone goes downtown, then I should be perfectly safe."

"So you think that the person doing these attacks is one of the guests?"

"I can see no other possibility." Luft continued to smile but the smile was a trifle condescending, as if he were instructing Charlie in one of life's little truths.

"And why do you think someone would be doing this to you?" asked Charlie.

Luft paused and turned toward Charlie. He had picked up a little stick and kept tapping it against his palm. "Clearly, Mr. Fletcher, there is no good reason. Perhaps I once gave the person a bad review or badly reviewed one of his or her friends. Perhaps the person simply objects to critics. Considering the violence of these attacks, such reasons are rather insubstantial. But you must remember that artists have a touch of—and please believe that I don't mean to offend—a touch of madness. At best they have a childlike streak, at worst they are insane. They are professional imaginers. That is what we value about them. But studies on creativity have shown substantial links to schizophrenia. On one hand, the activities of the artist can be seen as a form of play. This of course was Freud's idea. But the play can also become dangerous, can lead to psychosis. What has been happening to me here is that sort of play, that sort of violent creativity. It shows an artistic mind out of control."

"It seems hard to believe that one person is carrying out these attacks by himself. Do you think two people might be involved?"

"As you say, the fact of one person doing this is improbable. But once you accept the possibility that one person is mad, then you admit the possibility of two people being mad or three or even four. If one person can be crazy, then why not more? These attacks, Mr. Fletcher, are inspired by hatred, intense hatred. Please accept the truth of this. There is no reason why such hatred should be limited to one person."

The library at the Phoenix Colony was a one-story building entered through a kind of Greek portal. Most of the books were by guests who had stayed at the Colony over the past eighty years, but there were others as well. The ceiling was blue with murals of Greek gods and the muses, along with stars and constellations. All the chairs were set up facing one end, where there was a little podium and three chairs in a row facing at the audience. It hadn't occurred to Charlie that he would have to sit in front of the audience for the entire time. He was so nervous that he felt if he had a sudden heart attack he could only accept it as good fortune.

The room was already full when he arrived. People spoke to him but he hardly heard their words. Hercel Potter wished him good luck. Bobrowski said they would drink beer when it was over and have a good laugh. Alexander Luft once more repeated how he was looking forward to hearing about the exploits of Bill Doolin.

Again Charlie had to remind himself that he was a private detective and that he had work to do. He saw Frank McGinnis sitting toward the back and he walked over to him.

"This is a big night," said Frank. "I wish you luck."

The painter seemed perfectly relaxed. He was wearing a plaid Western shirt and a little black string tie. Could he really have attacked Alexander Luft? "Frank," Charlie began, "you said you went downtown to dinner the night Alexander was hit on the head. The guard at the gate said you never left the grounds. And there have been other times as well . . . ."

Charlie was surprised to see that Frank began to blush.

"Yeah, I was afraid there'd be trouble about that."

"What's been going on?"

"There's a girl who works in the kitchen," said Frank, lowering his voice. "She'd get fired if anybody knew . . . ."

Charlie found himself beginning to smile. It seemed that everything was falling into place. He reached out and touched Frank's shoulder. "Forget I said anything." Charlie turned and made his way to the front of the room where Ann Remington and Harry Rostov were already seated side by side. Seeing them, again filled Charlie with panic. He glanced toward the door, but there was no sign of Victor.

Arlo Webster got up to introduce the first reader. As usual he was graceful and courteous. He called Ann not only one of Colorado's finest poets, but one of the finest poets of her generation. He described her four books of poems, mentioned her Guggenheim fellowship and the prizes she had won. Charlie, facing the audience, saw how people looked attentive but not terribly enthusiastic. He thought again of Rostov's story of someone who had tried to commit suicide after reading in this very room. But I'm not a poet, Charlie told himself again, I'm a private detective. I have nothing to worry about. Even so, he wished the earth would swallow him up.

Ann Remington read in a high girlish voice. Most of her poems were love poems, although two dealt with the death of her mother. She had a funny one about a dog and several that Charlie didn't understand. He liked the dog poem and was pleased that people laughed. He was struck that even though the poems were quite emotional many people seemed not to be listening. One old painter in the third row had even fallen asleep and a novelist sitting right in front kept looking at her watch. They were all supposed to read for fifteen minutes, but Ann read for twenty. Her last poem concerned the trauma of divorce and Charlie was quite moved by it.

People applauded and Harry Rostov stirred in his seat. "Wish me luck," he told Charlie. "I've got one poem just for your buddy Windy Luft. You'll know it when you hear it."

Rostov stood up and Ann sat in his place. Charlie patted her knee and smiled at her. His hands were sweating and he felt that his heart was beating too fast. The difficulty with facing the audience for the entire time was that he had to look moderately alert and intelligent, while what he really wanted to do was to make terrible faces and weep. He thought how this was the end of his friendship with Victor, how it would be impossible to forgive him. Just to be safe Charlie had brought several of his own Bill Doolin poems but he had no illusions about them. They were awful.

Arlo Webster introduced Rostov. He described his books and prizes, mentioned that he taught in Brooklyn and had written an appreciation of Walt Whitman. Rostov looked nervous, which made Charlie feel even worse. After all, Rostov had read hundreds of times. How could he do it? How could he get up and submit himself to this attention? Rostov read in a great booming voice. Mostly he recited, only occasionally looking at the page. He read a poem about the homeless, then a poem about the need for debt forgiveness in our relationship with South America. Charlie thought it was quite good, or at least it struck him as an interesting subject.

Rostov glanced back at Charlie and winked. "Here's a poem called 'Utopian Melodies,' " he said. "It's about the place where I teach."

The poem dealt with a critic or post-structuralist who hated literature and wanted to replace it with his own criticism.

> *"His ambition,"* read Harry Rostov, *"is for*
> *a single emotion, a wintry one, and no lies,*
> *a life focused like a microscope upon a virus,*
> *and from his studies he will fashion a music*
> *from metal being twisted and breaking glass."*

Charlie kept his eyes on Alexander Luft sitting in the second row, but the critic's expression never changed during the reading of the poem. He looked attentive but distant, as if his thoughts were someplace else entirely. Charlie wondered again if Luft really liked poetry and, if he didn't, why he bothered with it. And he thought, too, of what it meant that Luft had once applied to the Phoenix Colony as a poet and how the rejection might have hurt him.

But it was impossible to think such thoughts for long. Rostov's reading was coming to a close. Charlie could feel his heart lodge itself high above his lungs. He was sure that if he tried to talk, he would only squeak. The library was stifling. Charlie loosened his tie, then worried that it might seem disrespectful. He kept wiping his palms on his thighs until his pants were damp. Every few seconds he glanced at the door, hoping to see Victor, but the door remained closed.

Rostov finished, then smiled and nodded to the applause. He came back and took his place next to Charlie.

"That was great," Charlie croaked.

Arlo Webster went up to the podium. "Our next poet," he said, "comes from the Detroit area."

Charlie listened as Webster described how the poet Charles Fletcher had worked for years in isolation, doggedly pursuing his craft but showing it to no one. Then, only recently, he had begun sending out his work and had met with great success. Webster mentioned several magazines that Charlie had never heard of. He guessed that Webster had invented them. Webster concluded by saying how the Phoenix Colony was committed to supporting new talent and how happy they were that Charles Fletcher had been able to leave his advertising agency on the spur of the moment and come to Saratoga.

People applauded and Charlie got to his feet. As he walked to the podium he was amazed that his legs were actually carrying him forward. He saw Frank McGinnis grin at him and there was Alexander Luft staring blankly, the same sort of look he wore when Charlie got ready to serve in Ping-Pong. Charlie glanced over at the door. It was still shut. Sighing, he pulled several scraps of paper from his pockets, then smoothed them out on the podium. He looked down at the words. One began:

> *Out of the night Bill Doolin came riding,*
> *Out of the night from his place of hiding . . .*

Another began:

> *Bill Doolin was a joker, Bill Doolin was a thief,*
> *Bill Doolin's bad behavior brought Bill Doolin to*
> *mischief . . .*

There were several others in the same vein. Charlie closed his eyes. Maybe if he concentrated hard enough he could make himself pass out. It was at that moment that he heard a noise like, "Psst, psst." Charlie opened his eyes and saw Victor standing in the doorway. "Excuse me," he said. Leaving the podium, he hurried to where Victor was standing.

"Hot off the press," said Victor.

Charlie took a manila folder. "I could kill you," he said.

"Just read them with lots of expression and you'll do fine. By the way, Janey's doing a great job."

Charlie returned to the podium. There was a certain amount of rustling as people waited for Charlie to begin. He opened the folder and looked down at the poems which Victor had brought. Words appeared to be scattered all over the page. They seemed impossible. With a sudden jab of fear, Charlie looked back at his own poem, "Bill Doolin was a joker . . . ." No, he was trapped. He would have to use Victor's. Charlie cleared his throat and began to read.

> BILL DOOLIN couldn't get NO satisfaction. NO, NO,
> Bill DOOLIN couldn't get NO
> SATISFACTION. He said to Heck Thomas,
> I DON'T WANT to SPEND the night toGETher.
> But Heck Thomas said,
> Paint it BLACK, Bill Doolin, TIME
> Is on MY side,
> You're just a STREET fighting man heading TOWARD
> Your NINEteenth nervous BREAKdown.
> What about DYNAMITE Dick with his HEART of STONE,
> Or Red Buck Weightman who was UNDER YOUR THUMB,
> Or Bitter Creek NEWCOMB, that TURD on the RUN?
> WILD HORSES, said Heck Thomas, couldn't BRING them to
> Help you RIP OFF THIS JOINT,
> You CAN'T always GET what you WANT.
> Oh no, said Bill Doolin, I may be TORN and FRAYED,
> But I got PLENTY of Sympathy for MY Devils
> So I'll just RAMBLE down PAST MIDNIGHT
> Toward that BROWN SUGAR in my FUTURE, because YOU'RE
> Just an UNDER assistant WEST COAST proMOtion Man.
> Listen HARD, said Bill, I'll HIP SHAKE my way
> through this CASINO BOOGie,
> Because it's ONly ROCK and ROLL but I LIKE it,
> Like it, YOU BET I DO.

Alexander Luft was not amused. After the reading he had congratulated the three performers with hearty yet noncommittal phrases. Then he stood aside to observe the congratulations of others. He wanted to seem friendly, not standoffish, but it was difficult. Such preposterous words of praise were being flung about. Such foolish accolades and compliments. Didn't these people have any sense of proportion? After about ten minutes more specific plans were made and several dozen people piled into a number of cars and rushed downtown to celebrate. Mr. Charles Fletcher appeared to be heading the expedition. Luft could hardly imagine that Fletcher needed more to drink than the amount already sufficient to bring about that display of shouting and caterwauling as he had buccaneered his way through the history of Bill Doolin. Song titles, that's all it was, although Alexander Luft hadn't quite caught on until "Bill Doolin the Pin Ball Wizard."

But now they were gone and Alexander Luft was left by himself on the path back to the mansion. The evening had worked out perfectly. This pleased him. His days at the Phoenix Colony were becoming burdensome and he was glad for the chance to bring his stay to a close. The reading itself had hardened his resolve. Look at those fools, those self-deluded pomposities. Such occasions only encouraged them to continue on their useless course. Well, if Alexander Luft couldn't get rid of them, he could at least get rid of the occasion. He began walking back to his room.

He reminded himself that he had to be careful. Even though the guests were gone, some of the guards were still about. He paused, but there was no sound of human activity, only the distant drone of traffic on the Northway. He walked to his Mazda, which was parked near the back door, and unlocked and opened the trunk. Then he removed his suit coat and put it around a small red can which he carefully lifted. After slamming down the trunk lid, he headed for the mansion. A brisk wind was blowing and its passage through the pines made a sort of a breathing noise.

Alexander Luft passed into the back reading room and continued down the hall. The building appeared empty. It was pleasant to have the place to himself. He paused in the front hall to look toward the fireplace. A Tiffany lamp focused on the mosaic showing the phoenix rising from the flames and the little red tiles seemed to sparkle in the glow. Luft thought of the expression about lightning not striking the same place twice. Surely, the same was true of the phoenix. It could not rise a second time.

Luft hurried up the stairs, his feet making dull thuds on the treads. The reading room was empty. He looked at all the stacks of poetry magazines and gave a little smile. He did not envy their future. Nor the future of all this heavy furniture and carved woodwork and the elaborate banisters going up to the third floor. But how pretty it would appear for a short time. Passing through the reading room, Luft continued down the hall until he reached his door. He unlocked it and went in. The light was on over the desk. Putting the red can next to the light, Luft quickly began packing a few papers, floppy disks, and some books in a dark gray attaché case. When it was full, he left the room, relocked the door, then hurried down the back stairs to his car. This was a weak link in his plan but he felt he had no option. After all, it would be foolish to destroy some of his best work. He locked the attaché case in the trunk of his Mazda, then hurried back to his room.

It was nearly ten o'clock. No telling how long the others would stay downtown but it would be best to get this business concluded as soon as possible. Putting on a pair of plastic gloves, Luft began grabbing handfuls of papers from the desk, then ripping them up and piling them on the floor. He tore books and journals as well. Their pages fluttered to his feet. When he had a pile that reached his knees, he unscrewed the top of the red can and poured most of the contents onto the pile. The smell of gasoline drifted across the room. Luft looked around him. It was a nice room and he had been moderately happy here. He only regretted that it had been under these circumstances. The fault, however, lay entirely with the Phoenix Colony. He thought of the poems he had written as a young man. That part of his life was finished, but who could tell how important a poet he might have become with the right encouragement? He had been vulnerable, perhaps even weak. Certainly, he was a different person today. He had been only in his twenties, hardly more than a child. How cruel for them to have hurt him so deeply. And for what? Just so they could accept these triflers, these purveyors of twaddle? Yet even so he had forgiven them, or almost. And perhaps his forgiveness might have been complete if they had invited him to read the application manuscripts. That, of course, would have given him some control over who was let in. Yet once again they had rejected him. Alexander Luft paused in his work. The insult was astonishing.

Looking around him, Luft grabbed a chair with both hands and held it up over his head. Then he swung it down upon the footboard of the bed with a crash. The chair splintered. He picked up one sturdy leg, then put the other pieces on the pile of paper. Going to the mirror, he studied his face. It was a thick face, with solid cheekbones and a large straight nose. His eyebrows were black and threatening. His eyes he found brilliant and unrelenting. He touched a place on his forehead near the temple. This would be the hardest part but he saw no help for it. Drawing back his arm, he struck himself in the head, then struck himself again. He reeled back across the room and fell against the bed. After a moment, he touched his fingers to his forehead. Good, he was bleeding. Not much but it would be sufficient. He removed his vest and wiped some of the blood on his white shirt.

Luft took more papers and twisted them into long spirals, making a chain that reached toward the door. It looked like a long white snake curving across the Turkish carpet. Luft stood up and surveyed his work, then went to close the window. The curtains had been blowing into the room and he didn't want the wind to disturb his trails of paper. The paper snake extended about a dozen feet from the desk to the door to the hall. Luft dropped more papers along the trail, then stripped the sheets from his bed and put them near the pile as well. He wanted a nice hungry fire, one that ate fast and energetically.

Walking to the door, Luft took a pack of matches from his pocket. He didn't smoke and had had to steal a pack from the drink room right before dinner. It had been a nuisance last night to lose his other pack of matches, but it was better now with no one around. Last night there had been too much chance of interruption, as had been proven when that greasy weight lifter tried to chase him. Luft paused to think of that. He was deeply offended by people's attempts to interfere with his plans. Luckily, he had a long memory and yesterday's interference would be replaced with tomorrow's retribution. Although in this particular case—here Alexander Luft looked at his watch—retribution would strike at ten-fifteen exactly.

Luft knelt down, struck a match and held it to a piece of paper. A corner flared, burned for a moment, then died. Striking another match, Luft held it to the paper again. It burned and ignited the paper next to it, but after another moment, it too died. Luft fetched the red can on the desk and shook it. There was about half a cup of gasoline left. Going back to the door, Luft unscrewed the top of the can. He would pour the remaining gasoline over some of the papers, light it, then have time to stagger from the building before the whole thing went up. Once outside he could cry for help and attract the guards, but by then the fire would be burning strongly. An old wooden building like this would go up in no time.

Luft upended the can of gasoline over the papers. But then a horrible thing happened. There must have been a spark, a smoldering corner, a tiny fire where he had seen nothing, because immediately the fire ignited with a whoosh and the flames leapt up toward his hand. Luft stamped at them, then jumped back.

"Ohh!" he cried.

The cuff of his pants was on fire and flames were moving up his leg. He threw the can away and tried to beat out the flames. The string of papers was burning rapidly and in only moments it would reach the large gasoline soaked pile by the desk. Luft grabbed the door to his room. "No," he kept shouting, "no!"

As he pulled the door open, he found someone pushing it from the other side. In his surprise he stepped back. It was that little Fletcher fellow. Luft raised a hand to push him away but Fletcher gave him a shove, sending him back against the wall. Before Luft could even protest Fletcher had elbowed his way past him and was stamping and kicking at the flames on the floor, disturbing that nice white snake of paper and pulling back the rug.

"Stop that!" demanded Alexander Luft. Then he saw that his pant cuff was still burning and he was forced to beat at it while that farcical Fletcher, that pretender to poetry, proceeded to destroy all that Alexander Luft had sought to create.

Fletcher put out the fire and kicked apart the string of papers. Luft watched horror-struck, then grabbed the leg of the broken chair.

Perhaps all was not lost. He could crush this Fletcher fellow, leave him in the flames, and make certain he took the blame for all that had happened.

Fletcher turned toward him. "It was you all along," he said. "You should be ashamed of yourself."

Luft lunged at him and swung the chair leg. Fletcher dodged back and the leg just grazed the front of his shirt.

"Stop," said Fletcher. "You'll get hurt."

Luft swung again and again he missed. Then he saw Fletcher step toward him and raise his fist. As the fist rushed through the air, Luft tried to find the words to encapsulate it, to verbally deconstruct it, to change it to language and so reduce it to nothing. But he was too slow. The fist made contact with his chin, his precious chin, and all went dark.

14

Janey Burris was washing her hair. Dressed only in her bra and a dark skirt, she stood at the bathroom sink of her room at the Bentley working the lather into her scalp with thin fingers. In front of her, the mirror was steamy and now and then she had to rub her arm across the glass in order to clear a space to see what she was doing, although why she needed to see herself washing her hair, she couldn't be sure. Habit, she supposed. It was nine o'clock Monday evening and she wanted to be nice and clean if there was to be any criminal excitement later on. In any case, Charlie had asked her to be ready.

She had hardly seen Charlie that day. For most of the morning he had been closeted with Chief Peterson and the director of the Phoenix Colony, who reminded Janey of a poplar tree, he was so long and bendable. Then, that afternoon, Charlie had gone down to Albany to talk to more policemen. Personally, Janey had had enough of Albany since she had already been down there three times to describe in great detail how Rolf Vinner had tried to kill her. She could only think herself fortunate that she had been unconscious for most of their ride in the golf cart, otherwise she would have had to talk about that too. All she remembered was being jounced awake and the sudden sensation of flying through black wet space, then hitting the sand and rolling. And just as she was trying to figure out what was happening, there was Charlie's nice face looking down at her, full of worry and concern. She still had various sore places, including a blue bruise on her hip in the shape of Brazil, but of course she was luckier than Rolf Vinner, who had lots of broken bones and a ruptured spleen. Both of his legs were in traction and he wouldn't be going any place for a long time.

And here she was at the Bentley pretending to be a morsel of cheese, which was an occupation that she could easily make her life's work. When she returned at four, she pretended she had been at the races. In fact, she passed through the lobby dribbling a large stack of useless pari-mutuel tickets for a series of anonymous losers, which Victor had nicely provided her with. Then she had changed and put on her jewels and had gone downstairs for a drink, which she had spilled in order to make certain that people were looking at her. Then she went back upstairs and changed again and put on even more jewels in order to have dinner. In the dining room she had sent back her steak as too well done and her wine as too sour and her vegetables as too cold. In no time she had had three waiters running laps to and from her table to the kitchen: poor haggard boys who kept tugging at their collars and wiping their brows with clean napkins. She had felt quite sorry for them and left a substantial tip. Afterward she had had coffee and brandy in the bar. Of course the coffee was too cold and the cream was a bit rancid, so she had the waiters running laps there as well. Then she had spilled her brandy just for good luck. There were about twenty people working in the hotel that evening and Janey felt she had made herself unforgettable to each of them.

And now she was giving her hair a good scrub just to relax and to get the cigarette smoke out of it. Soon she would change her clothes again, put on more jewelry, and go back down to the bar where she would have a little whiskey, read the *Racing Form* and draw attention to herself. Maybe she would spill her drink, although that trick was growing a trifle old. Maybe she would set her napkin on fire. She liked being the cheese, the tasty smidgin on the trap to attract the thief. She liked helping Charlie. She liked the food and drink and luxury at the Bentley. On the other hand, she also missed her kids and so she wished the thief would get off his butt and try to relieve her of her jewels, then she would give the alarm and about a dozen rough-looking fellows would come crashing down upon him. Ideally this would happen when she was down in the bar. She would set the electric eye and leave. The crook would come in, trip the eye, and get caught in the act, while she would have the glory but be spared the danger. Less to her liking was the thought that the thief might enter her room while she was asleep and that the rough fellows would do their work while she was hiding behind the bed.

Janey finished rinsing her hair and began drying it with a towel. The nice thing about having hair that was no more than two inches long was that the hair led its life and she led hers. How boring had been those years in high school and later in nursing school when she had felt in bondage to rollers and permanents and constant fussing. That was what was pleasant about life past forty: the useless stuff was just slipping away.

Giving her hair a quick brush, she inspected herself in the mirror. She was still holding her own in the aesthetic field: no beauty but pleasant to look at. Not only that but she could do fifty push-ups without even getting out of breath; well, maybe she would sweat just a little. She drew on a lavender silk blouse, then hung a fake emerald necklace around her neck. It was heavy and ugly and she liked it. Giving herself one last critical look, she turned away from the mirror, opened the bathroom door, and stepped into the bedroom. It was then that she received a nasty surprise.

Someone was standing by the bed and there was something awfully wrong with his face. No, it was a mask. Actually, it was the mask that frightened her more than the man himself: an over-the-head, white rubber Donald Duck mask. The man was holding her jewelry case in one hand and a small black pistol in the other.

"Quack, quack," said the man. Other than the Donald Duck mask, he was wearing a dark raincoat, sweat pants, and sneakers.

"You're not supposed to be in here," said Janey, trying to sound more outraged than afraid. On the bureau about five feet away was a little box about the size of a pack of cigarettes which contained the button that would summon Charlie. She was supposed to carry it at all times, but she hadn't thought that meant while washing her hair. And after all it was early, only a little after nine.

The man in the Donald Duck mask must have seen her looking at the remote control signal because he began to move toward it. Janey jumped for it first, grabbing it and pushing the button. The man was on top of her almost immediately, wrenching the box from her, then pushing her away so that she fell against the wall. He stared at the signaling device, then glanced at the door.

"You're in the hot seat now," said Janey.

"Shit!" said the man in the Donald Duck mask, then he ran for the door, still holding the jewelry case.

"Where's my poem?" said Janey.

The man threw down a piece of paper and dashed through the door. Already, out in the hall, Janey could hear shouting. Janey went to pick up the poem.

> *Some crooks rob stores, some crooks rob banks*
> *For which they get not a bit of thanks,*
> *But what rings this crook's particular bell*
> *Is to rob the rooms of a rich hotel.*
> *He likes to hear the fat cats scream,*
> *To shout, to curse, and otherwise blaspheme,*
> *When he rids them of their jewels so glittery*
> *And leaves them with their nerves all jittery.*

Charlie had just made it to the top of the stairs when he saw the man in the Donald Duck mask come running out of Janey's room.

"Hey!" he shouted. The man never paused and Charlie watched him rush down the hall toward the far stairwell. Immediately, Charlie began shouting into his two-way radio, directing Victor and Gillespie and Krause and even old Jimmy Hoblock to block the stairs at both the top and bottom. Then he ran toward Janey's door. He imagined her hurt and bleeding, or perhaps only scared. Again he felt guilty for putting her in danger. It was like some dreadful riddle. Question: how do you know if Charlie Bradshaw likes you? Answer: he risks your neck.

Janey was standing just inside her door calmly reading a piece of paper. "You better hurry, Charlie. He looks quite quick."

"Did he hurt you?" asked Charlie.

"No, he just quacked at me."

Charlie rushed off down the hall to the door of the stairway through which the man had already disappeared. There was shouting from the lobby, then from the stairwell itself came a gunshot that seemed huge, more like a cannon than a pistol. Charlie flung open the door. There was the smell of cordite and more shouting. He imagined guests all over the hotel rapidly stuffing their clothes in suitcases.

"He's up here, he's up here!" shouted Victor.

Charlie dashed up the stairs and found Victor just getting to his feet on the third-floor landing. Footsteps were rushing down from the floor above.

"Did he shoot at you?" asked Charlie.

"No, he punched me in the snoot and I dropped my fucking gun."

Charlie saw Victor's pistol in a corner and picked it up. "Are you okay?"

"My pride, Charlie. I feel like a dope."

Giving Victor the pistol, Charlie threw open the door to the third-floor hall. As the door slammed open, Charlie saw Eddie Gillespie fling open the door at the far end of the hall. Between them was the man in the Donald Duck mask. But only for a second. He opened the door to one of the rooms and disappeared. Charlie and Gillespie both ran toward it.

"I would have taken a shot at him, Charlie," said Gillespie, "if you hadn't been standing in the way."

"Thanks," said Charlie, "it's good to know you care. Which room did he go into?" Charlie began trying the doors but they were locked. It occurred to him that he ought to have a passkey. Maybe the room had been this one: 320. But it might have been 322 or even 318. He began hammering on the door. How did the man in the Donald Duck mask happen to have a key?

"I think it was three eighteen," said Gillespie, hammering on that door as well.

The door to 320 suddenly opened and a redheaded boy of about nine stared at Charlie. His freckled face bore alternating expressions of curiosity and alarm.

"Did you see a man wearing a Donald Duck mask?" asked Charlie.

The boy looked at Charlie in surprise. Next to Charlie, Victor was opening room 322 with a passkey.

"This room's vacant," Victor told Charlie.

"Why Donald Duck?" asked the boy.

Victor pushed open the door and Charlie glanced into the empty room. The window was wide open.

"Damn!" he said. "Get downstairs fast." He grabbed up his radio. "Get out to the alley behind the hotel."

Charlie ran for the stairs. There were guests in the hall and he had to push around them. Then there were more people on the stairs and constant shouting and questions. He shoved the radio into his pocket and galloped down the stairs, barely holding on to the metal railing. Behind him he was aware of Eddie Gillespie and Victor, while behind them both came the redheaded boy.

Charlie reached the bottom, then pushed through the emergency exit into the alley. The emergency horn began to ring, adding to the noise of the shouting and running feet. There was a rope hanging down from a third-floor window, presumably the window to room 322. It seemed that the rope must have been ready before Janey's room was robbed, which meant that the thief had known that room 322 was vacant. Charlie ran down the alley. There was no one in sight. Then Rico Medioli burst through the back door of the hotel.

"Did you see anyone?" asked Charlie.

"Nobody."

"Keep looking. Maybe someone out on the street saw something."

Charlie went back into the hotel by the rear entrance. The corridor ran between the kitchen and three or four storerooms. Glancing into the kitchen, Charlie saw Raoul talking to the cook. Apparently, he wasn't even aware that the hotel had been robbed. Charlie felt terrible. Here they had made this elaborate plan and it had failed. How stupid he had been. He continued into the lobby. It was full of guests and his mother was trying to placate them.

Charlie went behind the desk and looked at the register. The book made it quite clear that room 322 was vacant. Again he wondered how many people had known that. Charlie went upstairs to talk to Janey and to take a look at the poem. Why had the thief worn a Donald Duck mask?

Chief Peterson arrived about ten minutes later. By that time Charlie's various assistants had returned to the lobby. Several had even gone back upstairs just in case the thief decided to try again. The new detective hired by Charlie's mother and who Victor called Sherlock—his real name was Henri Bogan—kept asking everyone where they had been when the crime was committed. Uniformed police were everywhere and Janey was telling a couple of plain-clothesmen what had happened. People were upset about the gunshot and Victor had explained about twenty times that it was an accident. He had simply dropped his pistol. It happens. People make mistakes.

"After all, nobody's perfect," said Victor.

"Some people are less perfect than others," said Raoul.

Chief Peterson seemed amused. He stood in the center of the lobby rocking back and forth on the balls of his feet and with his thumbs stuck in his waistband. "So the guy tricked you too, did he, Charlie? What am I going to have to do, solve this case myself?"

But Charlie had been thinking quite hard in the few minutes before Peterson's arrival and he'd even had a chance to look around.

"Maybe so, Chief," he said, "but if you give me a little more time, I think I can give you the crook tomorrow."

"Oh yeah, and where do you plan to do that?"

"Come to my mother's apartment on the second floor around nine-thirty tomorrow morning. You can make the arrest there."

The horse's hooves were audible long before the animal could be seen, a rhythmic drumming on the soft dirt of the track. Then a dark chestnut filly with a white blaze on its forehead came rushing out of the mist with the exercise boy—or girl in this case—crouched over its neck. As the horse shot past the clubhouse, Victor heard the click of several stopwatches.

"Bad Britches," said Tony Geremiah. "She won the Ballerina Stakes the other day by six lengths. The big question is whether she'll make the Travers."

"Have a little more melon," said Victor. "Are you sure you don't want a Bloody Mary?"

"No drinking on the job," said Tony. "That's the rule."

It was early Tuesday morning and Victor and Tony Geremiah were having breakfast on the ground floor of the clubhouse. Victor had gotten up at six in order to meet Tony and he felt that Charlie owed him one. Although if it meant not getting fired from his job at the Bentley, then perhaps he was being well paid. They had a table right by the rail because Victor liked watching the horses being exercised. Around them about forty other people were having breakfast as well. A few worked at the track—Victor recognized the shiny bald head of the veterinarian—but most were either tourists or serious handicappers checking out the talent. It was a damp foggy morning and from where Victor sat it was impossible even to see the tote board—just grayness all around and the thumping of hooves as the horses galloped out of the fog.

Victor pushed another piece of melon in Tony's direction. It was a Hand melon from the Hand melon farms just across the river from Schuylerville, in Washington County. Maybe Hand melons were like other melons but Victor didn't think so. They were sweeter somehow and not as mushy. Not only were they a favorite with Victor, but Tony Geremiah seemed positively addicted to them, or at least he was willing to make a pig of himself. He had already eaten two large melons and he was reaching out to take half of another.

"When you set out to bribe a guy," said Tony, "you go first class all the way. I respect that in a person." Tony was a balding, prunelike man in his mid-fifties. Small and with dark leathery skin, he looked like a human version of beef jerky. One had the sense that twenty-four hours of soaking would restore him to his normal state: handsome, unwrinkled, and fully fleshed.

"Let's not call it bribery," said Victor.

"I could lose my job," said Tony. He took a bite of melon and chewed it slowly. His eyes rolled up to where the third floor of the clubhouse disappeared into the fog. His face, which had seemed pinched and careworn, grew peaceful. Tony worked as a clubhouse steward and wore a green blazer. His job was to stand at one of the clubhouse gates and make sure that the eager handicappers were properly dressed with jackets and ties and to see that they had their hands stamped.

"What's the harm?" said Victor. "We'll have it back by eleven."

"And this is for Charlie?"

"I wouldn't ask it for myself," said Victor. Another horse shot by. The exercise girl had long blond hair in a single braid that streamed out behind her. Victor liked the exercise girls. He would imagine their tremendous thigh muscles and his breath would quicken.

"Did Charlie ever tell you how he got me off after I'd knifed a guy in the old Turf?"

"I knew he'd helped you somehow," said Victor.

"Guy went crazy and jumped on me, was going to stick a broken bottle down my throat. I'd never seen him before. I didn't kill him or nothing, just cut a little window in him. But the prosecutor wanted to hang me. A lot of folks from the track got in trouble that summer— this was about fifteen years ago—and the prosecutor was all set to make an example of me. Then Charlie dug around, found out all about it, and told the prosecutor he was going to give everything he'd learned to my lawyer, some court-appointed guy. As a result I got a suspended sentence and two years of pro."

Victor leaned across the table and tapped Tony on the wrist with his fork. "It'd be a shame if you couldn't help Charlie now that he's in a fix," he said.

Tony's wrinkled face grew a little more wrinkled. "Is he really in a fix?"

"One of the worst."

"The cops?"

"His mother."

"And that machine could make it all right?"

"That's what he says. That and the ink."

"And you could have it back by eleven?"

Victor paused and thought of the kindly rabbis of his youth "That's not my promise," he said. "It's Charlie's."

"It would be mean of me not to let him have it, wouldn't it."

"I don't want to pressure you."

"But d'you think it would be mean?"

Victor remained silent while trying to contort his face into a expression that said, Yes, it would be mean.

"Okay," said Tony, "it's yours."

Victor grinned, then signaled to a waiter. "Have some mor melon," he said.

That night Victor met Maximum Tubbs at King's out by the track one of those dark cavernous bars that only seemed busy when th horses were running. This evening there were a few grooms playin pool and a girl wearing a dog collar who kept feeding quarters int the jukebox. Later Victor calculated that he must have heard Johnn Paycheck sing "Take This Job and Shove It" at least a dozen times

Tubbs was a little late and Victor had already finished his first Jac Daniels Manhattan when Tubbs showed up at his booth with a glas of ice and a bottle of Saratoga Vichy.

"So it's over?" asked Tubbs.

"Over and done with."

"And Charlie?"

"He's as pleased as punch."

It was drizzling outside and drops of water sparkled on th shoulders of Tubbs's dark blue raincoat. Removing the coat, h placed it on a chair. Then he took out a white handkerchief, carefull spread the handkerchief across the mustard-colored vinyl, and sa down on it. He wore a dark blue suit with a baby blue carnation in the lapel, and as he turned toward Victor he adjusted the knot of his tie then shot his cuffs.

"I was sorry to miss it," said Tubbs.

"You were invited."

"I had a crap game."

It seemed to Victor that if Frank Sinatra were older, smaller, and had more class, he would look a lot like Maximum Tubbs.

"So did he have all those people there?" asked Tubbs. He held his glass up to the light to make sure it was clean, then he poured it half full of Vichy.

"He sure did. He had about a quarter of the staff: the night bartender, Louie the chef, a couple of waiters, some maids, the wine steward, Zelda the dreamboat that works behind the desk, the head bellboy, Raoul, Sherlock the new detective, and even the fucking accountant. Then there was Chief Peterson, another cop named Novack, Charlie's mother, his cousin Jack, and Janey Burris. And he also invited that lawyer, Hamilton Bryan, who had made the offers on the hotel."

"I told him to get everyone he could think of," said Tubbs. "It tends to dilute the guilty feelings."

"The room wouldn't have held any more," said Victor. "Charlie got them there at nine-thirty and kept them waiting. Like he's busy someplace else. Right in the middle of the room there's this machine covered with a white sheet. Nobody knows what it is even though they're dying to ask. Louie the chef's complaining that he has to get back to the kitchen. Raoul is making indignant hayfever-like noises. One of the maids starts weeping for some reason I never figured. The accountant keeps looking at his watch. Hamilton Bryan looks at his watch. Peterson gets redder and redder. It gets to be quarter of ten, then ten of, then five of, and at exactly ten o'clock Charlie strolls in. Very efficient, very courteous. Raoul is sitting by the door and Charlie shakes his hand, then shakes Peterson's hand, then maybe Hamilton Bryan's and a couple more. He kisses his mother's cheek and then, although I bet I'm the only guy who saw him do it, he winks at Janey. Eddie Gillespie comes in with him and stays by the door."

Maximum Tubbs sipped his Vichy. "I told him to be late," he said. "I always do that for a big game. It puts the suckers off their luck. Was he boring? I told him to bore the hell out of them."

Victor called the waiter over and ordered another Jack Daniels Manhattan. "They nearly went to sleep," said Victor, raising his voice over the noise of the jukebox. "He described every robbery, gave the names and addresses of everyone involved; he read the poems; he said where people were at the time of each robbery. He took a good half hour to tell people what they already knew. The accountant was yawning. Raoul was rolling his eyes. The maid stopped crying. I guess Charlie must have spoken to Peterson earlier because although the steam was puffing out his ears, he kept his mouth shut."

"It's a pity that Charlie doesn't gamble," said Tubbs.

Victor was chewing some of his ice. "Nah, he'd be a terrible gambler. He cares too much. I mean, even this morning when he was looking cool and in control, I could see the sweat popping off his temples. Little drops of worry. The real reason why it all worked was because of the lying. Charlie can be a wonderful liar."

"It's a gift," said Maximum Tubbs.

"My sentiments exactly," said Victor. His drink arrived and he plucked out the maraschino cherry.

"You know those things are poison," said Tubbs.

Victor tossed the cherry into the air and caught it on his tongue. For a moment he held it between his teeth, then it disappeared into his mouth with a sucking noise. "Gotta die sometime," he said, "so why not die happy?"

"Anyway," Victor continued, "Charlie bores them till they're ready to scream, then he says, perfectly casually, 'Of course, the purpose of the robberies was not the jewelry, but the poems.' Well, that caught their attention and cousin Jack demands to know what he's talking about, so Charlie says that the purpose of the robberies was to make the hotel look bad and lose business, and what the poems do is give the robberies a lot of play in the papers and make the people at the hotel, like me, look like real dopes. So Cousin Jack plays straight man and says why in the world would someone want to hurt the hotel? And Charlie says that somebody is trying to make his mother sell the place. Well, at that point Hamilton Bryan jumps to his feet and says, 'I object,' just like in some Perry Mason flick. So Charlie gets all embarrassed and says how he's not trying to suggest that Bryan is a crook, although of course he is. And he says that just because Bryan made some offers on the hotel doesn't mean he's behind the robberies, and just because Bryan won't tell who his clients are doesn't mean they're crooks, and just because Bryan used to represent some of the worst crooks in Albany—here Charlie named off about ten names—doesn't mean he's representing them now."

"But the fact remains," said Tubbs, "that somebody wanted to buy the hotel."

"You bet," said Victor. "Someone wanted to kick Mabel out and take her place. And since she wouldn't sell, they'd make her sell. Maybe Bryan was involved and maybe he wasn't. Although now, of course, we know he was involved, or least his clients were, and he's going to have a hard time staying out of jail himself."

"Has he said anything?"

"He only opens his mouth to hiss," said Victor, "although this morning it was hard to shut him up, he seemed so mad. Anyway Charlie says he's sorry if he's hurt his feelings and he doesn't mean that Bryan is a crook, but he won't budge from the point that someone is trying to make Mabel sell. Then he starts talking about the robberies again, how the thief seemed to have keys and how he knew who had jewels and what rooms were empty and how to avoid getting caught. 'It seems obvious,' Charlie says, 'that either the thief had an accomplice in the hotel or was an actual hotel employee.' So now the chef gets indignant and the maid starts crying again and the bellboy starts snapping his toothpicks in half and throwing them on the rug and Raoul wants to know what proof he has. But Charlie ignores them. Instead, he says how these people were all in the hotel during each robbery. The chef was there, the head bellboy, Zelda the looker, Raoul, even the accountant was there during three of the robberies, even Charlie's cousin Jack. Well, Jack gets mad and says how he's never heard of such a crazy thing."

"And did Charlie get angry?" asked Tubbs. "I told him to lose his temper, to get really furious."

"You bet. He's not Mr. Softy anymore. Like he's Mr. Tiger. He tells Jack to shut up. He barks at the chef. He tells Eddie to guard the door. Then he goes over to the machine, you know, this mysterious thing covered with a white sheet, and he rips off the sheet and everybody stares at it wondering what the fuck it is. 'I'm not guessing about anything,' says Charlie. 'I know who committed the robberies. And I know the person's right here in this room.' "

"How'd they like that?" asked Tubbs.

"Nobody cracked a sound except that damn maid. Blubber blubber, blubber. I could of stuck a towel in her mouth. Anyway, Charlie then introduces Janey Burris and says how she was a plant and he explains how the jewelry in her room was dusted with a special powder and that even though the crook was wearing gloves he must have handled the jewels later and that the marks from the powder will show up under an ultraviolet light. And then everyone knows what that fucking machine is. They know it's the ultraviolet light they use at the track to see if you've paid your two bucks to get into the clubhouse. I could have laughed. Anyway, Charlie shouts at the chef and demands that he put his hands under the light. Of course, the chef's not happy but he puts his hands there and there's nothing. I can see he's relieved. Then he gets Zelda, then the bellboy, then one of the maids. Nothing every time. Then Charlie turns to Raoul. 'Okay,' he says, 'now it's your turn.' And Raoul gets all huffy and says how this is the most preposterous thing he's ever heard in his life, but I can see how he's rubbing his hands on his pants. Charlie again tells him to step right up and Eddie moves up behind him. So Raoul gets up. He looks at Hamilton Bryan but Bryan doesn't look back. He looks at Peterson and says, 'He can't make me do this.' And Peterson says, 'Yes, he can.' And I tell you, in all these years, that's the first time I've ever liked Peterson, although he's still a jerk and my one moment of weakness doesn't change that. So Raoul steps up to the machine and tries to look tough, although everyone can see he's about to wet his pants, and he sticks his hand under the light and it goes all purple. People make little gasps. Raoul yanks his hand away and there is a kind of moment."

"A long one, I bet," said Tubbs.

"Well, it was one of those short moments that seems about ten minutes long and nobody speaks and nobody moves and then Peterson says, perfectly calmly, 'It looks like you're in a lot of trouble.' In a fucking flash, Raoul pulls out this little gun. A maid screams. People jump back. I look at Charlie and he's looking so fucking relieved that he's just standing there smiling."

"Smiling?"

"He wasn't sure, you know. But that gun clinched it and I swear it was the same gun that the guy in the Donald Duck mask was waving around last night. So Raoul tells everyone to stand still and he starts backing toward the door, but he wasn't counting on one thing."

"Eddie Gillespie."

"You bet. Eddie fucking lives for moments like this. I mean, his whole life's a TV show. You remember those books they used to sell called stuff like *Boy Heroes* and *Boy Adventure* about little kids hurling themselves into raging rivers to save drowning pups, or leaping into the path of a locomotive to grab some poor blind lady who's gotten lost? That's Eddie. And he takes karate too, you know, or whatever that thing is where you make all these crazy poses like you're playing Mother, may I. So I look at Eddie and I see his eyes light up and his whole body starts to twitch like a dog that's just picked up the scent of something tasty and he pulls himself down into himself, getting smaller and smaller, somehow making himself all compact and then he goes off like a fucking spring, like he flies through the air, like he's fucking Clark Kent who can't be bothered to find a phone booth, he's a flying brick wall."

"Did Raoul see him?"

"Only at the very last moment. I mean, he saw something nasty out of the corner of his eye and he starts to spin and everyone takes a deep breath and everyone starts to speak or shout or gasp or hoot and then it's over. The little pistol goes sailing across the room and Raoul's just a heap on the floor."

15

The Scott Joplin song on the jukebox at the Spa City Diner was the same song that Charlie had heard tinkling out of the merry-go-round speakers just a little over two weeks ago. Had it only been two weeks? Charlie dropped a quarter in the slot, then heard it roll down various chutes and a light came on which told him that he could make one selection. He pushed the buttons. The song was called "The Entertainer" and it still sounded like musical yo-yos.

Charlie made his way back to the table where he and Victor were eating blueberry pancakes. Occasionally he had to step to one side as waitresses rushed past with great trays of food. It was eight o'clock Wednesday morning and the restaurant was packed. Charlie and Victor even had to wait in line, which was unthinkable for any time of year except August. There was the clatter of forks against plates, cups against saucers. Charlie had driven into town early to get a copy of the *Racing Form* and he figured he had about four hours of intense study in front of him before he had to make his pick for the first race. Right now Spanky's Pleasure looked pretty good with Cordero on top, but Charlie would have to look at the horse before he made a final decision. He would have to peer deeply into its brown eyes and inquire if it was true that Spanky's Pleasure loved him alone.

Charlie slid back into the booth. Victor briefly glanced up, then returned to the steady devouring of his pancakes. A snaky trail of syrup dribbled from his chin. Way in the distance Charlie could hear the Joplin rag, almost overwhelmed by the sound of eating. It struck Charlie that people were chewing exactly in time to the music. Then he shook his head to clear it of frivolous thoughts.

"What I still don't see," said Charlie, with what he realized were the last prickly remnants of a grudge, "is why you got me those darn poems so late."

Victor dragged his napkin across his chin. It was a bright sunny morning and streaks of sunlight slanted across their table. "I had to get them typed up," said Victor. "Besides, humiliation makes you strong. By the time you got those poems you were really ready to rip. It's one of the rules of the stage: adrenaline counts."

"They took everyone by surprise," said Charlie. He was still amazed by how people had enjoyed them.

"Did they like 'Bill Doolin in the Sky with Diamonds'?" asked Victor. "I'm a sucker for the sentimental ones."

"They liked them all," said Charlie, recalling how friendly people had been. "Arlo Webster even told me that I should apply sometime. I mean, as a regular poet."

Victor raised his eyebrows in a way intended to suggest that Charlie had just made an embarrassing remark. "And what happened to Alexander Luft?"

"They shipped him down to a mental hospital outside of New York yesterday afternoon."

"So he was really bonkers?"

"I guess so. He kept repeating the same thing over and over."

"What's that?"

"He'd say, 'There is only one poet and we are he.' I must have heard him say it a hundred times."

Charlie had visited him at a local hospital. At first Charlie had thought that Luft didn't recognize him, at least he didn't speak or make any expression that signified recognition. But then Luft began making a funny clicking noise with his tongue, first a high noise, then a low noise, over and over, like a clock ticking. Charlie had stared at him, trying to make sense of it, until, with a shock, he had realized that Luft was mimicking the sound of a Ping-Pong ball being hit back and forth across a table.

"He used to tell me," said Charlie, "that true artists were a little crazy. He must have been talking about himself."

Victor began to nibble a small brown sausage that was exactly the size of his little finger. "What made you figure out he was doing all this stuff to himself?" he asked.

"I'm not sure. I suppose I should have realized it earlier but I was distracted by having to write those Bill Doolin poems and then Luft was a kind of bully. He made me nervous. And then there was this painter who was having an affair with someone in the kitchen and was lying about where he had been. But, you know, once I realized that Rolf Vinner was behind that business at Long Meadows, it changed my thinking. I mean, Vinner seemed to have the most to lose from any scandal. He was one of the victims. And of course Luft was a victim, or apparent victim as well. So once I saw that the victim could be the attacker, everything changed. Luft had a lot of hatred and he never forgot a grudge. He was one of the most powerful critics in the country and he couldn't stand the fact that the Phoenix Colony accepted people who he had already judged as non-artists. Of course, these feelings had gone on for years and what began as a strong irritation eventually became an obsession. Also, he was obsessed by his own failure as a poet, and he had come to think that if the Phoenix Colony had accepted him and encouraged him almost thirty years before, then his life would have been different. He might have become the poet he had dreamed of becoming. In any case, the victim was really the villain."

Victor had stopped eating and leaned toward Charlie. The tip of his gray tie lay in a little pool of syrup. "Raoul, too, right?"

"Sure. It seemed that if the hotel closed, he would be out of a job, so he'd be crazy to try and make it close. As we know now, he'd worked out a deal so that not only would he be the manager of the new hotel, he would also be part-owner. But once I started thinking that the victim could be the person causing all the trouble, then I had a whole new list of suspects. Also, with Raoul, he hated you, and I was struck by how all those robberies made you look bad. But Vinner started it. Figuring out that one led to the rest."

"And what's happened to him?"

"He's still in the hospital. Six murders and two attempted murders will keep him in jail almost forever."

Victor took another bite of his pancakes, then he noticed the syrup on the tip of his tie and began washing it in his water glass.

"What about those bodies they dug up, did they find anything?"

The Joplin song had finished and Charlie considered playing it again. But who was he playing it for? Himself? For Blake Moss going around and around in the rain?

"They ran a toxicology, but it's extremely hard to find anything in a body that has already been embalmed. You have to know what you're looking for. Luckily the police had found several ampoules of Pavulon in Vinner's house."

"And what's that?" Victor began drying his tie with his napkin.

"It's the trade name for pancuronium, which is a derivative of curare, that stuff that South American Indians put on their arrows. Basically, it's something they use in surgery to relax the muscles. But if you use enough of it, it stops the heart."

"A heart attack," said Victor.

"More or less, at least that's what was given as the cause of death. After all, they were old people, so it was assumed they died of natural causes." Charlie sipped his coffee. It had gotten cold.

"And they found it in the bodies?"

"Only in the last one, Ted Davis. They found a trace in the vitreous."

"What's that?"

"The ocular fluid."

"Eye juice," said Victor. "But the cops think he dosed them all?"

"Sure, but pancuronium breaks down very quickly. Their main case against Vinner comes from the attempted murders of Janey and the old woman, Mrs. Preston, and the murder of Ted Davis. They can't really prove he killed the others, not even Blake Moss."

"But Vinner had fleeced those old folks? Can they prove that?"

Charlie glanced toward the door. Janey Burris had said she might meet them for breakfast and Charlie's whole body felt alert. He kept thinking that she was healthy and safe, and each time the thought came as a gift.

"Probably," said Charlie. "The first two he robbed till they had nothing left, then he killed them to get rid of them, just so he could have their rooms again. The second two he killed because they were suspicious, which was also why he killed Blake Moss and the nurse."

"How could he bring himself to kill six people?" asked Victor.

"Bit by bit, I suppose. Like that first person, Wilbur Potter: Vinner probably robbed him a little and nothing happened, so he robbed him some more and still nothing happened, and so he robbed him of everything and still nothing happened, after that he worked up his courage to kill him and nothing happened. From then on, it got easier."

"Is Vinner talking?"

"Nope, he just lies in bed and watches the sports channel on cable."

"That's sure not like Raoul," said Victor. "Nobody can shut him up."

Raoul had been talking nonstop ever since his arrest, apparently feeling that each small thing he could blame on someone else would reduce the time he spent in jail. Warrants had been drawn up for three men in Albany, while the lawyer, Hamilton Bryan, had been arrested and was already out on bail.

"Did you hear that they found a rhyming dictionary in Raoul's room?" said Victor.

That made Charlie feel good. "I never needed one," he said. "My Bill Doolin rhymes were entirely my own." He again glanced toward the door but there was still no sign of Janey.

"Maybe you and Raoul can join one of those poetry workshops," suggested Victor. "They got one at Skidmore. It'd be a good way to meet cute girls."

Charlie started to say that he already had a cute girl, but he just thought about her instead. Janey would go with him to the races that afternoon. He would advise her about the best horses, talk about training schedules and jockeys and how horses came into form. She would ignore his advice and bet birthdates, lucky colors, coin tosses. And at the end of the day, Charlie's careful evaluations would have cost him about forty bucks, while Janey would be a hundred bucks ahead. As Victor liked to say, the world exists to make you humble.

"What really impressed me," said Victor, "was how you fixed those jewels. I mean, I know that Janey was planted to tempt the thief, but it was sharp thinking to dunk the jewels in that ultraviolet stuff."

"No," said Charlie, somewhat sheepishly, "I didn't do anything to the jewels. I made it all up."

"What d'you mean?"

"Raoul out-tricked me, that's all. He got into Janey's room when we weren't expecting it and then had his escape all planned out. He completely got away with it."

Victor knitted his eyebrows. "But what about the stuff on his hands?"

Charlie felt a little embarrassed and lowered his voice. "Well, I'd already suspected Raoul and when we came galloping in from outside, there he was in the kitchen. Later I asked Louie the chef and he said that Raoul had showed up only a minute before."

"But that doesn't explain about the purple stuff," said Victor.

"I put it on his hands myself. I mean, I put the stuff on my own hands and when I went into my mother's room yesterday morning I shook hands with Raoul and got the ink all over him."

"But you shook hands with a number of people," said Victor. "I was struck by that."

"Yes, but I shook hands with Raoul first and none of the others put their hands under that light. If Peterson had put his hand under the light, it would have looked just as purple."

"But what if Raoul hadn't panicked, what if he had tried to tough it out?"

Charlie grinned. "Then I would have been in real trouble." He glanced up to see Janey entering the diner. She was wearing a blue polka dot dress and under her arm she carried a small white purse. Seeing her, Charlie felt a small electric shock. Then he got up and kissed her cheek.

"You're a pretty sneaky guy," said Victor.

Charlie stood by the table with his arm around Janey's waist. "I knew he was guilty," he said. "I just had to make him expose himself."

Victor put down his fork. He seemed both indignant and amused. "Do you know you're involved with a sneak?" he asked Janey.

Janey sat down and took a bite of Charlie's blueberry pancakes. "I wouldn't have it any other way," she said.